Highlander Seduced

Rebellious Highland Hearts
Book One

JAYNE CASTEL

WINTER MIST
PRESS

Published by Winter Mist Press

Edited by Tim Burton
Cover design by Winter Mist Press
Cover photography and thistle vector image courtesy of
www.shutterstock.com and www.depositphotos.com

Visit Jayne's website: www.jaynecastel.com

Can a simple chambermaid capture the heart of a proud laird? Passion, honor, and the power of destiny collide in Medieval Scotland.

Bonnie Fraser grew up in the shadows. A servant in Stirling Castle, she's invisible, ignored—even if her heart yearns for more. But when the king holds a masquerade ball, Bonnie decides to step out into the light for once. Masked and disguised, she tastes the excitement of another life—and that's when she meets a charismatic laird who sweeps her off her feet.

Iver Mackay has always been unlucky in love. Despite his obligations as chieftain of a vast holding, he's now sworn off marriage, content to let his younger brothers carry on the family bloodline. Yet when he dances with an enigmatic red-haired beauty at the king's ball, Iver forgets himself.

Their meeting leads to a steamy encounter that neither of them will ever forget.

But can there be a happy ending for two people from such different worlds?

Rebellious Highland Hearts is a four-book series following Iver Mackay of Dun Ugadale and his three brothers—Lennox, Kerr, and Brodie—as they meet women who will change their lives forever.

Historical Romances by Jayne Castel

DARK AGES BRITAIN

The Kingdom of the East Angles series
Night Shadows (prequel novella)
Dark Under the Cover of Night (Book One)
Nightfall till Daybreak (Book Two)
The Deepening Night (Book Three)
The Kingdom of the East Angles: The Complete Series

The Kingdom of Mercia series
The Breaking Dawn (Book One)
Darkest before Dawn (Book Two)
Dawn of Wolves (Book Three)
The Kingdom of Mercia: The Complete Series

The Kingdom of Northumbria series
The Whispering Wind (Book One)
Wind Song (Book Two)
Lord of the North Wind (Book Three)
The Kingdom of Northumbria: The Complete Series

DARK AGES SCOTLAND

The Warrior Brothers of Skye series
Blood Feud (Book One)
Barbarian Slave (Book Two)
Battle Eagle (Book Three)
The Warrior Brothers of Skye: The Complete Series

The Pict Wars series
Warrior's Heart (Book One)
Warrior's Secret (Book Two)
Warrior's Wrath (Book Three)

The Pict Wars: The Complete Series

On the Empire's Edge Duet
Taming the Eagle
Ensnaring the Dove

Novellas
Winter's Promise

MEDIEVAL SCOTLAND

The Brides of Skye series
The Beast's Bride (Book One)
The Outlaw's Bride (Book Two)
The Rogue's Bride (Book Three)
The Brides of Skye: The Complete Series

The Sisters of Kilbride series
Unforgotten (Book One)
Awoken (Book Two)
Fallen (Book Three)
Claimed (Epilogue novella)
The Sisters of Kilbride: The Complete Series

The Immortal Highland Centurions series
Maximus (Book One)
Cassian (Book Two)
Draco (Book Three)
The Laird's Return (Epilogue festive novella)
The Immortal Highland Centurions: The Complete Series

Guardians of Alba series
Nessa's Seduction (Book One)
Fyfa's Sacrifice (Book Two)
Breanna's Surrender (Book Three)
Guardians of Alba: The Complete Series

Stolen Highland Hearts series
Highlander Deceived (Book One)

Highlander Entangled (Book Two)
Highlander Forbidden (Book Three)
Highlander Pledged (Book Four)

Courageous Highland Hearts series
Highlander Defied (Book One)
Highlander Tempted (Book Two)
Highlander Healed (Book Three)
Highlander Sworn (Book Four)

Rebellious Highland Hearts series
Highlander Seduced (Book One)

Epic Fantasy Romances by Jayne Castel

Light and Darkness series
Ruled by Shadows (Book One)
The Lost Swallow (Book Two)
Path of the Dark (Book Three)
Light and Darkness: The Complete Series

***

To my wonderful readers ... and especially those of you who aren't ready to say goodbye to the Mackays. This series is for you!

***

It is never too late to be what you might have been.
—George Eliot

1: A LAIRD NEEDS A WIFE

Stirling Castle, Scotland

February, 1452

THERE WERE TWO questions Iver Mackay didn't like answering. The first was, why, at the age of five and thirty, he'd never married? And the second was, *when* was he planning on taking a wife?

But this evening, he hadn't been able to avoid either—especially since it was the king who was asking.

Iver stiffened in his high-backed chair, his fingers tightening around the cup of warmed spiced wine he held. He'd been enjoying the heat of the roaring fire, and only half-listening to the talk of politics from the others in the solar, when James had blindsided him.

Recovering, Iver favored the young king with a polite smile. "Clan matters have kept me occupied over the years, Sire. I've no time to look for a wife."

It was a weak excuse, and James snorted rudely. "Ye are at peace with yer neighbors these days, are ye not?"

"Aye, Sire."

"Well, ye are well overdue starting a family then." The king's deep-brown eyes narrowed. "A laird needs a wife ... and heirs to secure his line."

This comment brought murmurs of agreement from the others seated around the hearth. Iver's gaze traveled the chamber, and he noted his companions were now all staring at him.

After supper in the great hall, the clan-chiefs and chieftains who'd gathered at Stirling for three days of celebrations had retired to the keep. The spacious solar, with twin stag heads mounted on either side of the fireplace and hunting tapestries covering the damp walls, was big enough to accommodate them all.

The young king had taken the best spot, right before the hearth; he sprawled back in his high-backed, padded chair, booted feet up on a settle.

Iver kept smiling, even as anger quickened in his gut.

He wasn't going to argue with the king. Nonetheless, such a glib comment was easy for a man of two and twenty to utter—a man who'd married at eighteen, and who already had two bairns.

Life hadn't kicked James in the bollocks repeatedly the way it had Iver.

"Well said, My Liege." One of the clan-chiefs lifted his cup aloft in a mocking toast and flashed Iver a grin. "A man proves himself with his lineage, does he not?"

Iver clenched his jaw and took a large gulp of rich plum wine.

Christ's blood. Can they just change the subject?

He then silently cursed his own clan-chief for sending him in his stead. He hadn't wanted to make this trip to Stirling, yet it was Queen Mary's birthday and Lent was about to begin. A frugal period would follow—with no meat consumed and watered-down ale, mead, and wine. And so, before it did, King James had decided to host three days of celebrations and feasting.

Of course, Niel had known that the king would want to talk clan politics at some point over the festivities. As one of the most powerful Highland clans, the Mackays needed to be kept informed. So, although Niel was recovering from a harsh bout of the grippe and couldn't make the long trip himself, he'd chosen an emissary. Iver had been the obvious choice as he ruled the southern branch of the Mackays, at Dun Ugadale on the Kintyre peninsula. The trip to Stirling Castle wasn't as long for him—and he'd report back to his clan-chief afterward.

"I have three younger brothers," Iver replied after a lengthy pause, throttling his temper and focusing on keeping his tone smooth. "One of them will surely have sons. They shall keep the Mackay bloodline going."

"Aye, but they won't be *yer* sons," the king pointed out unnecessarily.

Iver inhaled deeply before answering. "Such things don't matter to me, Sire. I don't care if a nephew, or one of my brothers, steps into my role once I'm gone."

One of the clan-chiefs made a choking sound, while the man next to him muttered an oath under his breath. The tension in the solar was now palpable.

The embers smoldering in Iver's gut flared to life once more; it was an effort to keep his smile in place now. He was aware such sentiment wasn't popular. Many Highland lairds were obsessive about continuing their bloodline. His drinking companions likely thought he'd lost his wits.

Taking another gulp of wine, Iver cast a hunted look over his shoulder—to where his brother lounged.

Younger than Iver by three years, Lennox reclined near the window—out of the circle of warmth cast by the hearth—cup of mulled wine in hand, long legs crossed at the ankles.

Catching Iver's eye, he smirked.

Iver fought an answering scowl. Like him, Lennox was unwed. But *his* choice was never questioned. He could fight, drink, carouse, and sow his seed far and wide without anyone criticizing him, for he wasn't the chieftain of Dun Ugadale.

Iver had responsibilities, but Lennox didn't.

Turning his attention back to the king and the men seated around him, Iver drew in a slow, deep breath. Stubbornness tightened his gut then. *It matters not what the king, or anyone else, says.*

Aye, short of 'commanding' him to take a wife, he'd not be swayed from his decision.

Iver would never ask a woman for her hand again.

However, as everyone's focus remained on him, for they were waiting for Iver to elaborate on his unpopular decision, he decided it was time to steer the conversation to other matters.

Meeting the king's eye, he asked, "Will ye be gathering yer council tomorrow morning, Sire?"

James huffed a sigh while his gaze remained narrowed. "No ... the morning after. Mary has organized a masquerade ball for tomorrow, so we shall enjoy some revelry first ... before talking politics."

"A *masquerade* ball? I've never heard of such a thing, My Liege," a burly chieftain seated at the back of the group spoke up then.

The king heaved a sigh and pulled a face. The expression twisted the vermillion birthmark upon his left cheek.

"Aye," he muttered. "Mary tells me that these occasions ... where guests don costumes and masks ... are currently fashionable in France. She's been eager to host one for a while."

"Indeed, the queen and her ladies-in-waiting have spent the past moon fashioning masks for all the guests," Duncan Stewart, the seneschal of Stirling Castle, added with a smile. Seated at the back of the gathering of lairds, Stewart was a big man with red cheeks and a thick mane of greying black hair. "It should be quite an evening."

Iver's simmering irritation spiked once more. He didn't care if masquerade balls were popular elsewhere. Frankly, he hadn't come to Stirling for such foolish mummery. Yet, no doubt, he'd be expected to attend.

"There will be plenty of fine ladies in attendance tomorrow." James turned his attention to Iver once more, pinning him under a penetrating stare. "If a man can't find himself a wife amongst the best Scotland has to offer, he's a fool indeed."

Laughter rippled through the solar at this comment.

Iver flushed. He couldn't rouse a smile; instead, he fought a deep scowl. Not only had the king brought the conversation right back to the subject he wished to avoid, but he was now ridiculing him.

"The king was like a dog with a bone this eve."

"Aye ... he had his sights on me from the moment we entered." Iver stalked down the hallway toward the stairwell, hands clenched by his sides. They'd just left the king's solar and were making their way back to their bedchambers. "Just because *he's* happily wed, he thinks everyone else should be."

Beside him, Lennox snorted a laugh. "I wouldn't idealize it. I'd wager *Fiery Face* thinks his clan-chiefs and chieftains won't cause him trouble if they have a wife and a brood of bairns to contend with."

His brother's drawled comment made Iver's step falter. Glancing around him, lest there be anyone lurking in the shadows who might have overheard the insult, he scowled. "Christ's bones, Len. Lower yer voice when ye use that name."

Lennox wasn't the only one who called the king that behind his back. 'Fiery Face' didn't just allude to his birthmark but also his hot temper. However, none were foolish enough to say it in his company.

Shrugging, Lennox flashed Iver a grin. "Don't worry ... we're alone." He paused then. "Anyway, ye eventually managed to throw him off the scent."

"Aye, well, it comes from years of practice."

"Even so, it's not wise to rouse the ire of the king. Maybe ye *should* find yerself a wife."

Iver cut his brother a sharp look, yet Lennox just winked at him. "Ye're not getting any younger, after all."

Iver muttered a curse under his breath. "Don't *ye* start." It was bad enough that his mother continued to nag him about his unwed state whenever she got him alone. He didn't need his brother to join the chorus.

Lennox seemed to enjoy riling him—even more so these days. It was almost as if he was deliberately trying to antagonize his elder brother.

Iver suspected the reason—he'd become a reclusive laird of late, often locking himself away in his own solar so he could deal with clan matters and requests from neighboring chieftains. In the meantime, he'd left much of the management of his broch to his brother Kerr, who captained the Dun Ugadale Guard, and to Lennox, his bailiff.

And although Lennox hadn't openly complained, Iver suspected his brother chafed at having to collect the laird's rents. He didn't seem to enjoy overseeing Iver's lands, and those who farmed them, either. Of course, no one welcomed a visit from the bailiff.

Indeed, their strained relationship was why Iver had asked Lennox to accompany him to Stirling. He wished to sweeten his brother's temper and ease things between them a little. Yet he wondered now if Kerr wouldn't have been a better choice. Lennox was sharp-witted and an able negotiator, but Iver felt as if he'd just carried a cocked crossbow into the castle with him. Who knew what would come out of Len's mouth, or whom he'd offend, especially when he was in his cups?

"Don't mind me," Lennox drawled. "It's the king ye need to worry about."

"Aye, remind me to sit as far as possible from him at the banquet tomorrow."

Dread descended upon Iver then, at the thought of the coming festivities. He wished to avoid anything social and just attend the necessary meeting. However, James wouldn't look favorably on such behavior.

Right now, he wanted to be back in his solar, sitting by the hearth with his wolfhounds at his feet.

As if sensing Iver's darkening mood, Lennox slapped him on the back then. "Cheer up ... just two more days and we can go home."

"Aye," Iver muttered. "Although I wish it were tomorrow."

The brothers took the stairs to the guest floor then and walked along the corridor toward their bedchambers. Torches hung from chains on the walls, casting a warm light across the pitted stone.

A chambermaid hurried past them, carrying a huge pile of fresh linen. The lass kept her face downcast. All the same, Iver noted that she was a pretty wee thing with flame-red hair.

Lennox winked at her, yet the lass kept her head bowed and scurried on, her feet whispering on stone.

"Careful, Len," Iver murmured. "Try to keep yer slug in yer braies for once."

In response, his brother merely barked a laugh.

2: WOLFHOUNDS ON A SCENT

BONNIE FRASER REACHED the landing before realizing she'd forgotten to breathe.

Clutching the linen she'd collected for one of the guest bedchambers, she glanced over her shoulder at where the two men were disappearing into their respective quarters.

Bonnie's heart bucked hard against her breastbone.

They were both arrestingly handsome—although it wasn't the one who'd winked at her who'd caught her eye, but his companion.

Tall and heavily muscled, with a shock of white-blond hair that flowed over his shoulders, dark-blue eyes, and chiseled features, his beauty had struck her like a punch to the stomach.

The man he was with had similar looks, although his handsomeness was more rugged. His hair was a darker blond and cut short—and he walked with a swagger. She'd heard his companion's muttered reprimand, and her cheeks flushed hot at the crudeness of it.

The man who'd spoken had a low, gravelly voice that had made her breathing hitch.

All she could think about in the heartbeats that followed was how she wished she'd had the courage to meet his eye, and what it would feel like to have his gaze upon her.

Exhaling sharply, Bonnie drew in a large lungful of air.

Meanwhile, the two men had stepped from the hallway into their bedchambers, the doors thudding shut behind them.

Goose, she chastised herself. *Why the devil would he look at ye?*

She was a chambermaid—a shadow. And the man was clearly *somebody*. Dressed in chamois braies, expensive leather boots encasing muscular calves, and with a snowy léine of fine linen, topped by a padded gambeson to keep the winter's chill at bay—he had the air of a laird.

Indeed, Stirling Castle was full of them at present.

The king and queen were hosting three days of celebrations, and clan-chiefs and chieftains from throughout the realm had traveled here to attend.

The reminder made Bonnie swiftly turn and hurry down the twisting stairwell. Nearly all the guest chambers within the castle were now occupied—and she'd just been instructed to make up a bed for a latecomer on the floor below.

She shouldn't be dragging her heels.

Nonetheless, a familiar heaviness pressed down upon her as she made up the guest bedroom—a hopelessness that dragged at her limbs. Fighting it, she placed an iron warming pan full of hot coals from the glowing hearth inside the bedcovers. The weather had warmed a little recently—they were marching through February now—and the first of the snowdrops were peeking their white bonnets above ground in the castle's gardens. Nonetheless, the late arrival would appreciate a warm bed.

Leaving a lantern burning on the bedside table, Bonnie departed from the bedchamber and made her way downstairs to the kitchens. Although supper had been and gone for the rest of the keep, she'd yet to eat. Her belly was hollow, and her mouth watered at the thought of the mutton and turnip stew and bread she knew would be waiting for her in the Great Kitchens.

Pitted stone walls and an arched ceiling greeted her, glowing red-gold in the light of the huge hearths up one end. Located on the lowest level of the castle, the kitchens were the heart of the keep for many who resided there. A passage led out to the inner bailey so food could be carried with ease across to the great hall beyond.

During the day, it was a chaotic space filled with servants, and the noise could be deafening. But at this hour, only Lorna Fraser and her two daughters, Alba and Morag, were present.

"There ye are, lass," Lorna greeted Bonnie with a thin smile. "I was beginning to think ye'd forgotten about supper."

The head cook, a tall and angular woman with faded blonde hair, stood at the great scrubbed table in the center of the kitchens, kneading bread for the morning.

Alba and Morag worked alongside her. The twins didn't look anything like their mother. Instead, they favored their father. No one spoke of the man these days though. Lorna's husband, who'd once been the head groom of Stirling Castle, had run off when the twins were bairns.

Bonnie was five years older than her cousins. Morag and Alba were mirror images of each other in looks—sturdily built with brown hair and round faces—yet Bonnie had always been able to tell them apart. Alba was quieter and sweeter-tempered than her sister, while Morag scowled more readily and held her chin at an arrogant tilt.

Morag's chin jutted now, as she eyed her cousin. "She was probably idling, Ma."

"I was not," Bonnie replied, tensing. "With all the newly arrived guests, there have been many chambers to clean and ready. I haven't stopped all day."

Silence fell in the kitchen, broken only by the gentle crackle of the hearth.

Bonnie's chest tightened as she realized her mistake. She was tired and hungry and had forgotten herself, but that was no excuse.

Her aunt and cousin were like wolfhounds on a scent. Their gazes gleamed at her pert response.

Lorna drew herself up, her chin rising.

Meanwhile, Bonnie's stomach sank. *Here we go.*

"Unfortunately, Morag is right, lass." Lorna's voice was falsely sweet. "Ye pass most of the day in a dream."

"Aye, Ma," Morag dusted flour off her hands after covering the dough she'd been kneading, with a cloth. "I saw her earlier, singing to herself when she should have been emptying chamber pots. I swear it was as if she were away with the fairies."

Bonnie stiffened. That was a lie. She hadn't seen either of her cousins all day.

Morag and Alba knew it too—for the former smirked, while the latter glanced away.

Neither of their responses surprised Bonnie. Morag loved to torment her cousin, and although Alba didn't join her mother and sister when they ganged up on Bonnie, she'd never come to her defense either. Not once.

Bonnie was on her own—as she always had been.

"Aye, that's because yer poor cousin is a lackwit," Lorna replied gravely. "Her birth was a difficult one ... she was clearly starved of air."

A familiar, warm, prickling cloak of humiliation wrapped itself around Bonnie at these words.

Shame.

Her aunt wielded her cruelest words with a mild tone, as if she actually cared for her niece—which she did not.

Doing her best to hide her reaction, Bonnie raised her chin, meeting Lorna's eye. "Well, my chores are all done now," she replied. "And I haven't yet had any supper."

"No, ye haven't, lass." Lorna flashed her a smile, wiping her own hands on a damp cloth. "But fret not, Morag will fetch ye the stew we've kept back for ye."

"No need." Bonnie started toward the small iron pot that hung over the hearth. "I can do it."

"I insist, dear cousin," Morag replied in a sing-song tone that made Bonnie's hackles rise. "Ye must be *starving*." She stepped away from the table and crossed the floor to the fire, grabbing a thick cloth so that she could unhook it without burning her hands. But the lass had only just turned and taken a step toward the table when the pot slipped from her fingers and tumbled to the straw-strewn floor.

Bonnie's sharply indrawn breath reverberated around the kitchens in the moments that followed. She stared down at her ruined supper. And then, to her humiliation, her vision blurred.

She didn't want to weep in front of these women. But she was hungry and tired, and Morag had just deliberately spilled her supper all over the floor.

Blinking furiously, hands balled at her sides, she raised her chin and forced herself to face them.

Both Lorna and Morag were smirking now, although Alba's expression was pinched. Her gaze flicked between her mother and sister, as if she worried what they might do next.

Lorna tutted. "Oh dear, Morag, ye *are* clumsy."

"Sorry, Bonnie." Morag stepped away from the mess she'd made, making no move to stoop and clean it up. "It looks like ye won't be having any supper this eve."

Bonnie didn't answer immediately.

She was too intent on choking back tears. Meanwhile, helpless fury beat in her breast like a caged bird. And when she did answer, her voice shook with the force of the emotions she was still keeping locked down. "Ye did that on purpose."

Morag affected a shocked expression, slamming a hand to her breast. "Did ye hear that, Ma?"

"I did." Lorna's smirk disappeared now, replaced by a stern look. "I was going to see if I could dig up some scraps for her from the spence ... but not now." The head cook gestured to her daughters. "Come, girls ... let us retire."

Lorna moved across the floor, toward the stairwell that led upstairs. A moment later, her daughters followed. Bringing up the rear, Alba cast a glance over her shoulder, her gaze flicking from the mess at Bonnie's feet to her upset face. Alba's brow furrowed then. However, Lorna turned and flashed Bonnie a toothy smile. "Make sure ye tidy that up properly, lass. We don't want to attract rodents, do we?"

And with that, Lorna, Morag, and Alba departed from the kitchens.

Bonnie watched them go, her pulse pounding in her ears. "Too late," she whispered to the snapping hearth. "The queen of rats already presides over these kitchens."

Her hands clenched tighter then, her fingernails biting into her palms. *I should have said it to my aunt's face.*

God's bones, how she wanted to. But then she remembered the few times she'd stood up for herself over the years.

It always ended badly for her. Once Lorna had slapped her—had hit her so hard, she'd fallen to the floor. She'd done it in front of a kitchen full of servants, but not one had defended her. The head cook had a blistering temper and was known to lash out with a wooden spoon when vexed. The others had just been relieved they'd escaped her wrath.

If Bonnie gave her own temper free rein, if she said all the things were writhing in her chest, Lorna and Morag would make her life even more difficult than it already was.

Her existence here at Stirling would become unbearable.

Staring down at the ruins of her supper, while her empty belly growled, Bonnie's self-control frayed. There were times when the fear of reprisal almost wasn't enough to hold her back.

And this had been one such instance.

She'd been brought up by her aunt, had grown up alongside her cousins, yet despite that the four of them shared the same blood, there was no affection.

Family looked out for each other, cared for each other. But in her five and twenty winters, Bonnie had known very little kindness or warmth from her kin.

She knuckled away the tears that now trickled down her face. Then, trembling, she grabbed a ladle from where it hung on the wall and knelt on the dirty straw— and started to clean up the mess Morag had made.

3: SOME THINGS ARE BEST LEFT IN THE PAST

"WHAT ARE YE doing, lass?"

Bonnie glanced up, from where she was cleaning up the last vestiges of stew, to see a short, heavyset woman with greying black hair standing at the foot of the stairs.

"Ainslie," Bonnie greeted her, forcing a smile. "Don't mind me ... I just had a spill, that's all."

Ainslie Boyd, the keep's head laundress, made a clucking sound and bustled across the floor toward her. "What happened?"

"I dropped my supper." Bonnie's cheeks warmed as she lied. It was easier not to tell the truth. Ainslie was her friend—a kindly woman with a bawdy sense of humor that Bonnie had always appreciated—yet she didn't want to see pity light in her eyes when she told her of her aunt and cousin's bullying.

Ainslie halted, her warm blue eyes settling upon Bonnie's face. The way her expression clouded then made Bonnie's stomach clench. Of course, the woman knew she was lying—yet she was too kind to say so. "Oh, lass, so ye haven't eaten?" she asked softly.

Bonnie shook her head.

"And ye've been weeping," Ainslie observed.

Bonnie waved her concern away. "I'll be fine ... it's just been a long day."

"Well, ye can't go to bed hungry," Ainslie said briskly. She then headed toward the spence at the far end of the kitchens. "I'll fetch ye a morsel."

Bonnie rose to her feet, alarm rippling through her. "But my aunt—"

"Don't fash, lass ... Lorna won't notice anything's missing."

Bonnie wasn't so sure. Her aunt had an eye like a goshawk on the hunt for such things. Nevertheless, she followed Ainslie to the large room beyond the kitchen, where shelves covered the walls. The air was filled with the smells of ripening cheese and cured meats, and the musty scent of grain.

"Here, let's have ourselves some cheese and oatcakes," Ainslie announced, helping herself to a wheel of cheese that had already been started, and a basket of oatcakes that had been left over from the noon meal. The older woman then flashed Bonnie a cheeky smile. "I was feeling a bit peckish myself ... so I waited until I saw Lorna and the twins retire to their quarters before coming down here."

Bonnie's gaze widened.

Unlike her, Ainslie wasn't afraid of the head cook. Of course, she was older than Lorna, and her husband was chamberlain of the keep.

Following Ainslie out of the spence to the table that dominated the kitchens, Bonnie took a seat opposite her, watching as she cut a few thin slices of cheese. Her friend's hands were reddened and chapped—not surprising since she spent her days working with her team of laundresses. The mix of hot water, ash, and lye they used to clean clothing and linen was hard on the skin.

Nervousness fluttered in Bonnie's belly as she took an oatcake with a piece of cheese from Ainslie. "Are ye *certain,* no one will notice this?"

The head laundress met her eye before winking. "Don't worry, when I come down here tomorrow morning, I'll let Lorna know I raided her spence ... I don't want her blaming ye."

Bonnie's lips parted. Once again, Ainslie's boldness awed her—she wished *she* could be so daring.

Ainslie's gaze held hers then. "What *really* happened to yer supper?"

The moment drew out before Bonnie sighed, her shoulders slumping. There wasn't any point in hiding the truth. "Morag deliberately dropped it on the floor."

Ainslie's brow furrowed. Silence fell between the two women as they started on their oatcakes and cheese—but after she'd finished her second oatcake, Ainslie finally replied, "Someone should take a stick to that lass."

Bonnie snorted. "Aye, although she just follows her mother's example."

Ainslie's frown deepened. "I swear Lorna gets sourer by the year," she muttered. "She was always sullen, even when she was young. Yer mother was the prettiest of the two sisters, yet when Lorna wed the head groom, she was well pleased with herself. Meanwhile, yer mother ..." Ainslie's voice trailed off then, and a shadow fell over her blue eyes.

"Disgraced herself," Bonnie murmured, completing the sentence. She knew little of Greer Fraser, except that she'd been a lass of uncommon beauty, who'd foolishly had a dalliance with a man far above her rank. The liaison had ended with an unwanted pregnancy, and then she'd died shortly after giving birth. Bonnie had been saved, yet her mother had bled out. There hadn't been anything the midwife, or the healer, could do to save her.

Bonnie's oatcake turned to ashes in her mouth, and she swallowed with difficulty. "No one speaks of my mother," she whispered then. "It's as if everyone wishes to forget her."

Ainslie stiffened. "Some things are best left in the past," she replied, her voice unusually subdued. "It was tragic what happened to her ... and folk tend to get superstitious about such things."

Bonnie put down the oatcake she'd been eating, her gaze pinning her friend to the spot. "No one ever speaks of my father either," she pointed out. "I have no idea who he is."

"None of us know," Ainslie replied softly. "There were rumors, of course ..."

Bonnie's breathing quickened. This was a first—until now she'd heard *nothing* at all about her father's identity. Her questions usually met a wall of silence. She leaned forward. "Rumors of who?"

Ainslie's blue eyes unfocused then, as if she were suddenly back in the past, reliving the events of five and twenty years previous, when wee Bonnie Fraser had come squalling into the world, motherless and unwanted. "He" —Ainslie began, before catching herself. She shook her head then, a faint blush rising to her plump cheeks— "It's best not to indulge in idle speculation," she said quickly. "It won't help ye."

Disappointment pressed down on Bonnie's breastbone at these words. For a moment there, she'd thought Ainslie was about to reveal something important, yet—just like her aunt did whenever Bonnie questioned her about her origins—she went silent.

"God's troth," she muttered. "Everyone is so secretive ... ye would think my father was the King of Scotland."

The head laundress snorted at such a ridiculous notion. "Lorna wanted to give ye to the nuns at Iona, ye know?" She favored Bonnie with a brittle smile as she subtly steered their conversation in another direction. "But Duncan Stewart wouldn't hear of it. He insisted she take ye into her household and raise ye as her own."

Despite her simmering frustration, Bonnie's mouth curved. The seneschal of Stirling Castle was a good man; he'd always treated her well. Nonetheless, as much as a nun's life didn't appeal to her, she wondered if she'd have been happier growing up elsewhere.

"My aunt blamed me when Uncle Ennis left," Bonnie admitted then, her faint smile fading. "She said I put too much strain on their marriage."

Ennis would have stayed if it weren't for ye, her aunt had once raged at her. *What man wants a bastard supping at the same table as his bairns? Ye robbed my girls of a father!*

Bonnie lifted her oatcake to her lips once more. A moment later, she lowered it. Although she hadn't eaten much, talking about her aunt dulled her appetite.

"That had nothing to do with ye, lass," Ainslie replied softly.

Bonnie nodded. She appreciated Ainslie's candor. Despite the age gap, a strong bond had developed between them over the years. Nonetheless, there were certain subjects they rarely broached: one was Bonnie's parents. Yet Ainslie showed no such reluctance when it came to criticizing the head cook of Stirling Castle.

"Lorna has no power over ye these days," Ainslie went on, brushing crumbs off her ample bosom. "Remember that ye answer to the seneschal ... not to her."

Bonnie stifled a flinch. Ainslie meant well, yet her bluntness stung. "That's easier said than done," she murmured. "She's still my aunt, my elder ... and some chains are hard to break."

Leaving the kitchens behind, Bonnie climbed the stairs to the upper levels of the keep. After sharing the oatcakes and cheese, she and Ainslie cleared up the crumbs and wiped the table down. The head laundress had then returned to the chambers she shared with her husband, while Bonnie took a lantern and made the steep climb up the servants' stairs toward her own quarters.

Up and up, she went, making her way to the west tower. There she took another spiraling stairwell and finally reached the tiny attic—her sleeping space ever since she was old enough to leave her aunt.

Climbing the ladder into the loft, Bonnie shivered. There was no hearth up here, and the night outside was cold. Nonetheless, she was used to the cold and damp, and she put up with it gladly if it meant she slept apart from her aunt and cousins.

Moonlight filtered in through the tiny window, bringing with it an icy draft. The sacking Bonnie usually hung over it had come loose, and so she set down her flickering lantern, shuffled across to the window, and replaced the covering.

Then, sitting back on her heels, she surveyed her tiny chamber.

It really was cramped, yet it was her sanctuary.

From when she retired every evening, to when she rose with the dawn, no one made any demands on her. In here, she could float away on daydreams, could pretend she were someone else.

Bonnie had little in the way of possessions. A sheepskin and a pile of coarse blankets made up her bed. Next to it was a low stool, where a bone comb—the only thing of her mother's she owned—and a bouquet of dried lavender sat. Its sharp scent wafted across the attic, a familiar, comforting smell.

Bonnie moved over to the bed and placed the lantern upon the stool. She then unlaced her kirtle and wriggled out of it, hanging it up on the wall next to another, identical, plain brown kirtle. They were her only dresses. Clad in her léine and shivering from the chill, Bonnie hurriedly unbound her hair from where she kept it pulled back from her face during the day. She then combed out her red curls as best she could.

Teeth chattering, she pulled the shutter down over the lantern and climbed into bed, hauling the covers high up around her chin. She'd managed to get her hands on a few extra blankets this winter, and it made all the difference. The weight of them pushed her down into the sheepskin. The sensation was comforting; she felt cocooned, embraced.

Lying there, Bonnie heard the familiar pattering of tiny feet in the rafters above her head. The rats and mice who shared her attic were busy tonight. Her mouth curved. The rodents didn't bother her. At least *they* let her be.

And as she often did, when she was alone, Bonnie closed her eyes and imagined that she wasn't a lowly chambermaid tucked up in her cold and drafty attic. It was a habit she'd started years earlier, a way of escaping the drudgery of her life.

"Lady Fraser," she murmured, her mouth lifting at the corners.

Aye, instead of the bastard daughter of a disgraced cook, she was a lady-in-waiting to Queen Mary herself and resided in one of the comfortable bedchambers on the lower floors. A warm hearth would crackle all night, and she would recline on soft sheets with lilac-scented pillows. A maid waited on her, of course, brushing out her hair every eve, as the pair of them gossiped about the day's events.

"I shall wear the sea-green surcote today," she continued, as she imagined her maid helping her dress in the morning. "The one that matches my eyes."

She was now a well-dressed lady, walking through the hallways of Stirling Castle. And tonight, she passed the tall man with flowing white-blond hair—and this time, their gazes met.

She altered her fantasy then. Now they were wedded. They walked in the gardens of Stirling Castle together, arm in arm, supped together, and talked for hours. And then later, in the privacy of their bedchamber, Bonnie's laird peeled off her gown while murmuring endearments.

A sigh gusted out of Bonnie as she imagined what it would feel like to have his lips upon her skin—to have him kiss his way down her body.

4: A FOOLISH WISH

CARRYING A HEAVY basket filled with firewood, Bonnie crossed the inner close. It was a brisk morning outdoors, and the woodsmoke-laced wind that feathered across her cheeks held a sting. Above her reared the dun-colored keep, its battlements edging the pale-blue sky.

She and the other chambermaids had even more rooms than usual to service at present. It would be another exhausting day. The keep was abuzz, full of laughter and excited voices, while the inner close was a flurry of activity. Burly men carried barrels of mead, wine, and ale into the great hall. Page boys rushed by, running errands for the various lairds in residence, and servants bustled around the fringes of the courtyard, hurrying to make preparations for the night's ball.

A smile tugged at Bonnie's mouth. The excitement was contagious. It made her forget the weight of the basket that caused her arms to ache, and the tongue-lashing Lorna had given her earlier before Ainslie interrupted—informing her that it was *her* who'd helped herself to oatcakes and cheese from the spence.

But when she caught sight of a tall, broad-shouldered figure standing before the steps of the great hall, her step faltered.

Deep in conversation with an older man with grizzled dark hair, the stranger stood at the bottom of the steps leading up into the hall.

The Lord forgive her, he was a sight.

Bonnie couldn't help it—she gawked.

In daylight, the silver-blond of his hair gleamed, contrasting against the light tan of his skin and the dark leather gambeson and braies he wore. The man held himself with the easy confidence of someone who understood his own worth.

Someone who'd never lived in the shadows.

Of course, Bonnie had seen a few lairds grace the courtyards and corridors of Stirling Castle over the years, yet there was something about this man that scattered her wits and made her heart pound. Aye, he was handsome, but it was more than that. He had *presence*.

Oblivious to Bonnie's stare, he replied to something his companion had just said, the masculine rumble of his voice traveling across the cobbled space of the inner close. His expression was stern this morning, yet it didn't detract from his attractiveness.

Bonnie's heart kicked hard against her ribs. There was a maturity in his stance and in the low timbre of his voice; he was no callow youth. It was likely he had a wife and brood of bairns.

Did some lucky woman get to listen to that rich, deep voice every day?

Heat flushed over her then. Letting herself daydream when she lay abed in her attic was one thing. Yet she couldn't let fantasies take over while she was working. It wouldn't do to get caught staring at the king's guests like a mooncalf.

Yet she couldn't seem to drag her gaze away.

An instant later, her toe caught on the edge of a cobblestone—and the next thing she knew, Bonnie sprawled, face-down, in the yard. The basket flew from her hands, the wood spilling out.

Satan's cods! She couldn't believe she'd been so clumsy.

Knees stinging, for she'd surely skinned them, Bonnie pushed herself off the cobbles and scrambled forward, frantically retrieving the scattered wood.

Maybe if she kept her gaze fixed on the ground, no one would see her.

However, that wasn't to be.

"Are ye hurt, lass?" The deep voice she had been listening to just moments earlier intruded then—and Bonnie knew without even raising her chin that the handsome stranger was looming over her. "That was quite a tumble ye took."

"Fine, thank ye," Bonnie gasped, deliberately keeping her gaze downcast. Her cheeks were on fire now. As much as she'd fantasized about speaking with the man, she hadn't thought it would ever happen—especially in such embarrassing circumstances.

She couldn't look his way. Instead, she fervently wished the ground would open up and swallow her whole.

"Here ... let me help ye with those." There was a smile in his voice, and her cheeks burned hotter still.

And then, to her horror, the man hunkered down before her and started retrieving the logs. Shooting him a furtive glance, Bonnie saw that, indeed, his mouth was curved in an expression of wry amusement. Fortunately, he'd looked away at that moment, and so she was spared meeting his eye.

Heart pounding, she jerked her own gaze downward and continued collecting the wood.

Time seemed to slow down then, and her hands fumbled with the task.

And when the last of the logs and sticks were tucked back in the basket, Bonnie's heart was beating so fast that she was starting to feel dizzy.

"There ye go, lass," the stranger said finally. She could feel his gaze upon the crown of her head, yet Bonnie kept her face downcast. "Are ye sure ye haven't skinned yer knees?"

"No," she rasped. "Thank ye ... again."

With that, she grasped the basket and lurched to her feet. Then, clutching it to her breast, she fled across the inner close to the steps that led into the servant's entrance to the keep as if Satan's demons were at her heels.

It was nearing noon when Bonnie finished setting the last of the hearths in the bedchambers. Ash and flecks of wood dusted the bodice and skirt of her kirtle, and her hands were sticky with sap. Glancing down at herself, Bonnie's lips thinned. She'd have to wash off at the well outdoors before going down to the kitchens for the noon meal. Lorna and Morag never missed an opportunity to deride her, and she didn't want to give them an easy excuse.

Bonnie didn't need any further humiliation today; she was still smarting from the incident earlier in the morning.

Indeed, both her knees were grazed. She'd had to sponge away the blood before continuing with her chores.

But her sore knees didn't bother her as much as her bruised pride.

Coward. She'd fled like a frightened hare from the inner close. She hadn't even dared to meet the man's eye. The opportunity to meet him had been right there, yet she'd shied from it.

Did she believe herself so unworthy? Her daydreams were safe, of course. The reality of being in the proximity of the mysterious stranger had scattered her wits like the firewood strewn over the cobbles.

Her embarrassing reaction to the incident vexed her.

Inwardly berating herself, Bonnie exited the last of the chambers, empty wicker basket under one arm—and nearly collided with a group of ladies-in-waiting.

Clad in fine surcotes, jewels at their throats, with their hair swept into elaborate styles, the women resembled a flock of beautiful vividly-hued birds. Their voices were high and excited, their laughter tinkling like water from the fountains in the gardens encircling the keep.

"This will be a night to remember," one of them trilled to her companions. She didn't notice the chambermaid who flattened herself against the door to let them pass by. It was as if she were invisible. "The first masquerade ball ever to be held at Stirling Castle."

Bonnie's eyes widened. *A masquerade ball?* She'd never heard of such a thing.

The fact that the ladies ignored her wasn't surprising. In the years Bonnie had serviced the chambers of this keep, few high-born female guests acknowledged her. In contrast, she'd had to deal with lusty gazes and unwanted groping from various *male* guests many a time.

She noted then that the women's arms were full of baskets spilling over with colorful objects. Tassels and ribbons trailed behind them.

The ladies-in-waiting disappeared, leaving a cloud of expensive scent in their wake—and Bonnie was about to depart in the opposite direction toward the servants' stairs when a flash of pink and purple on the floor caught her eye.

One of the ladies had dropped something.

Putting down her basket, Bonnie stepped forward and stooped to pick it up.

It was a mask, one fashioned to cover just the eyes and the top half of the face. Covered in a dark rose-colored satiny fabric, the mask was decorated with two large purple thistles.

Breath catching once more, she tentatively ran a fingertip across the intricate embroidery. The mask was lovely, and she was loath to get it dirty.

She hesitated then and glanced after the ladies.

I should go after them and return this.

But she didn't. Instead, she stood there, her feet rooted to the spot.

Bonnie had never held something so fine before, and she didn't want to let it go. Her clothing was dull brown, and she'd never owned a brooch or jewelry of any kind. This was too beautiful to give up.

Magpie, she chided herself. *This isn't yers ... give it back.*

Yet still she didn't hurry after the ladies, didn't call out to them. Moments passed before she tucked the mask carefully into her apron. Then she turned, picked up her basket, and made her way toward the servants' stairs.

"The Virgin be praised, is this what folk wear to a masquerade ball?" Ainslie lowered the mask before giving a rueful shake of her head. "Angus has been telling me about the fuss the queen and her ladies have been making about tonight's festivities." The head laundress's mouth quirked then. "It will be quite a sight, I'd say."

Bonnie huffed a sigh. "If only I could attend ... and see it for myself."

Ainslie's expression sobered at this admission, her blue eyes shadowing. "Is that what ye wish, lass?"

The two friends sat in the chamberlain's quarters. It was shortly after the noon meal, and instead of retiring to her attic for a brief nap as she usually did, Bonnie had paid Ainslie a visit. They sat before the flickering fire enjoying a brief reprieve before the afternoon chores began.

Although Ainslie oversaw the team of laundresses and didn't have to work as hard as they did, she wasn't a woman to sit idle for long.

Bonnie had been relieved to find her here.

Favoring the older woman with an embarrassed smile, she shrugged. "Don't mind me ... it is a foolish wish, I know."

"It's not foolish," Ainslie murmured, running a fingertip over the embroidered thistles as Bonnie had earlier. "Every woman desires to step out of her life sometimes ... to be someone else for a short while. To be *admired*."

Bonnie arched an eyebrow.

Anslie's mouth curved. "Och, aye ... even me." She then glanced down at her plump body and sighed. "I was quite comely once, ye know ... with a figure much like yer own. Angus couldn't keep his hands off me."

Bonnie's cheeks warmed at this frank admission. Even now, after over three decades of marriage, Angus and Ainslie Boyd were a happy couple. Last Yule, the chamberlain had passionately kissed his wife before the Yule bonfire in Stirling town, for all to see.

Ainslie's attention dropped once more to the mask. "The kirtle and surcote I got married in were the color of thistle. They would have matched this perfectly."

"Really?"

"Aye, I still have the gowns too ... would ye like to see them?"

Bonnie's breathing hitched. "Ye still have yer wedding outfit?"

Ainslie flashed her a grin. "Of course." Handing back the mask, the head laundress got up and made her way across the chamber, ducking behind a hanging that separated the living and sleeping spaces. Bonnie heard her rummaging around in trunks, and a few muttered curses, before she exclaimed. "Here they are!"

Moments later, Ainslie appeared, shaking out two long purple garments. She made a tutting sound. "Heavens, the moths have been at the surcote!"

Bonnie's lips parted as she rose to her feet too and stepped forward to take a closer look. "Oh, Ainslie," she breathed, taking hold of the surcote's heavy damask skirt. Indeed, there were a few small holes there, yet they couldn't detract from the gown's beauty. "Ye must have looked like a princess wearing this."

"I did," Ainslie admitted, her blue eyes misting as she caressed the richly patterned silk that gleamed in the firelight. "I caused quite a stir wearing such a dress." She gave a soft snort then. "Although the kirtle *was* a bit tight across the bodice ... and I kept worrying my paps were going to burst free."

Bonnie, who was examining the long flared sleeves of the surcote now, snorted a laugh. She shifted her attention to the kirtle's bodice then. Indeed, it was low and daring and laced up at the front with rose-colored ribbons. "Did ye have these made in Stirling?"

"No, Angus used a seamstress in Edinburgh … cost him three months' wages, it did."

"I'm not surprised," Bonnie murmured. "How *I* would like to wear something so beautiful."

A pause followed, and when Bonnie glanced up, she marked the way Ainslie watched her, intently now. "Ye can try them on, if ye like?"

Bonnie waved her away and withdrew her hand from where she'd been tracing her fingers over the patterning that covered the bodice. "I should get back to work."

"Aye, and so should I. But not until I see what ye look like in these." Ainslie held up the surcote in one hand and the kirtle that went under it in the other and shook them. She then jerked her chin toward the hanging. "Go on … the quicker ye humor me, the quicker we can get back to our chores."

Inside the privacy of the chamberlain's sleeping area, Bonnie smoothed her hands over the skirt of the purple surcote she'd just donned over the kirtle of the same hue. Then, drawing in a nervous breath, she pushed aside the hanging and returned to where Ainslie was waiting for her by the fire.

Her friend's eyes snapped wide, her face slackening with surprise.

Bonnie halted, stiffening. Heat then flushed over her. "It doesn't suit me, does it?"

Recovering, Ainslie flashed her a beaming smile. She then stepped forward and deftly laced the front of the kirtle for Bonnie. "They fit ye like a glove … better than they ever did me, I'd warrant." She shook her head then. "I'm just taken aback, that's all. I've always known ye were comely … but in that gown, ye shine like a jewel." Ainslie recovered the mask from the chair next to the fire. "Here … put this on too, and I shall fetch a looking glass so ye can see what I mean."

Bonnie did as bid, even if she was starting to feel a little uneasy. As exciting as this experience was, she was skiving. Chambers had to be swept out and linen changed. She shouldn't be indulging in such frivolity.

Yet Ainslie seemed to have forgotten about the tasks that awaited them both. It was as if she were a lass again, preparing for her friend's wedding day. She bustled off, in search of a looking glass. In the meantime, Bonnie put on the mask, fastening it in place with the pink ribbons provided.

And when Ainslie returned, she grinned. "Mother Mary, ye are a sight! Here, see for yerself." She held up the looking glass before adding, "The gown looks as if it were made just for ye!"

Bonnie surveyed the woman staring back at her, and her breathing stilled.

She didn't recognize herself.

Ainslie was right. The surcote and the kirtle visible beneath it fitted her perfectly. The bodice skimmed low, showing far more cleavage than she'd ever dared to before. The garments hugged her mid-section and waist before flaring out into full skirts that rustled around her legs when she moved. The embroidered hems of the surcote's long sleeves brushed her knuckles.

And with the mask in place, she looked as if she were ready for the masquerade ball.

As if reading her thoughts, Ainslie gave a wistful sigh. "Looking as ye do, ye wouldn't be out of place tonight, dancing with the lords and ladies."

Bonnie's pulse leaped, and she glanced the head laundress's way. Ainslie wore a wistful expression.

Pulse fluttering, Bonnie looked back at her reflection. And then, just for a few moments, she imagined what it would be like to grace the interior of the great hall of Stirling Castle, to dance the evening away with the guests.

It had seemed like an impossibility just moments before—but now, dressed as she was, could she wish it into reality?

She tore her gaze away from the looking glass then and met Ainslie's eye. "What if I did?"

5: IF WISHES WERE HORSES, BEGGARS WOULD RIDE

FOR A MOMENT, Ainslie merely stared back at her. And then her smile faded. "Och, lass ... some things should remain fantasy. It's safer that way."

The fragile flame of hope that had flickered to life in Bonnie's breast guttered.

Of course, as much as Ainslie had enjoyed this game, she'd known it was just a bit of entertainment. It reminded her of her youth, of the excitement of being a bride and feeling like a princess in a beautiful dress.

But Bonnie had gotten carried away.

Swallowing, she glanced back at her reflection, committing the sight of the lovely gown and the mask that, indeed, matched it perfectly, to memory.

"Of course," she whispered, her voice catching. "Forget I said that ... my aunt is right about me. I'm a goose-wit, and my head is full of foolish notions."

"Lorna talks rot," Ainslie replied, her voice tightening. And when Bonnie glanced back at her, she saw that her friend was frowning. "But to disguise yerself and attend a masquerade ball is too great a risk." Tension flickered across her face. "What if ye were discovered?"

Bonnie managed a wan smile. "Aye ... forget I ever said anything, Ainslie," she murmured. She then reached up and untied the mask. "I suppose I should return this."

Something tugged deep in her chest at the thought, yet she chastised herself. *It doesn't belong to ye!*

The head laundress nodded. "Leave the mask with me, lass ... I'll see that it finds its way to the ladies' solar." Her mouth curved then, although her gaze remained somber. "No one shall know it went missing."

Bonnie handed the mask over, even as her shoulders slumped.

She knew her friend was just looking after her—Ainslie was practical, not a dreamer like Bonnie—even so, disappointment crushed her throat.

The mask wasn't hers, yet she longed to keep it.

Ye have yer mother's reckless spirit. Her aunt's shrill voice tormented her then—as it had two winters earlier when Bonnie formed a liaison with one of the men-at-arms. Their dalliance was short-lived, especially when the guard was posted elsewhere. Yet when Lorna had heard of it, she'd upbraided Bonnie in front of the whole kitchen. *She too was impulsive, and it was her ruin. It will be yers too, mark my words.*

Bonnie's belly clenched.

As much as she resented her aunt, Lorna did have a point. She wished for things above her. For years, she'd thought her daydreams harmless, yet she realized now they weren't.

They made her long for things she could never have. She often got so lost in her fantasies that the boundaries between what was real and what was make-believe got blurred. She came to believe certain things were possible—when they weren't. Scrubbing chamber pots, emptying hearths, and making beds were her world. There was no escaping it.

Reaching up, she started to loosen the laces of her bodice. "Thank ye, Ainslie," she murmured. "Now, I really *do* have to get back to work."

Bonnie heaved a sigh of relief as she carried the last load of dirty linen down to the laundry.

Finally.

Since dallying with Ainslie earlier, she'd had to make up for lost time, and was now exhausted after hurriedly changing beds and sweeping out chambers. The keep was so busy now that it had been difficult to keep out of the guests' way. One of the lairds' wives had just scolded her for not having her bedchamber serviced early enough for her liking.

Entering the laundry—an annex on the ground floor of the keep—Bonnie peered through the clouds of steam at the flushed cheeks of the lasses who were busy scrubbing clothes on wooden wash boards or pummeling them with a laundry bat.

Ainslie was instructing one of the laundresses, but upon Bonnie's entrance, she glanced over and caught her friend's eye. She then smiled before favoring her with a conspirator's wink.

Bonnie tried to smile back, even as a sickly sensation washed over her. That wink likely meant that she'd managed to replace the mask in the ladies' solar without being spotted. Suddenly, it felt as if a stone lay in Bonnie's belly; a moment later, the back of her eyes started to prickle.

Curse it, she wasn't going to weep over such a thing, was she?

She was even more addlepated than she thought.

Keeping a brave smile plastered upon her face, while she blinked rapidly to stop the tears from spilling over, Bonnie grabbed a stack of clean linen, swiveled, and marched out of the laundry.

She needed to get ahold of herself.

Even so, as she made her way across the inner close, back toward the keep, Bonnie spied page boys traipsing in and out of the great hall. Those going in were carrying armloads of decorations—bunting and streamers to festoon the cavernous space. A woman's laughter filtered out from inside the hall, echoing across the courtyard.

No doubt some of the queen's ladies-in-waiting were overseeing the decorating within.

The weight in Bonnie's stomach grew heavier still, and her vision blurred.

What she would give just to have a glimpse inside the hall this eve, to see the splendor within. Those born into a higher rank took all of this for granted, for it was their right to enjoy such luxury, yet she wouldn't.

She'd commit every detail to memory to be cherished for the rest of her days.

Bonnie sighed then. What was it that her aunt often said when one of the twins wished for something beyond her ken?

If wishes were horses, beggars would ride.

Aye, some things were impossible, and it was foolish to yearn for them.

Jaw clenching, Bonnie turned her gaze from the yawning doors of the great hall and hurried on.

"The guests will be arriving soon, Ma," Morag's voice carried through the busy kitchen. "Can Alba and I go out to watch them?"

The head cook turned from where she'd been directing two lads who were spit-roasting a suckling pig over one of the great hearths. Both boys wore pinched expressions, for Lorna had been criticizing them. Her long face was flushed from the heat, her expression harassed.

Nonetheless, her features softened just a little as her gaze settled upon her daughter. "Aye, lass ... don't take too long mind." She then glanced over at where Bonnie was vigorously stirring batter for honey cakes that would be served for the banquet. She didn't usually help in the kitchen, yet with such a large banquet being served, every spare servant had been enlisted to assist. "Yer cousin will finish making those tarts."

Morag gave a high-pitched squeal of excitement at this news and cast aside the bowl of winter-store apples she'd been peeling for the pies. She then wiped her hands on her apron and grinned at her twin. "Come on!"

Around them, some of the kitchen hands stopped working; their expressions tightened in resentment none of them would dare to voice.

Oblivious, Morag cast Bonnie a triumphant look, her gaze gleaming. "We expect all the tarts to be filled by the time we return."

Bonnie stiffened. It was bad enough that her aunt treated her like a minion to be ordered about at will. Yet she balked at her cousin doing the same.

"I'm busy making honey cakes," she replied, her tone clipped.

"Hand that over to Malcolm, and do as my daughter says," Lorna instructed, her tone distracted as she moved over to inspect the spit-roasting pigs once more.

Bonnie stopped stirring the batter. She then reluctantly passed the bowl to the lad who'd been feeding wood onto the fires. Malcolm didn't look any happier than she was about this.

Actually, most of the kitchen servants were now favoring Alba and Morag with jaundiced looks as they abandoned their work, stripped off their aprons, and hurried from the kitchen.

Like Bonnie, they were *all* curious to see the costumes and masks that the guests would don for this evening. There would be many attendees, and those who lived nearby were arriving by carriage now.

But only the head cook's daughters were allowed to view the spectacle.

Mouth compressed, Bonnie started work on the apples. There were many tarts to fill, and she had to work quickly lest the fruit turn brown.

Wordlessly one of the kitchen lasses, Fiona, stepped up to help her.

"Ye aren't needed there, Fi!" Lorna had just turned from the hearth and spied the girl reaching for one of the apples. "The boiled turnips are ready. Get to mashing them ... and make sure ye add a decent amount of butter and cream."

Abashed, Fiona slunk off to do as bid.

Bonnie was sliding the first batch of sealed pies into the oven when the twins returned to the kitchen.

"Oh, Ma, it was splendid," Morag chimed as she replaced her apron.

"Aye, ye should see their masks," Alba added. "One of the lairds wore one that made him look like a barn-owl."

"And his wife had eagle feathers on hers."

These comments made gazes swivel in the twins' direction. Bonnie glanced their way too.

Morag met her eye then, her attention going to the neat rows of pies ready to go in the oven. Her mouth pursed as if she was disappointed to find that Bonnie had indeed completed the task.

"I'm surprised to see only the first batch in," Morag sniped before casting Lorna a sidelong look. "We don't want to keep the king waiting for his apple tarts, Ma. What if Bonnie has put us behind?"

"If the king has to wait for his sweets, it'll be yer doing, not mine." The words slipped unbidden from Bonnie's lips before she could help herself. "Ye could have helped me, but ye preferred to idle instead."

Silence fell in the kitchens.

Moments earlier, it had been a flurry of activity—the clang of iron pots, the rhythmic thud of blades chopping, and the sizzle of roasting meat had filled the space.

But not now.

Bonnie's heart beat like a smith's hammer as she stared down her cousin.

It wasn't wise to speak up thus, and she knew it. Yet she'd been unable to stem the resentment that bubbled up inside her. The events of the past couple of days had frayed her patience. Suddenly, she could no longer hold her tongue.

The moments slid by before Morag shattered the quiet, her voice shrill. "Did ye hear what she said to me, Ma?"

6: PROVOCATIVE TALK

"WHAT A FEAST," Lennox murmured, his gaze traveling down the table to the array of platters the page boys were setting out before them. "I don't think I've ever seen the like … even at Castle Varrich."

"Neither have I," Iver agreed distractedly. Actually, he'd been wishing he was enjoying a quiet supper back in his chamber—but even he had to admit the banquet was a lavish one. Blinking, he too surveyed the spread before them. Two suckling pigs with apples stuffed into their mouths, venison pies, and braised lamb all graced the table, with a magnificent roast swan taking center stage. There were also baskets of different kinds of breads, tureens of spiced stews, buttered and mashed turnip, and platters of braised greens.

Aye, it was impressive, yet he still wished he could have begged off attending.

"Just as well I haven't eaten much today then." Lennox rubbed his flat stomach before holding up his pewter goblet so that a passing page boy could fill it with rich French wine. "This should be a banquet to remember."

"It should." A big and broad-shouldered man with an unruly mane of black hair, shot through with grey, and penetrating grey-blue eyes seated next to Lennox spoke up then. Colin Campbell, the Lord of Glenorchy, was well into his fifth decade yet as hale as a man half his age. His gaze narrowed as he swept it down the rows of trestle tables that filled the great hall. "Especially since the king has invited a traitor to the crown."

Despite his distracted mood this eve, Iver frowned. He knew that Campbell was loyal to the Stewarts, yet making such comments in public was inflammatory.

Tensing, he glanced around, preparing himself for someone to take offense at Campbell's comment. Fortunately though, the din of conversation and the music that drifted down from the minstrels' gallery drowned out the man's words. Also, the 'traitor' in question—William Douglas—was seated well out of earshot.

The clan-chief, tall and lean with hawkish features, sat near where the king reclined in a high-backed chair. He and James were currently talking, both their expressions unreadable.

Shifting his gaze from the pair, Iver lifted his own goblet to his lips, welcoming the wine's warmth. He then glanced back at Campbell. "The king has decided to leave off talking politics until tomorrow," he reminded his companion.

The laird snorted. "Aye, well, if it were up to me, I'd strike off the conspirator's neck now and be done with it."

"I'm surprised Douglas agreed to attend these celebrations ... or the council," Lennox replied, inclining his head. "He knows the king doesn't trust him."

Iver stifled a sigh. Couldn't they leave off discussing politics, for once?

Campbell's mouth pursed. "James has promised him 'safe conduct' during his stay." His gaze shifted once more across the hall to where the Earl of Douglas was nodding at something the king had just said. "Look at him ... the treacherous bastard."

"Enough provocative talk, Colin," Iver answered, his exasperation surfacing. God's blood, this conversation was wearying. "Let's just enjoy this evening, shall we?"

Their gazes fused before Campbell's mouth curved, his gaze glinting. He then nodded. "Aye, let us appreciate this banquet ... and the fine company." His smile widened then. "There are a number of pretty lasses present, I note." He glanced over at a well-built woman with straw-colored hair, her formidable bosom spilling over the edge of her low-cut kirtle and surcote. Like many of the ladies present, she'd entered the hall wearing an elaborate mask, yet she removed it for the banquet. "Perhaps tonight will be the right occasion for ye to find yerself a wife, Mackay."

Iver took another gulp of wine, even as irritation spiked through him. *Not again.* Campbell hadn't been present the eve before when the king had questioned him. Nonetheless, it seemed that everyone in Scotland had an opinion about his position as an unwed chieftain.

He wasn't blind—he'd noted there were dozens of pretty women present this evening. But many of the younger ones had a hungry gleam in their eyes. They were husband-hunting, and Iver wouldn't be caught.

"I hear ye have become a bit of a recluse," Campbell went on, seemingly oblivious to the fact that Iver was now scowling. "A dance or two with a comely lass might sweeten yer mood."

"I don't need my mood *sweetening*," Iver growled back, even as his temper simmered. He'd been distracted and wishing he were elsewhere earlier, yet now he was vexed.

"Aye, ye have a point there," Lennox quipped. "My brother even shuns his family's company these days. He's at risk of turning into a curmudgeon." He smirked then, meeting Iver's eye. "Colin's right, why don't ye relax a little this eve, brother?"

Iver glowered back at him, his fingers tightening around the stem of his goblet. Curse Lennox, he was deliberately goading him again. Aye, it was true that Iver had started to spend increasingly more time alone over the past couple of years, but that was *his* business and no one else's.

He was tired of others having an opinion about how he lived his life. At home, his mother wouldn't stop nagging him about taking a wife every time she cornered him. Was it any surprise he sought solitude these days?

What did it matter anyway? His broch and lands prospered. Iver's kin and retainers didn't need to see his face every day. Lennox dealt with any disgruntled or feuding tenants, while Kerr kept the broch's defenses strong. And if important decisions had to be made, Iver was always available.

"There will be more guests arriving after the banquet concludes." The Lord of Glenorchy winked at Lennox. "And even more beauties to flirt with. As a widower myself, I shall be on the lookout."

Lennox's expression sobered. "I heard about yer loss, Colin," he replied, "and was sorry to learn of it."

Campbell shrugged. His heavy-featured face tensed. "Aye, well ... Aileen was always sickly." An uncomfortable silence followed before Campbell cast a lingering glance over at the well-endowed blonde once more. "I shall ensure my next wife is sturdier."

A moment later, he shifted his attention back to Iver.

Tensing, Iver took another sip of wine. He didn't like the calculating glint in the man's eye. He was beginning to rue the fact that Colin Campbell had seated himself next to them—actually, he was deeply regretting leaving home at all.

"Of course, if ye find no woman fine enough for yer tastes here, I can offer ye my daughter's hand," Campbell went on, holding Iver's gaze. "Ye would be well matched ... and fear not, Davina is a comely lass."

A shadow passed over Campbell's face then. It was brief, yet Iver marked it all the same. Mentioning his daughter had hit a nerve, yet Iver wasn't interested in discovering the reason for it.

"I told the king, and I shall repeat myself for ye, Colin," he said, allowing displeasure to creep into his voice. "I'm not looking for a wife. Not tonight. Not *ever*."

Campbell's greying brows crashed together.

"I hear that building work has been completed at Kilchurn," Lennox said then, smoothly interjecting as tension rose between the two lairds. "Is that true?"

Campbell glanced over at Iver's brother. A moment later, his disgruntled expression smoothed, and he smiled. "Aye. The castle is quite a sight too. It's a great five-floor tower house … with its courtyard protected by a high outer wall."

Despite himself, Iver was intrigued. "It's well-defended then?"

Campbell nodded. "Kilchurn perches upon a small island at the northeastern end of Loch Awe. The only way to reach it is by a low-lying causeway. If anyone wanted to lay siege to my fortress, they'd have trouble."

Lennox's gaze widened. "It must be quite a sight."

The laird of Glenorchy nodded, grinning now. It was clear he was proud of his castle. "Why don't ye lads stop off for a visit on yer way home, after these celebrations? I have some business to conduct in Stirling, yet if ye are willing to wait a few days, we can travel back together."

Iver tensed at the invitation. After Campbell's description of the castle he'd recently finished building, he did have a hankering to see it. However, the Lord of Glenorchy had just tried to push his daughter at him, and he was wary of going anywhere near her.

Iver's lips parted as he prepared to decline the offer. But his brother spoke first. "That sounds like a fine idea." Lennox flashed Iver a wide smile then. "Does it not, brother?"

Heat ignited in Iver's belly. *The devil take ye, Lennox.* Why couldn't his brother keep his mouth shut? He'd effectively backed Iver into a corner. Campbell was watching him now, his expression expectant—and since they were neighbors, it wouldn't do to upset him. As such, Iver forced a benign smile and nodded. "Aye, thank ye, Colin."

A trumpet echoed through the great hall of Stirling Castle then, cutting through the roar of excited voices. Conversation and music died away, all gazes swiveling to where King James the Second had risen from his high-backed chair.

Raising a slender hand, he waited for the last of the chatter to quieten. He then smiled. Clad in a crimson surcote, his flame-red hair brushed out around his shoulders, the young king was a striking sight.

"Lords and ladies of the realm." His voice carried across the cavernous space. "I thank ye all for gracing me with yer company on this winter's eve to mark the start of Lent." He paused then, motioning to the woman seated next to him. "And to help me celebrate my queen's nineteenth birthday."

Mary favored her husband with a gentle smile.

Lithe and as pale as moonlight, Mary was a beauty. She'd been a fine choice for a Scottish king, for she was the daughter of the Duke of Guelders, and their marriage had formed an alliance between Scotland and Flanders.

James picked up a jewel-studded goblet then and held it aloft. "Please join me in a toast to wish the queen the merriest of birthdays."

A chorus of well wishes rumbled through the hall as the guests, including Iver, obliged.

"Feast and drink to yer heart's content," the king continued. His cheeks were flushed with wine, and he was clearly enjoying his speechmaking. "And then we shall be hosting a masquerade ball … a spectacle none of us will ever forget."

More cheers followed this pronouncement, while Iver's mouth pursed. *Find someone else to attend these meetings in the future, Niel Mackay,* he thought sourly. Next time his clan-chief made such a request of him, he'd ensure he got out of it.

Of course, Niel's insistence that Iver act as his emissary was a compliment. His clan-chief appreciated the blend of diplomacy and toughness the chieftain of Dun Ugadale employed at meetings. The Mackays were a powerful Highland clan, and relations between the king and the north were often tense.

Once, Iver had enjoyed the cut and thrust of negotiations—but that seemed a lifetime ago now. He didn't have the patience for all this pomp, and he didn't want to don a mask and dance either.

James had reseated himself now, and all gazes remained upon the king while he helped himself to a sliver of swan breast.

No one would eat before he did. But the moment James took his first bite, his guests fell upon the banquet with relish.

Iver ate slowly, listening as his brother and Colin Campbell chatted like old friends. It appeared they shared a passion for boar hunting and dog breeding. In contrast to Iver, Lennox wasn't irritated by the man. Instead, he seemed charmed by him.

Yet Campbell wasn't trying to make a match between his daughter and Lennox. As the second-born son, he'd been spared all that.

Like Iver, Lennox was unwed by choice. But whereas Iver's decision was a result of disappointment, his brother's choice had more to do with his need for freedom. Lennox had no interest in shackling himself to a wife and bairns.

Brooding over the invitation his brother had just accepted on his behalf, Iver helped himself to a spoonful of rich venison stew. He'd hoped to travel directly back to Dun Ugadale after Stirling, yet a detour to Kilchurn would lengthen their journey by days.

Not only that, but Campbell would likely make another attempt to foist his daughter upon him.

7: FEAR NOT, LASS

BONNIE WAS SITTING in the empty laundry, playing with kittens, when Ainslie found her. Smoky, the keep's mouser, had just had a litter. The kittens were all varying shades of grey. Some were as pale as woodsmoke while others were the color of wood ash or pewter.

"There ye are," Ainslie halted in the doorway and braced her hands on her hips. "I've been looking for ye everywhere ... I even made the climb up to yer attic. Nearly killed me too, it did."

Bonnie managed a tight smile. She'd just finished scrubbing the last of the mountain of dirty pots and pans Lorna had given her to clean. Of course, the pert answer Bonnie had given Morag hadn't gone unpunished. Her back now ached, her hands were chapped—and hopelessness dragged down at her.

This was her life, and there was no escaping the drudgery of it.

"I didn't feel like retiring yet." Bonnie lowered her gaze then, stroking the kitten that was rolling about her lap. "I thought a visit to Smoky and her brood might cheer me up."

"And have they?"

"Aye, a little."

"I heard about what happened earlier."

Something in her friend's voice made Bonnie glance up.

Ainslie shook her head. "Och, lass, ye are a woman now. Lorna Fraser isn't yer mistress." Bonnie's mouth thinned, although Ainslie hadn't yet finished. She took a step inside the laundry, folding her arms across her ample chest. "Bullies can sniff out weakness ... they can only grasp power if ye give it to them."

Bonnie stiffened. It was easy enough for Ainslie to stand up to Lorna. The cook had no sway over her at all. Plus, she couldn't imagine anyone ever trying to boss Ainslie Boyd around; even her own husband wouldn't dare.

Heaving a sigh, Bonnie shifted her attention back to the wriggling kitten that was now trying to sink its tiny needlelike teeth into her wrist. "Ye are right," she muttered. "If things are to change ... I must be the one to act."

"Aye, lass. It's a battle only ye can wage." Ainslie pulled up a stool opposite Bonnie while the kittens tumbled between them. They sat in companionable silence for a short while before Ainslie cleared her throat. "Ye know, I have been thinking about what ye said to me earlier ... when ye tried on my wedding gown ... that ye wished to attend tonight's masquerade ball."

Bonnie huffed a bitter laugh, her gaze lifting to meet Ainslie's. "Aye, and I'm embarrassed I said something so foolish."

Ainslie's round face tensed, her brows drawing together. "It wasn't foolish, Bonnie. I was just a little taken aback. The notion was ... shocking."

"Aye." Bonnie shook her head, even as something tugged deep within her chest. "Just forget I ever suggested it."

"I'm not sure I can." A slow smile stretched Ainslie's mouth then. "They're in the midst of their banqueting ... there's still time for ye to ready yerself."

Bonnie stilled. "What?"

"Too long have ye hidden in the shadows, Bonnie Fraser. Before ye know it, life will slip by, and ye shall be an auld woman full of regrets. Tonight, I shall help ye create a memory ye will cherish for the rest of yer days." Ainslie's smile widened, even as Bonnie's heart started to pound. "Fear not, lass, ye *shall* go to that ball."

Bonnie's breathing quickened as she descended the steps to the entrance hall.

Excitement fluttered up. She couldn't believe she was doing this. She was desperately trying to keep her nerve, yet her heart was beating so hard, it felt as if it were about to take flight. Her palms were slippery with sweat, and she was breathing so shallowly that she now felt lightheaded.

Calm down, Bonnie counseled herself, *or ye shall faint before ye set foot in the great hall.*

The heavy wooden doors that would lead her out of the castle's main entrance loomed ahead now, flanked by liveried guards.

She swallowed hard and squared her shoulders as she stepped out onto the wide atrium and headed toward them.

Now was the moment of truth.

Would her disguise fool these guards, or would they see right through it and realize she was an interloper?

A chambermaid in disguise.

Lord forgive me for this deception, she thought, resisting the urge to curl her fingers into her palms. *Just give me this one evening.*

Both the guards watched her approach, their gazes glinting.

She started to sweat then. Her long skirts—which Ainslie had mended—rustled around her ankles. The kirtle, which fitted so snuggly under her surcote, suddenly felt overly tight around her ribcage. And she was aware of just how much flesh she had on show.

Ainslie had tied the rose-colored ribbon that laced the bodice into a neat bow. However, it drew the eye straight to her cleavage.

The head laundress hadn't given that mask back, after all. Instead, Ainslie had handed it over to her with a wide smile. She'd then brushed Bonnie's hair out for her before rubbing a little rose-scented oil through it. Her hair now fell in heavy, gleaming waves around her shoulders. Bonnie had suggested it was more fitting to pin it up, yet Ainslie had clucked her tongue and shaken her head. "There's no need for that, this eve … everyone is in costume. Ye look like a fairy that lives amongst the heather with yer hair tumbling over yer shoulders."

Ainslie's words had bolstered Bonnie's self-confidence. Even so, it was hard not to feel uncomfortable under the hot male stares that tracked her path now.

Bonnie lifted her chin into the air and sailed past the gawking guards. If she was pretending to be a high-born lady this eve, she needed to act the part; it wouldn't do to round her shoulders and avert her gaze as if she were ashamed of herself.

Raising her skirts a little to prevent herself from tripping, revealing the embroidered purple and pink slippers Ainslie had also loaned her, Bonnie made her way down the steps into the inner close.

It was a surprisingly mild night out. Often, a bitter wind gusted in from the north, biting through layers of clothing. But this evening, it almost felt warm, as if spring had embraced Stirling early.

Bonnie was glad it wasn't cold, for she hadn't brought a shawl with her. She had nothing fine enough to use as a wrap and had forgotten to ask Ainslie if she could borrow something.

Music drifted out of the open doors of the great hall just a few yards away. The lilting strains of a lyre and a pipe soared high into the still night.

Bonnie's heart continued to beat a tattoo against her ribs as she crossed the courtyard toward the hall.

She remembered Ainslie's parting words then.

"For this to work, ye have to be canny, lass," she'd murmured, her gaze spearing Bonnie's. "Best ye enter the hall once the banquet is done and the ball is well underway. Ye should be discreet. Say as little as possible. Tonight, ye are Lady Adair Farquharson ... of Braemar Castle." Ainslie had paused there, a smile tugging at her lips at her own cleverness. "The clan-chief is red-headed, so it should seem plausible that ye are one of his brood. If anyone asks, ye are staying with relatives in Stirling."

Bonnie had flashed her a nervous smile in reply. "Ye seem to have an answer for everything."

"I do ... but pay attention, lass. As I said, ye are to slip in when the dancing has started, and ye are to remain mysterious. Don't, for the love of our Savior, take off yer mask ... for any reason. Don't linger too long either. Leave well before the witching hour, while the revelry is still going on, and return to yer attic unseen."

Ainslie was right, of course. She had to be careful. Bonnie climbed the steps to the great hall while nerves danced like overexcited sprites in her belly. Her heart was beating so hard now, she was starting to feel nauseated.

This was it—she really *was* going to the ball.

Two more guards flanked the entrance. They nodded at Bonnie as she walked by them.

An instant later, she stepped into another world.

Bonnie gazed around her.

Of course, having grown up within the walls of Stirling Castle, she'd been inside the great hall before—and had scrubbed its floors several times. Yet she'd never seen it like this.

Wonder tightened her throat as she took in the brightly colored streamers that cascaded from the heavy beams arching overhead, and the swirling crowd of costumed lairds and ladies that filled the hall.

She hadn't expected to see such elaborate costumes and masks. A woman, dressed like an ice-queen in flowing silver and a glittering mask, floated past her, on the arm of a hulking man with a wolfskin about his broad-shoulders and a matching mask.

Gazing around, Bonnie suddenly felt under-dressed. Earlier, she'd thought Ainslie's thistle-colored gown was splendid, yet it seemed drab compared to the costly fabrics, jewels, exotic feathers and furs, and fanciful designs that surrounded her.

Bonnie's lips parted slightly before she realized she was gawking like an idiot. Shutting her mouth, she moved around the edge of the hall. In the past, she'd cringed before these people, had lowered her gaze, and shuffled out of their way.

But even in her fine surcote, it was hard to pretend to be one of them.

The embarrassing memory of how she'd reacted that morning in the inner close, when she'd tripped, resurfaced then, and heat flushed across her chest.

Inhaling deeply, Bonnie drew her shoulders back and lifted her chin. She then took a goblet of wine from a passing page boy.

Raising the goblet tentatively to her lips, she sipped the wine. An instant later, she stifled a gasp of pleasure. Lord, she'd never tasted something so delicious. It was light and fruity, and danced on her tongue.

Bonnie took another sip. The wine steadied her nerves. Maybe, after a goblet or two of this, she'd no longer be a blushing lass, cowed by her betters.

Perhaps then, she could pretend she belonged here.

"Ye look utterly ridiculous."

"So do ye."

Iver scowled, even though he knew his brother couldn't see. Curse it, he didn't even want to attend this ball. The last thing he wanted was to don a mask—yet here he was.

Earlier in the day, when two of the queen's ladies-in-waiting had accosted him and Lennox, bearing a basket of masks, and insisted they choose one each for the ball after the banquet, he'd wanted to refuse.

But the ladies had been so enthusiastic, their faces glowing with excitement, that it seemed churlish to do so. All the same, Iver had chosen the simplest mask he could find—it was the color of pewter and satiny with winged edges. In contrast, his brother had taken the opposite approach. Lennox had selected one that was black and feathered with a huge beak.

Both the Mackay brothers had worn clothing to match their masks. Lennox was clad head-to-toe in black leather, while Iver wore dark grey.

"Ye resemble a crow," Iver muttered, running a disparaging eye over his brother. "And an evil-looking one at that. If ye were hoping to frighten women off this eve, ye might well succeed."

"I hope not." His brother grinned then, his mouth just visible under the protruding beak. "I intend to entertain myself tonight."

Iver stiffened at this declaration. As much as he wished to retire at the first opportunity, he was loath to leave his brother to his own devices down here. Lennox had downed around twice the quantity of wine he had during the banquet, and although he showed no sign of inebriation, there was a wicked edge to his voice that often crept in when he was in his cups.

Grinding his teeth together, Iver wished, once again, that he'd asked Kerr to join him on this trip. Lennox was exhausting him.

Oblivious to his brother's weariness, Lennox raised his goblet of wine to his lips and drained it. He then slammed it down on the table and pushed himself to his feet. "I'm joining the dancers."

Iver stood up as well, casting Colin Campbell a sidelong look. The Lord of Glenorchy had made a special effort for the ball, donning a stag's head cloak and a mask covered in deerskin. He looked like the ancient god Cernunnos himself. "Are ye joining us?"

Campbell huffed a laugh and held up the goblet he'd just refilled. "Unlike ye youngsters, I need a bit more drink in me before I take to the floor."

Iver snorted. He was hardly a youngster himself these days, and was only venturing out into the fray to keep an eye on his brother.

"We'll see ye later then, Colin." Lennox flashed the laird a grin before sauntering off in the direction of the swirling dancers.

The minstrels had just finished playing a collection of slow, courtly dances, but had now changed tempo, abandoning the *basse danse* for a lively Scottish jig.

Lennox threw himself into the crowd, taking the arm of a tall, curvaceous woman wearing a mask decorated with peacock feathers.

Iver didn't join him. He wasn't going to dive in like his younger brother. Iver had learned all the dances over the years, and a decade earlier, he'd been one of the first to take the floor. He'd loved the fire festivals or any occasion that brought folk together. It had been an opportunity to flirt, to get close to a woman he'd desired from afar.

He'd been a different man then—carefree and a little careless.

But not any longer. Tonight, the gaiety and loud music just made his head hurt.

Just clench yer jaw and suffer it, Mackay, he counseled himself as he wove his way through the press toward the edge of the hall. *The eve will pass soon enough.*

8: AN ACCIDENT OF BIRTH

THE MASQUERADE BALL was quite a spectacle—it was like being transported into a fairy realm.

No, Iver didn't want to be here—but he had to admit he'd never seen such pageantry. His gaze swept to the heart of the dancing, to the king and queen. James was in a red and gold mask and a great horned headpiece that made him appear like a mythical beast, while Mary looked like a fairy queen with her pale hair and silver mask studded with gems.

Iver's attention alighted then on a tall, lithe man with long dark hair shot through with grey standing nearby. A slender woman with silvering brown hair stood at his side.

Tavish and Robina Gunn.

The clan-chief spied Iver then, and the two men's gazes fused.

Moments passed, and then Tavish's mouth lifted at the corners. A heartbeat later, Iver returned the smile before favoring the clan-chief with a respectful nod.

The Gunns and the Mackays were old rivals, and for years, the two clans had been locked in a bloody feud. There was a time when the sight of a Gunn made Iver's blood heat, his right-hand itching to reach for his dirk. But things were different these days.

Over a decade had passed since they'd united against the Sutherlands in battle, and in the years following, relations had healed.

Nonetheless, the sight of Tavish Gunn reminded Iver of the man's youngest brother, William Gunn, and the humiliation he'd once suffered at the bastard's hands. And like many disputes, this one had been over a woman: the lovely Eilidh Munro.

It was water under the bridge now—for William and Eilidh had long been wed and had three children—yet Iver had never forgotten the incident.

Even so, he couldn't blame Tavish for it.

The dancers had formed a ring now, linking arms as they spun around the floor.

Wary of being drawn into the revelry, Iver quickened his step, moving to the edge of the hall. A crowd had formed there, as many of the revelers chose to watch rather than participate.

A woman standing a little apart from them caught Iver's eye.

Dressed in a becoming gown, the color of blooming heather, with a matching mask, her flame-red hair cascading over pale shoulders, she looked a little different from those around her. The woman's costume was less elaborate than the other ladies—and yet, to Iver, she outshone them all. And that low-cut kirtle and surcote hugged every lush curve of her small body, revealing deep cleavage.

Iver's breathing grew shallow as he observed her. His swift, visceral reaction surprised him. The woman was a temptress indeed.

She noticed his stare then—and a pair of sea-green eyes met his own gaze. The moment drew out, and neither of them looked away.

An odd sense of recognition fluttered up within Iver, as if they'd met before. Yet he was sure they hadn't. He'd have remembered.

Perhaps there was something about her that reminded him of the comely, yet cripplingly shy, chambermaid he'd assisted that morning, for her hair was of the same fiery hue. But the similarity ended there. That poor lass hadn't even been able to meet his eye.

Iver's breathing stilled for a moment, heat igniting in his belly, and his senses sharpening. Suddenly, the heaviness that had dogged his steps all evening lifted. It had been a long while since he'd responded like this, and it was discomforting.

Cynicism was usually his first response to a comely lass these days—and he preferred that.

Beautiful women are the most dangerous, he reminded himself, his hands clenching by his sides. Aye, Eilidh Munro had been lovely—and so had Flora MacPherson. But his dealings with both ladies had left scars.

Tension rippled through him as he fought the pull.

Fought and lost.

As the music soared high into the rafters of the great hall of Stirling Castle, Iver stepped forward. And still holding the red-haired woman's eye, he crossed the floor toward her.

He's coming my way.

The Lord help her, she hadn't meant to stare at the man—but she'd been unable to help herself.

Bonnie had been watching the dancers, marveling at what a striking pair the king and queen made, when she'd felt someone's gaze upon her. Tearing her attention from James and Mary, she'd discovered that a man across the crowd was watching her.

And her heart had leaped into her throat when she recognized him.

Wearing a mask the shade of storm-clouds, he was distinctive. His hair, almost as pale as sea-foam, flowed over his shoulders. Tall and clad in form-fitting grey leggings and a jerkin of the same hue that left his arms bare, the stranger she'd admired from afar over the last two days was now striding across the floor toward her.

Like her, he was dressed more simply than many of the other guests. And yet, he stood out. Even masked, she'd have recognized him anywhere.

Bonnie's pulse started to hammer in her ears.

What will I do?

She considered turning and running away, yet her feet had grown roots.

Unlike the two previous times she'd encountered him, Bonnie held the man's gaze. It was as if he'd cast some enchantment over her; she couldn't seem to look away. And as he drew near, she noted he had dark-blue eyes— the color of the sky, just before night's curtain fell.

She couldn't believe he was heading her way.

A wave of panic hit Bonnie then as her heart started to kick against her ribs. Ainslie had warned her not to speak to anyone.

What if he recognizes me?

Lord, what if he had already? Maybe he was on his way over to demand what a lowly chambermaid was doing at the king's masquerade ball.

Bonnie started to sweat. She even managed to unfree her slippered feet from the wooden floor and take a step back.

But it was too late, for the blond stranger had reached her. Halting, he stared down at her, and Bonnie raised her chin to hold his gaze.

They shouldn't stare at each other like this. It was too intense.

The moment drew out, and when the man spoke, the low warmth of his voice wrapped itself around her. "Would ye like to dance?"

Bonnie's breathing hitched. *Remember, ye are pretending to be a lady,* she reminded herself. *Speak like one.* "Aye," she whispered. "I would."

His mouth curved, and he held out a hand to her. "Shall we then?"

Bonnie nodded and raised her own hand, placing it over the top of his, as she'd seen the ladies around her do.

She could dance—and had attended enough fire festivals in Stirling to feel confident to take the floor. Fortunately, the minstrels were playing a lively jig, music she was used to. The courtly dance they'd been performing earlier would be another matter. Although it was slow, the *basse danse* appeared to have many carefully planned moves.

Bonnie wouldn't be able to hide her lack of expertise in such a situation.

However, it was too late to worry about that, for he was drawing her into the dancing. And the moment after that, Bonnie was twirling around him.

Joy fluttered up, causing her panic to subside. Moments later, the nerves knotting her stomach loosened. Never had she felt like this. Beautiful. Free. When the music caught hold, it was as if nothing bad could ever touch her.

She was smiling so widely that her face ached, her feet flying over the floor as they linked arms, and he swung her in the other direction.

Bonnie guessed it wasn't seemly for a lady to openly express such delight, yet she couldn't help herself. When she'd stepped inside this hall, she hadn't dreamed she'd end up dancing with the blond stranger who'd intrigued her so—and yet here she was.

Her happiness must have been infectious, for when she glanced her dance partner's way, she saw that he too was grinning.

Bonnie's breathing caught. Heavens, she'd thought him handsome before, but when he smiled, he was devastating. It lit him up.

The song ended then, and disappointment constricted Bonnie's chest as she drew to a halt, breathing hard.

Yet, an instant later, the minstrels in the gallery above struck up another fast tune—and they were off again.

Bonnie whirled around her partner, the joyful sound of her laughter joining the lilt of the lyre and pipe.

"We shouldn't be here," Alba hissed, tugging at her sister's sleeve. "If Ma finds out, she'll take a wooden spoon to us both."

Morag snorted and wrested her arm free. "Nonsense. We're too old for that. Plus, she'll never know."

Alba's mouth flattened, yet she didn't argue. They were twins, and physically identical; nevertheless, Morag was the bold one. The leader. Alba was forever the follower.

It was no surprise then that this escapade was her sister's idea.

They'd sneaked into the great hall via the servants' entrance while the dancing was in full swing and then crept up the wooden stairs into the minstrels' gallery.

From here, they'd be able to see the dancing.

Fortunately for the twins, it was chaos down there, and the music was loud. The din of merrymaking echoed through the cavernous space—and all eyes were on those dancing.

The minstrels, two lyrists and two pipers, hadn't seen the twins, who'd halted at the top of the stairs and were now pressed up against the banister. Sweat beaded on the men's brows as they played, their gazes also trained on the revelry below.

Alba's breathing quickened as she peered down at the brightly colored sea of figures beneath them. "Look," she whispered. "The king and queen."

Indeed, it was impossible to miss them. James and Mary danced at the very heart of the crowd and with as much vigor as the other guests. They were both young and full of energy—the queen herself was three winters younger than the twins, although she'd already given birth to two bairns.

"What a spectacle," Morag breathed. "How I wish *we* could don costumes and join them."

Alba marked the envy in her sister's voice. Morag had reacted in a similar fashion earlier when they'd gone out to see the guests arrive. Like some of the stable hands who'd gathered around the fringes of the inner close to watch the costumed lords and ladies file into the great hall, both the sisters were enraptured. Yet Morag had muttered something about how they were invisible to these people.

Her sister was right—they were—but Alba didn't let that bother her. "It's like watching a fairy gathering," she whispered, focusing on the dancers once more.

Morag didn't reply. But a moment later, she caught hold of Alba's arm with one hand while she pointed with the other. "Look at that handsome man ... if only *I* were his partner."

Alba's gaze traveled to where her sister indicated, to see a tall, broad-shouldered man clad in grey. He was eye-catching indeed, with long pale-blond hair, although the small woman dressed in a purple gown with whom he was dancing stood out just as much. The lady had bright red hair the same color as their cousin's. Laughing, she pivoted on her heel, ducked under her partner's arm, and then changed direction.

"I always wanted hair that color," Morag muttered. "It's not fair that Bonnie was blessed with a fiery mane, while ye and I have hair the color of mud."

Alba's mouth pursed. She wouldn't have described their hair in such a fashion. The masquerade ball had indeed turned her sister as bitter as their mother.

There was no denying their cousin was a comely lass. Bonnie's loveliness seemed to bloom brighter with each passing year, but their cousin also had a gentle, sweet nature. She worked hard and never complained.

In truth, Alba didn't like the way her mother and sister harassed her. They'd gotten more vicious recently too, more personal. Bonnie weathered their bullying with grace, yet it was often difficult to bear witness to.

There had been many times when Alba wanted to extend the hand of friendship toward her, but Morag wouldn't have stood for it.

"It's just an accident of birth," her sister grumbled then. Her gaze was riveted upon the dancing couple, high spots of color upon her cheeks. "If I'd been born under a different star, that could be *me* down there."

Alba raised an eyebrow. No, she and Morag weren't the daughters of a clan-chief or even a chieftain. Instead, their parents were a cook and a feckless groom who'd abandoned his family.

"Ye two!" An angry voice intruded then, and Alba saw that one of the musicians, a man holding a lyre, had spotted them. "What are ye doing?"

9: A PLEASURE TO MAKE YER ACQUAINTANCE

LIKE TWO HINDS cornered by hunters, the twins stared back at the lyrist.

An instant later, Morag dove for the steps.

Panic kicked in Alba's chest as the minstrel lurched in her direction and made a grab for her.

Reeling backward, Alba narrowly avoided the man's grasping hand before she half-stumbled, half-fell down the wooden stairs. Curse Morag, she was nowhere to be seen. Her sister had fled without a thought for her twin.

Breathing hard now, Alba reached the foot of the stairs. She slipped around the edge of the hall and through the servant's entrance. Outside, a full moon sailed high in the sky, illuminating the inner close where the light from the blazing torches hanging on brackets around the perimeter didn't reach.

Hand placed upon her chest, as she willed her galloping heart to slow, Alba hurried toward the kitchens. That was where her sister would have headed— and when she found her, she'd give her a piece of her mind.

Alba wouldn't have abandoned Morag like that.

"Where are ye off to in such a hurry, Alba Fraser."

A man's voice, young and faintly amused, intruded then.

Alba skidded to a halt, looking wildly around. An instant later, a well-built young man with sandy hair stepped out of the shadows.

Alba's lips pursed, her panic subsiding. "Rory Comyn," she muttered. "What the devil are ye doing sneaking up on folk?"

The man's mouth quirked. "Sorry if I startled ye ... but I just saw yer sister race past and worried there was trouble."

Placing her hands on her hips, Alba frowned. It was a discomforting fact that Rory always knew who she was—even when she and Morag dressed identically.

Comyn, who'd been apprenticed to the blacksmith at Stirling Castle for a year now, folded heavily muscled arms over his chest. "Ye look all flustered, and yer cheeks have gone a bonnie shade of pink." He then inclined his head, his smile widening. "What *were* ye up to, lass?"

Heat flushed through Alba. She barely knew the blacksmith's apprentice and didn't appreciate his teasing.

Trying to ignore her burning face, she drew herself up. "None of yer business," she snapped. With that, she swept past Rory and stalked back to the kitchens.

"Apologies, but I need a breather," Bonnie gasped. The last of the jigs had ended, and the minstrels now struck up a slow, lilting tune.

It was time to bow out.

Her dance partner flashed her a grin. "Ye don't wish for a courtly dance?"

Bonnie's belly fluttered at that smile, yet she wouldn't be swayed. Unlike the ladies surrounding her, she didn't know the steps of the *basse danse*—trying to fumble through was too risky.

"Later perhaps," she replied. Bonnie had exchanged only a few words with this man, and she was careful to speak formally, not to let the rough vernacular used by the servants in this keep slip in.

Her partner dipped his head and held out an arm to her, indicating that he'd lead her from the floor. Bonnie took it, keenly aware of the heat of his body, of the iron-hard strength of his arm against hers.

"I think we should introduce ourselves," the man murmured as they reached the crowd looking on from the fringes of the great hall. "I'm Iver Mackay, laird of Dun Ugadale ... whom have I had the pleasure of dancing with?"

Bonnie met his dark-blue gaze, and for an instant, she longed to blurt out the truth.

I'm Bonnie Fraser, a chambermaid in this castle.

Fortunately, she had the wits not to do anything so idiotic. Instead, she used the identity Ainslie had created for her. "I'm Lady Adair Farquharson ... of Braemar," she murmured, lowering her gaze. It was impossible to hold his eye while lying, and she hoped he'd merely think her shy. Her pulse quickened then. What if this laird knew the Farquharsons of Braemar? If he did, she was in trouble.

"It's a pleasure to make yer acquaintance, Lady Adair," he replied.

Bonnie glanced up to see Mackay smiling down at her. There was no suspicion in his gaze, only appreciation. She was safe.

"Pardon my ignorance," she murmured then, "but I have no idea where Dun Ugadale is."

His sensual mouth curved once more. "It's on the Kintyre peninsula ... my stronghold is an ancient one that looks out to sea."

Bonnie's gaze widened. "I thought the Mackays resided in the far north of the Highlands."

"Most of my clan do, but the Mackays of Dun Ugadale have held lands in Argyll for the last hundred years." There was pride in his voice, and Bonnie was intrigued. It made her forget her nervousness and how out of place she was here. Her world was narrow indeed, and this man was an opportunity to learn about another part of Scotland, somewhere far beyond the walls of Stirling Castle. She was fascinated to discover more.

"Ye said yer stronghold is ancient," she began hesitantly. "Do ye know just how old it is?"

He shrugged. "My grandfather told me that the people who dwelled here, long before the Norsemen started raiding, built a stone roundhouse to watch over the sea. It was a ruin when my great-grandfather was gifted the lands, but he repaired it, added on to it. Dun Ugadale is a blend of old and new now."

"Dun Ugadale," Bonnie murmured the name. "Valley of the Owl."

"Aye, although ye see more seabirds than owls these days," Mackay replied. "The land is bare and windswept." He paused then, his expression softening. "But it's home."

His tone turned wistful then, those midnight-blue eyes shadowing just a little.

"Ye would rather be there right now than here, wouldn't ye?" she asked, forgetting herself for a moment.

His gaze widened at the directness of her question before he huffed a wry laugh. "Is it that obvious?"

"Only just then," she admitted, suddenly shy. Bonnie wasn't sure what had come over her, only that there was something about Iver Mackay that made her feel comfortable, almost as if she'd known him forever.

What an irony that before meeting him properly this evening, she'd been unable to even look at him squarely. Now that they'd shared a few words, her timidity had eased. After all, she was in disguise. She had to keep reminding herself that she was Adair Farquharson, not Bonnie Fraser.

"I *was* wishing I was back home," he admitted then. "The Mackay clan-chief asked me to attend these celebrations on his behalf ... but I'm not overly comfortable at court these days." He paused, his gaze fusing with hers. "But that was *before* our paths crossed." He favored her with a slow smile then, one that made Bonnie's pulse stutter. "For now, this eve has taken a turn for the better."

Bonnie smiled back. She was enjoying his flirtatious manner and being the object of admiration. When she'd stepped into this hall, she hadn't imagined for an instant that the man she'd admired from afar would ask her to dance, or that they'd be standing here on the edge of the hall talking afterward.

Around them, the dancing continued, but Bonnie barely noticed.

Mackay took two goblets of wine from a passing page boy and handed her one.

Bonnie was grateful, for she was thirsty after the dancing. She lifted the goblet to her lips and took a couple of sips, aware that Mackay was watching her.

"And what of ye, Lady Adair," he asked after a brief pause. "Do ye enjoy these events?"

"Well, I've never attended a masquerade ball before," she admitted, taking another sip of wine. The warmth of it sliding down her throat and pooling in her belly helped to settle the nervousness that still fluttered there.

"Neither have I," he replied. "Although I hear it is a first for the Scottish court."

"It really is something to behold." She gave an awkward laugh then. "I feel a little underdressed."

"Aye, there are some spectacular costumes and masks," he agreed, his gaze never straying from hers. "Yet I prefer yers." To her surprise, he reached up then, his fingertips tracing the detailing on the edges of her mask. "Thistles remind me of home ... there are clouds of them carpeting the hills behind Dun Ugadale in summer."

They were standing close, so close that Bonnie inhaled the scent of him: he smelled of woodsmoke and leather, with a fresh hint of something like pine.

His nearness was heady, and Bonnie couldn't help it: she sucked his scent deep into her lungs. A man had never smelled so good.

"And yer gown is the color of heather," he continued. "It's bonnie, indeed."

Bonnie.

Heat flushed through her. Bonnie's name was a dying gift from her mother. The tale went that Greer Fraser hadn't survived long after birthing her daughter—yet even in her weak state, she'd managed to bestow a name upon her. It was pretty, yet it wasn't a fashionable one among the high-born. She wondered then if he'd think it low-class.

"Aye, well ... like I said, it's a simple dress compared to some in here," she murmured, taking another fortifying sip of wine.

In truth, she was starting to feel out of her depth. She wasn't used to flirting with men. She'd fought off a number of wandering hands over the years, but most men weren't interested in talking to her, let alone flattering her.

Mackay drank from his own goblet, his expression turning thoughtful. "Are ye here with yer kin, Adair?"

Bonnie's pulse quickened. Lord, she and Ainslie hadn't come up with a story about that. She'd have to think on her feet. "No," she replied, favoring him with a tight smile. "My father sent an escort with me." She made a gesture. "Our steward is somewhere in here, amongst the revelers."

Mackay inclined his head. "The laird didn't accompany ye?"

Bonnie cleared her throat as nervousness assailed her. "Aye, well ... he's keen for me to find a husband," she replied, using the first excuse that came to mind. "And thought I needed a little freedom to do so."

To her surprise, a shadow passed over Iver Mackay's gaze then. It was like watching a cloud dim the sun for an instant. Likewise, the fingers wrapped around his goblet of wine tightened, and his tall frame stiffened just a fraction.

Warmth flushed across Bonnie's chest. Did he think she'd set her sights on him?

Mackay had been attentive and flirtatious, yet he clearly hadn't attended these celebrations in search of a wife. In fact, the very notion appeared to panic him.

"Fear not," Bonnie said quickly. "My father may be desperate to see me wed, but I couldn't care less. I love living at Braemar too much to ever leave."

She was surprised how easily the lie slid from her lips.

Mackay's gaze widened just a fraction, the tension easing in his broad shoulders. "Aye, well, it's difficult to be uprooted from everything ye know," he replied. "Folk should leave well alone. There are plenty of us who don't wish to be shackled to another."

"Shackled?" Bonnie's mouth curved. Suddenly, the urge to challenge him a little, to know why he'd say something so cynical, rose within her. "Is that how ye see marriage, Mackay?"

10: APPEARANCES DECEIVE

DAMN IT, HE was starting to sweat.

Things had been going well. For the first time in years, Iver had let himself go a little. He'd enjoyed dancing with Adair Farquharson and even flirted a bit.

He had to admit, he was fascinated by this woman. Their conversation had been enjoyable too, until she brought up the subject of marriage. At that moment, it had felt as if an icy bucket of water had been emptied over his head.

Adair's comment about not wanting to leave her home had eased his panic a little, although the directness of her sea-blue gaze now made him squirm.

Suddenly, Iver wished he hadn't been honest with her.

As much as her presence made him want to lower his shields, there were some things best not spoken of. His attitude toward marriage wasn't a popular one, and the bitterness of such a sentiment now cast a shadow over their conversation. It was at odds with the gaiety around them.

Why couldn't he have kept their exchange light?

God's troth, he *was* turning into a curmudgeon. Nonetheless, the steadiness of Adair's gaze made him want to answer her honestly. "Aye," he murmured. "I'm afraid I've had a run of ill-fortune when it comes to women and proposals of marriage."

Her lips, lush and bow-shaped, parted slightly. "I find that hard to believe," she replied. Adair's voice was low and husky. Yet the tone wasn't affected in the slightest; it was as if she didn't have any idea how sensual she was. "A man like ye could have his pick of any maid."

He gave a soft snort. "Appearances deceive, Lady Adair. The women I've set my heart upon over the years didn't share yer opinion, alas."

Her gaze remained steady. "Why not?"

Iver raised his goblet to his lips and drained its contents. He beckoned a page over who was circuiting the fringes of the revelry, ewer of wine in hand. The lad filled his goblet and then his companion's as well. Meanwhile, Iver wondered how on earth he'd answer that question.

He suddenly felt out of his depth with this woman. Her question was direct, probing—too much so—yet he didn't want to withdraw from her.

Across the floor, he spied his brother then. Lennox had taken a short break from the dancing and was now sculling mead from a great ox horn—a difficult feat indeed considering he was still wearing his beaked mask—while two young courtiers cheered him on with whoops and shouts.

Iver's brow furrowed. *Christ's bones, don't encourage him.*

Sucking in a deep breath, Iver then shifted his attention back to Adair. She was watching him, awaiting his reply. "I wish I could blame the ladies in question," he replied cautiously. "Yet I fear it was my doing ... looking back, I can see a pattern. I went after women who didn't want me." He paused then, a sour taste flooding his mouth as unwelcome memories surfaced. "I believed that a true lady is coy in her affections, and that it was up to me to pursue her."

He halted then, heat flushing through him once more. He couldn't believe he'd blurted all that out—and to a stranger. He'd never actually articulated his thoughts so honestly before. He'd never been candid about the reason why his proposals had always ended in disaster.

Sweat now trickled down his back, between his shoulder blades. There were some subjects he avoided for good reason.

"I've heard some men like a challenge," Adair replied, her tone veiling. "There is a thrill in the hunt I suppose."

"There is." His gut clenched. Curse it. He wasn't giving a great account of himself. There had to be some way to disentangle himself from this conversation. "Or so foolish lads, like I was once, believe."

Bonnie's brow furrowed. She wasn't sure what to think of this laird. She appreciated how honest he'd been with her—and understood why past experiences might have tainted his view of women.

Nonetheless, the cynicism in his voice took the shine off the enchantment of this evening. Earlier, she'd been caught up in the excitement of meeting, and dancing with, Iver Mackay. But his admission hinted that despite the wealth and opulence that surrounded her—happiness didn't come any easier to lairds than it did to common folk. Mackay was charming and handsome, yet he didn't appear to be happy.

The laird flashed her an embarrassed smile, raising the goblet he held to his lips and taking a deep draft. "I've said too much." His voice roughened. "And I apologize, Adair ... ye didn't need to hear all that."

"Don't apologize," she replied, stepping closer to him. Aye, the real man beyond the handsome façade had taken her aback, yet she wasn't cowed. Instead, she wanted the magic that had wrapped itself around them earlier to return. She wanted to see him smile again.

Seeking to put Mackay at ease, she reached out then and placed a hand upon his forearm. "Sometimes it's easier to unburden yerself to someone ye don't know." Her mouth curved. "Carrying around a heavy heart does ye no good."

Although her touch was light, he stiffened under it. Chastened, Bonnie was about to remove her hand when he reached up with his free one, placing it over hers.

"Thank ye," he said softly, his voice barely audible over the clamor of music and laughter that surrounded them.

Bonnie paid none of that any notice though.

All she was aware of was Iver's hand on hers, the strength and warmth of his touch. It both reassured her and knocked her off-balance.

A strange excitement fluttered low in her belly.

Suddenly, their surroundings disappeared. The music and laughter faded—and all that existed was the intensity of his dark-blue eyes and the feel of his hand on hers.

The moment stretched out, and then, to her disappointment, Mackay removed his hand and stepped back. Never breaking her gaze, he lifted his goblet to his lips. Bonnie mirrored the gesture. It gave her something to do, for at present, she was tongue-tied.

His touch had unbalanced her.

The laird cleared his throat. "Ye are somewhat of an enigma, Adair," he said, the corners of his mouth lifting.

Bonnie gave a soft laugh, even as her pulse sped up.

His words reminded her of something Harris, the man-at-arms she'd fallen for a few years earlier, had said once. "Ye are a riddle, Bonnie," he'd crooned after they'd tumbled in the hayloft above the stables. "One I long to solve."

But Harris hadn't meant those words, for he'd taken a position elsewhere within the moon and departed without even saying goodbye. In the days that followed, Bonnie had struggled with grief and panic. Sorrow that her lover had abandoned her, and fear that her womb might have quickened. When her courses arrived a few days later, she'd wept with relief.

And ever since Harris, she'd been careful with men. When the male servants or men-at-arms flirted with her, they were met with a cool response.

And the reminder made her cautious now. "Am I?" she replied softly. Her stomach tightened then as her earlier anxiety resurfaced.

Once again, she felt like an imposter—as if one misspoken word would unmask her.

There was a reason why Ainslie had cautioned her against speaking to anyone.

Silence swelled between them once more, an awkward one. Meanwhile, another lively jig had begun. The king and queen, after a brief rest, were in the midst of the dancers. The king's russet hair flew behind him like a flag as he and Mary swung around each other.

Bonnie kept her gaze upon the dancers and wished she felt more at ease. Her mind had gone blank; earlier she'd had plenty to say to this man, but now she was at a loss for words.

"Ye have the air of an only child, Adair," Mackay said finally. She glanced back at him to see he was watching her intently. "But surely, that isn't the case?"

Bonnie favored him with a brittle smile. "No ... I have two younger sisters." That wasn't a complete lie, for she saw Morag and Alba as sisters rather than cousins. Perhaps because they'd grown up together and weren't that much younger than she was.

"Are ye close to them?"

Bonnie kept her smile in place as she shrugged. "Not particularly ... they are twins and are so fond of each other that I've always felt like an outsider." She inclined her head then, eager to shift the conversation away from herself once more. "And do ye have siblings, Iver?"

It was bold to call him by his first name. However, since he'd already done so with her, she decided to be brave. She found she liked how his name sounded, how it rolled off her tongue.

And he did too, for the laird's mouth quirked. "Aye, three younger brothers." He paused then, scratching his chin. "As bairns, we were always close ... although less so these days."

Bonnie inclined her head. "Why is that?"

His smile faded. "I'm not sure really ... maybe we're all too different. Lennox is the wild one. Kerr is old beyond his years. And Brodie has a dour way about him."

Shouting reached them, cutting through the rise and fall of the lively music.

Tearing her gaze from Mackay's, Bonnie shifted her attention to the other side of the hall, where a tall man clad in black leather, wearing a terrifying mask of inky feathers and a sharp beak, had just launched himself at another of the guests—a burly man dressed in a wolf's pelt.

Excitement rippled across the great hall as the two of them, both clearly in their cups as they staggered and bellowed slurred insults, slugged at each other.

Mackay growled a curse, and Bonnie shot him a sharp look. "Ye know them?"

"Aye," he muttered. "The one dressed like Satan's crow is my brother Lennox." With a sigh, he handed Bonnie his goblet. "I'd better sort this out." He met her gaze then. "Will ye wait for my return?"

She stared back at him a moment before murmuring, "Of course."

Yet even as she assured him that she wouldn't leave, her belly clenched. She'd lost track of time since entering the great hall; nonetheless, the eve was drawing out. Ainslie had advised her to leave while the ball was still at its height.

But she couldn't bring herself to. Surely, it wouldn't hurt to linger just a little longer.

Iver Mackay favored her with a nod—and then he was gone, striding across the floor, weaving his way through the crowd toward where his brother had just driven his fist into his opponent's gut.

11: THE KELPIE'S CALL

IRRITATION SPIKED THROUGH Iver as he bore down on where his brother and Malcolm Sutherland were pummeling each other.

Aye, he'd recognized the huge man in the wolfskin earlier. The Sutherland clan-chief's eldest son was impossible to miss in a crowd.

Since his arrival at Stirling, Iver had avoided the Sutherlands. Relations between the two clans had been strained for years, and he hadn't missed the baleful looks Malcolm had been flashing him across the hall during the banquet.

Iver's jaw clenched.

Curse ye, Len ... couldn't ye have picked a fight with someone else.

Reaching his brother's side, Iver grabbed him by the arm and hauled him back. Lennox cursed and swung a fist in his direction before realizing it was his brother who was manhandling him. He pulled the punch at the last moment; nevertheless, his fist grazed Iver's ear.

Shoving Lennox behind him, Iver stepped forward, eyeballing Malcolm Sutherland.

The clan-chief's son was bleeding from a cut lip, while his gaze, unfocused from drink, still managed to spear Iver like a pike.

"Stand down, Sutherland," Iver greeted him. "The fight's over."

"Out of the way, Iver," Lennox slurred, trying to elbow his elder brother aside so he could reach his opponent again.

But Iver stood firm. Lennox couldn't budge him.

Sutherland's bloody mouth twisted. "Yer wee brother has an insolent tongue," he growled. "He needs teaching some manners."

"Ye are right, he does," Iver replied, holding the huge man's eye. "But let me be the one to do it."

The wolfskin-clad warrior took a threatening step toward him. "I don't think so. Get out of my way, Mackay."

"No," Iver replied, his fists curling at his sides. "Do ye really want to brawl here ... under the king's gaze?"

A muscle bunched in Sutherland's heavy jaw. Nonetheless, Iver knew he'd gotten through to him. Indeed, many of the dancers, the king and queen included, had stilled, their gazes swiveling their way.

Like his father before him, James took a hard line with the Highland clan-chiefs and chieftains, and he had a low tolerance for their feuding.

Sutherland spat a gob of blood on the floor between them. With a muttered curse, he then pushed his way past the Mackay brothers and headed toward the doors of the great hall.

Iver watched him go, his own temper simmering. Sutherland had an insolent mouth on him.

Shifting his attention back to Lennox, Iver shoved him toward the tables at the other end of the hall, where some of the older guests reclined with goblets of wine, watching the revelry—and the fight.

"Come on," he grunted. "Time to cool yer heels."

"Sutherland insulted Niel," Lennox growled back. "Are ye going to let the slight lie unanswered?"

"Aye."

"I had him." Lennox staggered then. He would have fallen too, if Iver hadn't caught him by the arm and hauled him upright.

"God's teeth, ye've had a skinful," Iver grunted.

"I was about to best the bastard," Lennox went on, his voice rising. "Until ye threw yer weight around. Ye always ruin my sport." All the same, his brother rubbed at his jaw, where a bruise was already forming.

"Shut yer gob and keep walking."

On the way back to the table where they'd banqueted earlier, they passed William Douglas. A solitary figure this eve, James's special guest sat alone at the king's table, nursing a goblet of wine. Like Iver, Douglas had opted for a simple mask—one the color of peat that matched his clothing. The earl's gaze tracked the Mackay brothers as they passed him, his mouth curving. "Enjoying yerselves, lads?"

"Aye," Lennox slurred. "No gathering is complete without a few punches."

Douglas laughed. "Aye ... too right."

Iver managed a smile that felt more like a grimace, pushing Lennox back to their table. Colin Campbell was still there, a row of empty ewers in front of him. The laird's cheeks were flushed with wine as he greeted Lennox. "That's a strong right hook ye have on ye."

"Don't encourage him," Iver replied, shoving Lennox down onto the bench seat next to the laird. "He always thinks he has the strength of ten men when he's had a few."

Campbell snorted. "Aye ... we all think that, especially when we have more years before us than behind us."

"Cods ... I think I'm going to be sick," Lennox announced then.

Iver's gaze narrowed as he surveyed his brother. Indeed, Lennox's face had gone pale under that ridiculous beak, and he was swaying dangerously in his seat. "Here." He grabbed an empty ewer and shoved it at his brother. "Use this."

Clutching the ewer to his chest, Lennox nodded. His shoulders hunched then, and he made a soft gagging sound.

Mouth thinning, Iver shifted his attention to Campbell. "Could ye watch over him for me?"

The laird flashed him a sly smile. "Eager to return to the revelry, are ye?"

Iver frowned at the insinuation in the older man's tone, although Campbell's smile merely widened to a wolfish grin. "Can't say I blame ye though ... I saw that bonnie woman ye were dancing with earlier." He nodded toward the dance floor. "She's waiting for ye."

Heaving in a deep breath, Iver glanced back at where he'd left Adair Farquharson.

And as Campbell had stated, she stood at the edge of the crowd, still holding their goblets, her gaze resting upon him.

Shifting his attention back to the Lord of Glenorchy, Iver stiffened. He had that look that men got when they were both envious and encouraging. It was clear from his grin that he reckoned Iver would get a hot, sweaty tumble before the night was out.

Campbell's presumption irritated Iver.

He didn't like the man paying such close attention to his business—especially since Iver had just turned down his offer to wed his daughter earlier that evening.

"Don't worry," Campbell said then, raising his cup in a mocking toast. "I'll make sure Lennox doesn't get himself into any more trouble ... go on, forget about us."

Iver was drawn back to her like a moth to a flame.

The knowing edge in Campbell's voice had galled him. Yet he'd agreed to keep an eye on Lennox—and Iver didn't want to throw his offer back in his face.

And so, he'd left Campbell and Lennox with a brusque nod and returned to Adair's side.

Meanwhile, the disruption that the Sutherland-Mackay fight had caused had been forgotten.

The minstrels had shifted pace to a slow, romantic dance, and when Iver neared Adair, he saw that she was swaying slightly in time with the beat, a smile curving her pretty mouth.

"Do ye wish for another dance?" he greeted her.

To his surprise, she shook her head. "I prefer the jigs to courtly dances," she replied. "However, this is a lovely tune."

"It is." He halted next to her and took the goblet she handed him.

"Ye were brave to insert yerself between two brawling men like that," she murmured. "I thought that huge warrior was going to take a swing at ye."

Iver snorted. "The Sutherlands are troublemakers," he replied with a shake of his head. "Malcolm Sutherland thought he'd speak ill of our clan-chief, and like the drunken fool he is, Lennox rose to the bait."

He lifted his goblet to his lips and took a deep draft. Unlike his brother, he'd consumed only enough wine to mellow his mood and relax him. Len always had to take everything to the limit.

Nonetheless, the noise and activity around him were starting to weary Iver. The great hall of Stirling Castle felt oppressive. The crowds of drunken revelers pressed in, and the air—warmed by two great hearths at either end of the space and the heat of many bodies—was stiflingly hot.

The urge to be outdoors, breathing in the night air and enjoying some peace, descended upon him, and he met Adair's eye once more. "Would ye like to take a stroll outdoors?" he asked. "It's a mild night out ... and the air in here is suffocating."

His companion hesitated, and Iver wondered if he'd overstepped. Despite Campbell's insinuation, he had no ulterior motive. Of course, many ladies would worry about the danger to their reputation if they took a moonlit walk with a man.

In other circumstances, he wouldn't have suggested it. Yet this eve, he felt as if he'd strayed into another world—one where the usual social rules didn't apply.

All the same, he didn't intend to take advantage of her. The truth was, Adair Farquharson fascinated him. He wasn't yet ready to bid her good eve.

But the delay in her response checked him. He was about to retract his offer when Adair replied, "Aye, I too could do with clearing my head. I've had more wine than I'm used to ... and it *is* hot in here."

An odd wave of relief crashed over Iver. Smiling, he took her goblet from her and placed both vessels on a ledge behind them. He then held out his arm to her. "Well then, My Lady, let us depart."

Bonnie descended the steps outside the great hall and tried to ignore the wild beating of raven wings in her chest—as both excitement and anxiety fought for dominance.

What are ye doing?

Something she'd likely regret in the morning.

The attraction between her and Iver Mackay was strong enough that good sense warned her it wasn't wise to be alone with him. And yet she couldn't help it. Being near him was thrilling. The desire to remain in his company was a kelpie's call.

Heaving a deep breath of cool air, laced with the scent of woodsmoke, Bonnie glanced up at the full moon glowing overhead. "What a lovely night," she breathed. "It almost feels as if spring is here."

"It's too early for that," Iver replied. "And considering how cold it was a few days ago, I'd wager that it's the deep breath before winter hits us with one final flurry."

Bonnie nodded. He was likely right. The bitter weather gave up its grip reluctantly here; they often had snow even into March.

Reaching the bottom of the steps, they cut right, crossing the inner close and heading toward a stone archway. Torches hung from brackets on either side of the arch, illuminating the figures of helmed guards standing watch. Mackay nodded to them as they passed.

More torches blazed from the walls in the outer close, although the shadows were longer here.

"The rose garden is a tranquil spot ... even this time of year," Mackay said. "Shall we walk around it?"

Bonnie smiled. She'd ventured into the garden rarely over the years—access was restricted to the gardeners, high-ranking servants, and nobility. The few times she'd visited had been in secret when she was a lass.

The idea of taking a stroll through it now thrilled her. "Aye," she replied, attempting to keep the excitement out of her voice. "I'd like that."

And so, they crossed to the arch-shaped arbor that led through a high hedge into the garden, feet crunching on gravel. Beyond, it was much darker than the outer close. Few torches burned here, although the full moon shone down, casting its hoary light upon them. It frosted the proud lines of Iver Mackay's masked face and glinted upon his pale hair.

Bonnie's pulse quickened. The Saints forgive her, she could have stared at him forever. Now that they were outdoors, it was as if a veil had drawn itself around them. The rest of the world, and the revelry in the great hall, all ceased to exist.

Arm in arm, they circuited the garden, passing neatly pruned rose bushes. This time of year, the thorny bushes were bare, but come spring, they would burst into life, and soon after, the garden would be decorated in shades of pink and red.

At the heart of the garden, they stopped before a large statue: the rearing head of a horse. The statue was quite a sight at night, for it was made of a pale sandstone that glowed in the moonlight.

Bonnie raised her chin, gazing upon the kelpie's wild face. "It almost looks alive," she whispered.

"Aye, as if it's about to grab hold of ye and drag ye into the deep," her companion murmured.

Bonnie glanced his way to see the laird was gazing up at the statue.

"There is a darkness in ye, Iver," she observed softly. "A shadow that not even a magical evening like this one can lift."

He glanced her way, his gaze widening. "I didn't realize I was so transparent."

"Aye, ye are."

He huffed a wry laugh. "My brothers tell me I'm at risk of turning into a bitter old mon." His expression sobered then. "I've tended to brood of late ... sorry about that."

"Don't apologize," she murmured. "I just find ye full of contradictions ... that's all."

His mouth curved, and he stepped forward, reaching out and brushing a lock of hair off her forehead. Bonnie's breathing caught as the veil drew closer still. Her world shrank to this man, this moment. "As are ye, Adair Farquharson. Ye are a clan-chief's daughter, and yet there is something refreshingly earthy about ye. There have been moments over the last few hours when I feel as if I've known ye all my life, and then others when I wonder if this" —his fingers slid over the top border of her mask— "isn't the only mask ye wear."

12: DANGEROUS WATERS

BONNIE'S HEART KICKED against her breastbone.

If only he knew.

To hide her discomfort, she gave a light laugh and stepped back, creating a much-needed gulf between them. His nearness was heady, distracting—as were his observations. "My mother often complains of my lack of refinement," she replied, focusing on the 'earthy' comment. It was easier to answer than the others.

Her response wasn't a complete falsehood either. Her aunt Lorna, who'd brought her up in lieu of a mother, had told Bonnie numerous times over the years that she was 'common' and 'graceless'—an unfortunate consequence of being born a bastard.

Mackay snorted. "I like how natural ye are. It puts me at ease. I feel as if I can be myself with ye."

Their gazes held, and warmth curled in the pit of Bonnie's stomach. Her breathing quickened, and she cleared her throat. It was time to speak of other, safer, subjects. "Have ye seen 'the King's Knot?" she asked huskily.

He inclined his head. "No ... although I've heard of it. Isn't it where the king goes hawking and hunting ... and holds jousting tournaments at midsummer?"

"Aye." Bonnie gestured to the wall that edged the north of the garden. "There is a fine view over the Knot from up there ... it should be visible in the moonlight."

Bonnie had climbed up to the wall once as a bairn, after one of the stable lads had dared her, and marveled at the view over the grounds that spread out to the north of the castle.

Mackay flashed her a grin. "I should like to see it." He held out his arm for her to take hold of once more. "Lead the way."

Bonnie did. They circled the kelpie statue, their feet crunching on the fine pebbles underfoot, navigating the twisting paths of the garden until they reached the steps leading up to the high wall.

Wordlessly, they scaled them, side by side, and walked along the top of the wall, edged in high merlons. They then climbed another set of stone steps to a narrow terrace. Encircled by walls on all sides, it was a secluded space. However, the parapet that faced north was low enough to give them an uninterrupted view. Halting at the edge of it, Bonnie and Iver looked down upon a vast grassy space, illuminated by the starlight. At its center was a large octagonal mound.

"That's quite a view," Iver said after a lengthy pause.

"Aye," Bonnie replied softly, as entranced as he was. It looked as if a heavy frost lay upon the ground, yet it was just the moonlight. She remembered then what Ainslie had once told her about the grounds. "Folk say that the mound is an ancient one ... and that King Arthur's round table lies beneath the Knot."

"Aye, I'd believe it." Iver leaned against the wall then, turning to her. "I'm fond of the old tales ... my grandmother used to tell me a few."

Bonnie smiled. "Such as?"

He scratched his jaw. "Aye, well, there were many I loved ... but as a bairn, I especially enjoyed listening to the legend of Dunadd fort in Kilmartin Glen."

"The birthplace of Scotland ... isn't that where the first kings were crowned?"

"Aye, so ye have heard of it then?"

Bonnie shook her head. "The place ... but not the stories behind it."

His mouth curved. "Well, at the top of the fort, there's a rock with an impression of a footprint ... where kings would place their foot when they were crowned. There are plenty of theories on how it got there, but my grandmother always insisted it was made by Oisín, son of the giant Fingal. He was hunting on the hills above Loch Fyne when he was attacked by a great wolf. To get away, he took a big leap to Rhudle Hill, and then landed heavily on Dunadd Hill, creating the indent."

Bonnie's smile widened. "I like that story too." Indeed, listening to him talk delighted her. She'd never had a conversation like this. Most of the men she'd known over the years weren't eloquent, and the talk around the table in the Great Kitchens at mealtimes was mostly gossip and complaining—not folk tales.

Silence fell between them then, and Bonnie leaned up against the wall beside him, her gaze traveling north. It was such a clear night that she could see the outlines of the snow-capped mountains in the distance.

Moments passed, and then she became aware of Iver's gaze upon her.

Iver. She'd started thinking of him in familiar terms rather than by his clan-name. They'd only known each other one evening, and yet she felt so comfortable with him that she didn't want to think of him as 'Mackay' any longer.

Even so, the weight of his gaze made her breathing grow shallow, awareness prickling her skin.

She'd brought him to this spot, for it gave the best view of the King's Knot—and yet they were now shielded from prying eyes.

He knew it, and so did she.

Turning from the view, she raised her chin and met his eye.

He'd been smiling just moments earlier, yet he wasn't now. Instead, he was staring down at her with an intensity that made Bonnie's breathing quicken.

The moment drew out, and neither of them spoke.

Bonnie didn't move. To do so would break the enchantment that wreathed around them. Instead, Iver stepped close and raised a hand to cup her cheek.

And then, without another word, he lowered his mouth to hers.

His kiss was gentle—yet there was a question in it. He wanted to know if she would welcome his embrace, if he was going too far.

Bonnie stilled, breathing in his scent as his lips brushed across hers once more.

Step back, the voice of common sense whispered in her ear then. *Ye are straying into dangerous waters, lass.*

But Bonnie didn't move. Instead, she leaned forward slightly, her lips parting as his mouth found hers once more.

With a groan low in his throat, Iver placed his hands upon her shoulders and deepened the kiss.

His tongue slid into her mouth, caressing her own, and Bonnie's belly tightened, heat igniting in the cradle of her hips.

Lord, she liked that. She wanted more of it.

A sigh escaped her then, and she leaned into him further, kissing him back. He tasted of wine, with a hint of spice that made hunger spike through her.

Raising a hand, she caressed the strong line of his jaw, her fingertips running over rough stubble.

Iver's grip on her shoulders tightened, and he stepped in closer still as his mouth mated with hers. He was both gentle and passionate, a combination that made something inside her catch fire.

Bonnie's heart started to pound.

Eyes fluttering shut, she yielded completely to the kiss, to the taste and feel of his mouth.

She'd never been kissed like this—didn't know it could transport her so.

She sighed once more, her fingers trailing down his throat to the hollow between his collar bones. There, she felt his pulse fluttering against her fingertips.

Need arched up inside her, and her own heart started to hammer.

Despite the languorous way he was kissing her, Iver was holding himself in check.

Lord help her, she wanted to know what would happen if he lost control—if they both did.

Not questioning the impulse, she entwined her arms around his neck and stepped into him. Her teeth then grazed his bottom lip.

Another groan rumbled across his chest, and suddenly, he was kissing her wildly. An instant later, Bonnie found her back up against the wall, while his body pressed hard along the length of hers.

She answered his fierce hunger with her own as their tongues tangled and dueled. Iver tore his mouth from hers then and trailed kisses down her jaw to her throat.

Bonnie's head fell back. Heat pulsed in her lower belly at the feel of his lips sliding down her throat to where her breasts strained against the tight bodice of her gown. His tongue slid into her cleavage, tasting her there, and then his hands were on her, pushing down the already daring neckline.

The cool, silky night air whispered against her naked breasts—and then Iver's hot, hungry mouth was on them.

He'd cupped her breasts in his hands, lifting them to him wantonly.

Eyes flickering open, Bonnie lowered her gaze, watching as he feasted on one nipple and then the other. Her breasts, which gleamed in the moonlight, felt heavy, aching for his touch. He suckled her softly at first, yet quickly worked himself up into a frenzy, his teeth grazing the sensitive tips until she writhed against him.

Bonnie bit her lip, her fingers tunneling through his hair as he suckled her. Sensation arrowed straight down from her breasts to her womb with each hard suck—and the sensitive flesh between her thighs had started to pulse in time with her heartbeat.

When Iver finally tore his mouth from them, her nipples were swollen and glistening.

His gaze kicked up then, fusing with hers once more.

"Do ye want more of this, lass?" he murmured. His voice was husky, breathtakingly sensual. "I can stop now. The choice is yers."

Breasts heaving, Bonnie stared up at him. Framed by the dark-grey mask he wore, his eyes gleamed. In this light, they didn't look blue but inky black.

Her mind was muddled, her body trembling, desire pulsing through her, and he was asking her if she wished for more.

Harris hadn't ever checked that she was willing. The first time he'd taken her, she'd been a maid and he'd been eager. It had hurt.

But Iver was an altogether different man than the only other one she could compare him to—and despite the intimacy of what they'd already done, and the naked hunger on his face, he wanted this to be her decision.

"Don't stop," she whispered back, thrilling at her own boldness. "I want more ... I want *everything*."

13: FORGETTING

IVER'S BREATHING HITCHED as if her response shocked him.

Bonnie wouldn't have been surprised if it had, for she couldn't believe she'd uttered those lusty words.

Nonetheless, he recovered quickly. Growling an oath, Iver turned her around and pushed her heavy mane of hair to one side as his mouth explored the line of her neck and shoulder. He cupped her breasts once more, kneading them gently as his teeth grazed the sensitive skin of her neck.

Bonnie trembled against him, craving more.

His touch turned her inside out; it made her forget everything except this wild hunger. Excitement clenched deep inside her.

As if sensing her desperation, his hands slid from her breasts and down her torso. He then hiked up her full skirts.

Once again, the soft night air—so mild for this time of year—feathered against Bonnie's naked legs.

With one hand grasping her skirts, he explored the skin of her belly and thighs—and the soft nest of hair between them—with the other.

And when his fingers slid between her legs, parting her wide for him, Bonnie gasped. Dizziness swept over her, and she collapsed against the hard wall of his chest.

"It's all right, lass," he whispered. "Just brace yerself against me." With that, his leg slid between her thighs so she could lean on it. "Is that better?"

Bonnie gave a guttural moan. At present, she was beyond speech—for he was stroking her gently in a place that made her legs go weak, made the aching pleasure between her thighs intensify.

"Iver," she whimpered.

"Aye," he groaned. "Open yerself up to me ... that's it."

And, the Virgin forgive her, she did. Her thighs spread wider still as he stroked her, his fingers playing her as if he were a minstrel and she his lyre. She was so sensitive down there, the sensations he roused were almost unbearably delicious—yet he continued, relentless now.

Bonnie was aware of how wet she was, how the friction of his touch altered to a glide as her arousal deepened. Her breathing grew shallow, her bare breasts heaving. She was losing control, unraveling.

Her legs trembled under her, jerking as something hurtled toward her. If Iver hadn't been supporting her, she'd have collapsed in a heap at his feet.

But he held her fast in his arms, stroking her until warm, languorous pleasure pulsed between her thighs. Bonnie bit down hard on her bottom lip to stop herself from crying out. She barely managed to choke it back though, for the delicious sensation almost undid her.

She hung in Iver's arms, weak and quivering, in the aftermath, dimly aware that he'd removed his hand from between her slick thighs and was unlacing his leggings with the other.

And then, she felt his shaft, hot and hard, slide between the cleft of her buttocks.

Bonnie gasped once more, and the same heady excitement as earlier arrowed through her. Grabbing hold of the wall to anchor herself, she lifted her hips to him, offering herself.

His hot breath caressed the back of her neck as he positioned himself. An instant later, he slowly sank into her, and Bonnie let out a long, shuddering sigh.

Her legs started to shake once more at the delicious sensation of being filled. She couldn't help it, she rolled her hips, encouraging him to slide home fully.

Iver groaned another curse as he did just that.

Bonnie moved her hips in another languorous circle, her breathing catching as a melting sensation began in her womb. She then whispered his name.

He gripped her hips and withdrew in a long, sensual drag, almost to the tip, before sliding deep once more.

Bonnie writhed against him.

An instant later, Iver was plunging into her in measured, hard, determined thrusts.

Bonnie's lips parted, and she hung her head between her arms, giving herself up to pure sensation. He was so big, so hard—and he felt so good. Pleasure rippled through her whole body now, every nerve alight.

Suddenly, he pulled out of her.

No! A cry of disappointment rose in Bonnie's throat. However, Iver spun her around and pressed her back against the wall, spreading her against it before thrusting into her once more.

Now that they were facing each other again, his mouth captured hers, his tongue sliding rhythmically into her mouth as he plowed her.

And if Bonnie had thought the last position was going to send her spiraling off the edge of a cliff—this one was even more exquisite, even more intense.

Every time he slammed home, he touched a place that made her writhe, that turned her wild. She clung to his broad shoulders, her fingers digging into leather.

Moments later, she shattered for a second time, shuddering against him. She couldn't help it, she did cry out then, yet the sob was muffled by his mouth.

Iver held her tight as he continued to thrust into her, his movements jerky and frenzied now. Bonnie could do nothing but cling to him, tears of ecstasy leaking from her eyes and soaking into her mask.

A few moments later, Iver tore his lips from hers and buried his face in her bare shoulder. He then gave one last powerful thrust and went rigid against her.

Bonnie gasped at the sting of his teeth biting down on the tender skin where her shoulder met her neck. His rod pulsed inside her, spilling its liquid heat.

And after that, all she could hear was the rasp of their breathing and the thunder of her heart.

It took Iver a while to recover his wits.

His climax had sent him free-falling down a tunnel, and when he'd landed, it had knocked the wind out of him.

Face buried in Adair's shoulder, his arms wrapped around her trembling body, he waited for his heart to slow. At present, it was pounding like a hunting drum. Sweat slicked his skin, and it was fortunate that he was leaning against the wall, for his legs had gone weak in the aftermath of taking Adair.

Christ's blood, he hadn't meant for things to go that far.

He hadn't even meant to kiss her, yet standing together in the moonlight, a madness of sorts had come over him. He'd suddenly *had* to know what her lips tasted like—and then once he'd begun kissing her, he hadn't been able to stop.

Adair had been willing, yet that was no excuse. *He* should have been the one to pace things.

Gradually, his pulse settled, and he became aware of his surroundings once more: the cool air on his heated skin; the warm, musky scent of his lover's arousal; and the whisper of her breath in his ear.

Still holding her tightly, he raised his face.

In the moonlight, he could see a red mark on her shoulder. His stomach contracted then as he remembered sinking his teeth into her flesh. It was the only thing that had stopped him bellowing like a stag in rutting season, yet guilt speared him now.

"I'm sorry for biting ye," he whispered huskily. "I forgot myself."

Adair raised her hand then and caressed his face. "We both did." Her breathing was ragged, her gaze dark and limpid. Like him, she was still reeling from what they'd just done.

Iver was no untried lad, yet he'd never experienced anything like this. He'd lost control, as had she. He remained buried deep inside her, and Adair's legs were still entwined around his hips, her naked breasts pressed up against his chest.

Despite that the wall shielded them from view, they were exposed up here—and yet neither of them moved.

The moonlight highlighted Adair's face as she stared up at him. Her lips were slightly parted, and her gaze now gleamed. Releasing one of his arms from behind her, Iver raised a hand to her face. He then huffed a soft laugh. "Can ye believe, we're both still wearing masks, lass?" he murmured.

She swallowed. "Aye, well ... our attention was elsewhere."

Iver's mouth curved. It certainly had been. This woman was delicious. He wanted to take her back to his bedchamber and feast on her sweet, soft body for the rest of the night. His pulse quickened once more at the thought.

An instant later, he wrenched his attention back to the present. He needed to get ahold of himself. Such things could wait—first, he wanted to see the face of the woman who'd enchanted him.

"I think it's time we revealed ourselves then," he said softly, his fingers grasping the edge of her mask.

Adair's breathing caught. "I—"

The tinkle of feminine laughter interrupted them, followed by the rumble of a male voice.

Iver froze. They were no longer alone—someone else was approaching their sanctuary.

Lowering his hand from her mask, he withdrew from her, sliding from her heat. Disappointment arrowed through him as he did so, although he pushed the sensation aside. There would be time for more intimacy later.

First, he needed to deal with the intruders.

"Wait here," he murmured. "I shall see whoever it is off."

Adair nodded. She was adjusting her gown, pulling the bodice up over her magnificent breasts and smoothing her rumpled skirts.

Iver did up his leggings and turned away, taking the steps toward where the woman's laughter, louder now, drifted across the wall.

Halfway down the steps, his gaze alighted on a tall, lean man dressed like a jester, and a woman in a flowing gown wearing a feline mask with long whiskers. They walked hand in hand toward him.

"Good eve," Iver greeted them smoothly.

The couple halted, their gazes lifting to him.

"A bonnie night it is too," the man replied, his tone guarded.

Iver leaned up against the wall, folding his arms across his chest. "And it is a fine view from up here."

"It is."

"Nonetheless, I hear the vista is even better from the northwest lookout," Iver added lightly.

The moment stretched out, and when it became clear that Iver wasn't moving aside to let the couple pass, the man cleared his throat. "Aye, well ... we shall take in the view from there." He nodded to Iver. "Good eve."

"Good eve."

The couple turned and walked away. Iver watched them go, and when he was satisfied that they were indeed leaving, he turned and retraced his steps back up to the terrace.

But when he returned to the wall where he'd left Adair, she was gone.

14: A FADING DREAM

BONNIE'S LEGS WOBBLED under her as she hurried through the garden, yet she didn't slow her step. And all the while, warm stickiness—Iver's seed—trickled down her thighs.

She didn't want to leave him, yet she had to.

He'd been about to remove her mask, and once he dealt with their intruders, he would.

Bonnie couldn't let that happen.

Until now, she'd been pretending to be someone else, but once Iver saw her face, he'd remember it. Perhaps then, he'd recognize the chambermaid who'd tripped in the inner close the day before.

Bonnie almost broke into a run then. However, she couldn't panic. She had to remain composed. She'd shortly be passing in front of the guards who watched over the outer close.

She couldn't draw attention to herself.

Bonnie swallowed hard, not daring to look over her shoulder.

He'd come after her; she was sure of it.

She'd slipped down the steps that led from the eastern side of the terrace as soon as he disappeared—yet it wouldn't be long before he returned to the wall and discovered her missing.

Bonnie passed out of the garden, under the archway.

Her heart was beating so hard, she felt as if it would explode from her chest.

Suddenly, the archway that led into the inner close seemed leagues distant.

She hurried her step further, panic clawing up her throat.

I can't let him catch me.

An enchantment of some kind had fallen over her this evening. When she'd danced with Iver in the great hall and spoken with him afterward, she'd let herself get carried away. Once she'd mastered her nerves, she seemed to have forgotten this wasn't one of her fantasies. It was real—and reality had consequences.

Ainslie had issued her a few stern warnings, but she'd completely disregarded her friend's advice.

Worse still, she'd coupled with a stranger on the castle walls.

Bonnie's throat constricted then, tears stinging her eyelids. Indeed, she'd inherited her mother's recklessness.

No woman with any sense of self-preservation would have let herself go like that.

I want more ... I want everything.

Heat flushed through Bonnie at the memory of her gasped words.

Did she have no shame at all?

It was just as well she'd never have to face Iver Mackay again.

Reaching the inner close, and passing by the guards flanking the archway, Bonnie crossed to the kitchens. She ducked inside the warm space, glancing around as she did so to make sure that no one was about.

Fortune was with her, for the large space was empty.

The hearths at one end burned low, the red-gold embers casting a soft light over the shadowy kitchens.

Bonnie didn't linger there. Instead, she retrieved a bowl, a drying cloth, and a jug of water. Then, hooking a lantern over one arm, she hurried up the stone steps. As always, she took the servants' stairwell to her attic.

She met no one on the way, for at this hour, most of Stirling's servants, except for the guards and those serving in the great hall, were tucked up in their beds.

As she should have been.

Bonnie had never scaled the stairs so quickly, and by the time she reached the attic, her pulse was pounding in her ears.

Climbing into the loft, and careful not to spill the water, she set down the items she'd brought with her. Then, she stripped off her mask and gown. Her hands trembled as she did so, and she fumbled with the laces, yet eventually, the damask pooled at her feet.

Worry tightened Bonnie's ribcage then. She and Iver had been careless. What if she'd damaged Ainslie's gown? She held it up before the glow of the lantern, inspecting it. However, she couldn't see any tears or stains.

Huffing out a relieved breath, she carefully folded the garment, smoothing out any creases. She then placed the mask on top of it.

Naked, she crouched before the bowl, wet the cloth she'd brought from the kitchen, wrung it out, and washed herself.

Part of her, the traitorous part that lacked good sense and modesty, didn't want to wash Iver's seed away. She could still smell him on her skin, and she longed to crawl into her nest of sheepskins and fall asleep enveloped in his scent.

Her skin prickled then. What if her womb quickened? Her courses were due in just a couple of days—but if they never arrived, she'd be in deep trouble.

"Foolish chit," she muttered between gritted teeth. "Ye must act sensibly from now on."

Something deep inside her chest twisted then. Lord help her, she didn't want to let go of this evening's magic. Aye, she'd felt like an imposter amongst those lords and ladies, but that hadn't stopped her from walking in their world for a short while—a world where a man like Iver looked her way.

But the truth was *this* life was all she had, and there was no escaping it. She was trapped within the walls of Stirling Castle, bound to a chambermaid's existence.

Tears blurred her vision once more as she finished washing and pulled on the scratchy léine she always wore for bed.

He'll still be searching for me.

The ache under her breastbone intensified. He'd be alarmed that she'd run off into the night; he'd want to know she was well.

Lying amongst her sheepskins, staring up into the darkness, Bonnie reached up, her fingers tracing the spot on her shoulder where he'd bitten her.

It *had* hurt—and yet at the same time, she'd welcomed the pain, the feeling of possession.

Heat ignited low in her belly as she recalled how she'd unraveled, twice, in his arms.

It's over … let him go.

And yet she couldn't. Not yet.

Squeezing her eyes shut, as hot tears scalded her eyelids, Bonnie rolled onto her side. Tonight, she wouldn't let herself dream about the forbidden. No, those days were over. Such fancies were dangerous, for they blurred the edges between fantasy and reality.

And Bonnie had just learned that reality had sharp edges—ones that left bruises.

"Brother?"

Blinking, Iver glanced up from his untouched bannock. He'd spread it with butter and honey yet hadn't taken a bite. Lennox's voice sounded as if it were reaching him from afar. "What?" he asked distractedly.

His brother made an irritated noise in the back of his throat. "Were ye actually listening to anything I just said?"

Iver sighed and forced himself to focus on Lennox.

The two of them sat at the small table in Iver's bedchamber. Servants had just brought in bannocks and a jug of watered-down ale for them to break their fast with. However, neither man had touched the food.

In the silvery light filtering in from the open window, Lennox's face was pale and drawn, his dark-blue eyes bloodshot.

He looked rough, although Iver wagered—despite that he hadn't overindulged in drink like his brother—*he* didn't look much better.

He hadn't slept at all the night before.

"No," he said with a sigh. "Sorry. Could ye repeat yerself?"

Lennox muttered something under his breath before raising his cup of watery ale to his lips and gingerly taking a sip. "I was saying that we need to hurry ourselves up," he replied. "The king's council starts shortly."

Iver grunted, raking a hand through his hair. Satan's cods, he'd almost forgotten the meeting they'd all been bid to attend in the king's solar. It was the reason Niel had sent Iver here in the first place.

Yet, Iver was so preoccupied this morning—his thoughts upon the woman he'd met the night before—the council had completely slipped his mind.

Across the table, Lennox frowned. "What is wrong with ye?"

"Nothing."

His brother's mouth pursed. "Liar." He leaned forward then and raised both hands to his temples massaging gently. "Curse it," he muttered. "I'm in no fit state for this council either ... it feels as if a tribe of vicious imps has taken hammers to my thought cage."

"I'm not surprised," Iver replied. He then lifted his cup to his lips and drained it. "Ye overdid it last night."

Lennox snorted. "Ye enjoyed yerself too if I recall. I was sober enough to see how taken ye were with that red-haired beauty ye were dancing with." His brother's mouth quirked then. "And Campbell and I both saw ye leave the hall with her."

Iver tensed, casting his brother a scowl. He pushed himself to his feet, massaging a tense muscle in his shoulder.

However, Lennox was favoring him with a speculative look now. "I expected to see ye with a spring in yer step this morn, brother. Yet ye look as if someone just pissed in yer porridge."

"Leave it, would ye," Iver muttered.

The scrape of wood echoed through the bedchamber as Lennox pushed back his chair and rose to his feet. He winced then. "The Devil take me, that was loud."

Together, the brothers left the chamber and made their way to the spiral stairwell that would take them down a level. It was still early, yet already the keep was busy.

Servants hurried past carrying chamber pots that needed emptying and sheets to be laundered.

Iver and Lennox paid them little notice.

Instead, as Iver made his way down the stairs, his thoughts turned inward once more.

Why did she run?

He'd searched for Adair in the garden and the outer and inner close courtyards before he entered the keep and scoured each floor. Nonetheless, he'd known it was futile. He couldn't go around door-knocking, and Stirling Castle housed a great number of people.

Even so, he'd been so desperate that he'd asked some of the guards if they'd seen her. None had.

Eventually, Iver had given up and returned to his chamber.

There, he'd flung open the window and gazed out at the moonlit night, trying to make sense of things. He'd never felt so comfortable with anyone as he had with Adair Farquharson. For a short while, he'd forgotten his vow never to expose his heart again, never to take a wife. And in the aftermath of their tryst on the walls, he'd been determined to get to know her better.

Maybe fate was done tormenting him.

And yet, Adair had melted into the night like a shadow the moment his back was turned.

The sting of old hurts had risen then, as Iver stared up at the moon. He'd suffered a few rejections over the years—and two, in particular, had left a scar—but he'd never actually had a woman flee from him.

It was tempting to withdraw, to lick his wounds in private and put the encounter behind him.

And yet, he couldn't. The events of the night before had jolted him out of the malaise that had plagued him over the past years. This morning, it was as if his old self had just awoken from a deep slumber. Suddenly, he no longer wanted to hide away.

Iver ground his teeth together. *Curse the king and this council.*

He wasn't in the mood for it. He wanted to find Adair instead.

Reaching the floor below, he headed toward the open door of the solar. The growl of male voices drifted out, warning him that the room was rapidly filling up.

As much as it chafed him, he needed to put Adair out of his mind for the moment; nonetheless, now that the magic of yestereve had gone, something niggled at him. An odd disquiet. Adair wasn't like any laird's daughter he'd ever met.

I have to find her.

And as soon as he got this council out of the way, he would.

15: NOT OUR QUARREL

TENSION CRACKLED THROUGH the large solar. The air felt heavy, as before a thunderstorm. This council was highly anticipated, and clan representatives had traveled from every corner of Scotland to attend.

And as Iver had predicted, the room was nearly full. Servants had brought in a few trestle tables and pushed them together to form one large meeting table, which they'd then covered with a blood-red velvet cloth. They'd removed much of the furniture from the room, to make space, and carried in long benches for the clan-chiefs and chieftains to sit upon.

King James had already taken his place at the head of the table, seated upon a high-backed chair with courtiers flanking him. The queen wasn't with James this morning—indeed, there were no women present.

Only men were invited to political councils such as this one.

Taking one of the few spaces remaining, next to Colin Campbell, Iver nodded to him.

In response, the Lord of Glenorchy flashed him a knowing smile. "Enjoyed yerself last night, did ye, Iver?"

"Aye," Iver grunted, pretending not to notice the glint in the older man's eye.

Sensing Iver's mood, Campbell cast a questioning look at Lennox, who'd squeezed onto the end of the bench seat next to his brother. "Looking a little peaky this morn, lad," he observed.

Lennox pulled a face. He glanced then over the table at where Malcolm Sutherland glowered across at him. The two men locked gazes, their stare drawing out before Iver leaned into his brother and growled. "Let it go."

A muscle flexed in Lennox's jaw, yet he obeyed, cutting his gaze from Sutherland and focusing instead on where the king had risen to his feet.

The rumble of conversation inside the solar died.

"Good morning," James greeted them. "I take it ye all enjoyed yerselves yestereve?" A chorus of 'ayes' followed, and the king smiled. "I thank ye for being my guests, and for rousing yerselves from yer beds for this early council. We have much to discuss."

Iver inwardly groaned at this news. In contrast to his early days as chieftain, where he'd enjoyed the verbal sparring of such meetings, they just exhausted him now.

Nonetheless, he'd have to suffer through this.

The bench he sat on was hard and uncomfortable, and despite that one of the windows was open, letting in a fresh breeze, the smell in here was rank. There were too many bodies, many of whom needed a bath, pressed in close together. The odor of stale sweat mixed with the pungent reek of wine and ale.

In contrast, the king was bathed and coiffed, and dressed in a fresh crimson surcote. He didn't look like he'd made merry the eve before with his guests; although at two and twenty, Iver also could drink a skinful and then wield a broadsword in the morning without batting an eye.

"We shall begin our council with a report from each of ye," James announced, settling back into his chair and picking up a goblet of wine. His gaze then cut right to where a tall, lean man with dark greying hair sat. "Let us start with the Gunns."

Tavish Gunn rose to his feet and began his report. However, as the clan-chief's voice rumbled across the solar, Iver found his thoughts returning to the lovely Adair.

Where was she right now?

Most likely with the queen and her ladies-in-waiting. As soon as this council was done, he'd seek her out in the ladies' solar.

Gunn's summary was brief. Answering a question from the king, he then settled back into his seat and let the man next to him heave himself to his feet and say his bit.

But now that Ian MacLeod—a red-faced, loquacious clan-chief from the Isle of Skye—was the center of attention, he was determined to hold it. After a few words about general business, he started on about how the MacDonalds were stealing his sheep. Eventually, James brought his complaints to a halt with a dismissive wave of his hand and the muttered the words, "I've heard enough."

A few minutes later, it was Iver's turn. Rising to his feet, he relayed the words Niel had sent him. There wasn't a lot to say as the clan was indeed peaceful and prosperous these days.

He finished speaking and was about to sit down when James forestalled him. "Why isn't yer clan-chief here to speak for himself? Is he too busy to meet with his king?"

"He's recovering from the grippe, Sire," Iver replied. It was the truth. Illness had raged through Castle Varrich all winter.

James's brow furrowed. "But he is on the mend?"

"Aye."

The king's full lips pursed. "It's a pity Niel isn't here. He holds much power in the north ... and I wish to seek an assurance from him."

Iver inclined his head. "I am my clan-chief's emissary, Sire ... as such, ye may ask me. He has given me leave to speak on his behalf."

James huffed a sigh. "Very well. Can ye reassure me that the Mackays are wholly loyal to the crown?" He cut a veiled glance to where William Douglas sat. "And that he will not seek alliances with other Highland clan-chiefs."

Tension coiled in Iver's gut, his own gaze resting upon Douglas's face. The older man's expression was shuttered. Of course, everyone here knew what James was alluding to. The king suspected that some of the Highland lairds were moving against him.

It was concerning that James's distrust extended to the Mackays.

"Niel Mackay is loyal, Yer Highness," Iver replied after a brief pause. "As are all his chieftains ... I swear it."

James stared back at him. His expression was inscrutable, yet his brown eyes were hard. "Good," he said, his tone clipped. "Nonetheless, I will need confirmation from the clan-chief himself. Ye are to send word to Niel and inform him I require a signed declaration of his loyalty."

"Aye, Sire," Iver replied, even as heat flickered to life under his ribcage.

James was his king, yet Iver didn't appreciate the man's tone. His lack of trust was insulting. He hadn't demanded such a declaration from the other clan-chiefs who'd spoken so far—and his order made it look as if James had a problem with Niel specifically.

The king's interrogation ended there, but even as Iver sat back down—exchanging a look with his brother as he did so—his anger still smoldered. Niel would likely comply with the order, but he would chafe at it.

James's aggressive stance risked making him more enemies than friends. Indeed, the king seemed in a testy mood this morning.

Colin Campbell stood up then and made his report. And when he was done, Iver noted that the king didn't seek any assurances from the Lord of Glenorchy either.

Slowly, the talk edged around the table, and eventually finished with William Douglas, who sat directly to the king's left.

Douglas didn't waste words. His report was terse and lasted only a few lines.

When he was done, James's gaze narrowed. "Is that all, William?"

"Aye, Sire."

James inclined his head. "Are ye sure ye aren't leaving anything out?"

The earl shook his head, his face unreadable.

A heavy silence fell across the table, while the tension in Iver's stomach tightened once more.

Of course, the king had been building up to this moment.

James leaned back in his carven chair, tapping his smoothly shaven chin with a fingertip. "Interesting ... for I've heard that ye have been busy indeed recently."

"I have told ye all my news, Sire," Douglas rumbled.

James's eyes glinted. "And yet ye left out yer recent meeting with John MacDonald and Alexander Lindsay."

Murmurs rose then, although James silenced them with a sharply raised hand.

"I might have," Douglas replied, his expression still veiled. "But surely, that's my business. John and Alex are old friends of mine."

Iver shared another look with Lennox then. A groove had furrowed between his brother's eyebrows.

MacDonald, the Earl of Ross, and Lindsay, the Earl of Crawford, were two of the most influential men in Scotland. Lindsay was known as the 'Tiger Earl', while MacDonald held a second title of 'Lord of the Isles' and could trace his ancestry back to the times when the Norse had raided these shores.

"Perhaps," James replied, his voice hardening. "But they're not *my* friends. MacDonald and Lindsay rule like kings in the north ... and make no secret that they see me as a 'lowland' king with no power over them."

Douglas held James's stare. "Ye're mistaken, Sire ... neither would presume to ignore yer authority."

James took another sip from his goblet before setting it down on the table in front of him. "Yer assurances are empty, William. I have eyes in the Highlands ... and I know those two are plotting against me." A nerve flickered on his left cheek, making his red birthmark twitch. "And I ask ye to break yer bond with them."

Iver's breathing grew shallow. James wasn't bandying words this morning. Here was the reason he'd called this council—the reason he'd given Douglas safe conduct to

Stirling. He wanted *all* the Highland lairds to kneel before him.

However, the king's request clearly didn't sit well with the earl, for his mouth compressed. His dark brows then drew together as he folded his arms across his chest. "I will not."

Silence fell in the solar, shock rippling through the stuffy air.

The king's long face stiffened, his cheeks flushing. "Is that yer final word on the matter?" There was a rasp to his voice, as if he was struggling to control his temper.

"It is."

"False traitor," James spat. "Since ye will not, I shall."

And with that, the king catapulted from his chair and launched himself at Douglas.

Steel glinted, and the earl reared back. Not in time though, for the blade of the jeweled dirk the king had just drawn sank deep into his shoulder.

A roar went up around the table, and the clan leaders and representatives lurched to their feet—Iver among them.

But the king and Douglas were now on the floor.

And as they looked on, James lifted his blood-stained blade high before plunging it deep into the earl's neck.

Douglas's raw cries filled the room, joining the muttered oaths from some of the gathered men. He was trying to fight the younger man off, yet the king had straddled his chest, pinning him to the ground.

And when James brought his dirk down once more with a meaty thud, Iver's heart lurched into his throat. Alarm propelled him forward, and he moved toward the two struggling figures.

King James had lost his wits. He had to stop him before he killed Douglas.

But Campbell grabbed Iver by the arm and held him back.

Snarling a curse, Iver tried to twist away, yet Campbell's fingers bit into his flesh, his grip like iron. "Stay out of this, Iver," he growled. "This isn't our quarrel."

"Christ's blood," Lennox muttered. His gaze wasn't on his brother but on where the king continued to drive his blade into the earl's shoulders and neck. Lennox's face was now taut and pale. Like Iver, he'd seen, and dealt out, death many times. However, witnessing their king attack an unarmed man—seeing him lose control—was shocking.

James was in a frenzy.

William Douglas's cries had stopped now, replaced by wet choking sounds.

Bile surged, stinging the back of Iver's throat. This was obscene.

And then, if the king's savage attack wasn't enough, one of the king's courtiers, a tall man with close-cropped yellow hair, grabbed a poleax, from where it hung on the wall, and rushed forward, bringing it down upon the earl's head.

16: THERE WILL BE REPRISALS

BONNIE WAS CARRYING a pile of freshly laundered sheets out of the laundry, and was about to cross the inner close back to the keep, when the screaming started.

Skidding to a halt, heart lurching into her throat, Bonnie glanced around. "What the devil?" she breathed.

The screams, hysterical and female, echoed off the surrounding stone. However, after a moment, she realized they were coming from the garden behind the chapel.

Forgetting her chores, Bonnie turned and hurried toward the passageway that led between the castle's chapel and the keep. An archway took her through to a small garden.

Bonnie had never set foot in this space before, for servants weren't usually permitted inside. But since the screaming had now disintegrated into shrieks and sobs, she forgot all about propriety.

Something was wrong, and she had to help.

But when Bonnie rushed into the secluded garden, framed on one side by a high wall where ivy climbed, and on the other by the keep, a grisly sight greeted her.

A man's body lay spread-eagled on the pavers. His right arm was twisted at an impossible angle, blood slicked his neck, and he appeared to be missing part of his face.

Bonnie came to an abrupt halt, clutching the sheets against her chest, her gaze riveted upon the mangled corpse.

A group of ladies dressed in jewel-colored surcotes, the queen amongst them, had gathered in a terrified knot a few feet away from the body. Many of them were weeping, although Queen Mary kept her composure. Nevertheless, her lovely face was ashen as she stared at the dead man lying nearby.

Swallowing down bile, Bonnie looked up at the open window far above. She then whispered an oath.

Someone had thrown the man from there.

If the women had been standing just a few feet closer to the keep's wall, he would have dropped onto their heads.

"Who was it?"

"William Douglas." Hands trembling, Bonnie lifted the cup of wine to her lips, taking a fortifying gulp.

Her admission caused one or two of the servants gathered around her to cross themselves, while others muttered oaths under their breaths.

"The queen recognized him," Bonnie continued shakily. In truth, she was surprised Mary had managed to, for the poor man's head had been a mess.

She took another large gulp of wine before a tall figure elbowed her way through the press of servants inside the kitchen.

Lorna ripped the cup from Bonnie's hands. "Who gave ye that?" she snapped.

"I did," Ainslie admitted, scowling at the head cook. "Go easy on the lass, Lorna. She's just had a terrible shock." Ainslie stepped closer to Bonnie and placed a comforting hand on her shoulder. "Do ye know what happened?"

Bonnie shook her head. "There was shouting coming from the solar window upstairs. Someone threw Douglas out of it."

"The king did it!" A young male voice, high with excitement, intruded then. The crowd of servants parted to allow the page boy through. "I was there," he announced, wild-eyed. "I saw it all."

Everyone's gazes rested upon the lad, Bonnie forgotten.

"The king and Douglas argued ... and then the king drew his dirk and attacked him."

Gasps reverberated around the smoky kitchens in response.

Before Bonnie had rushed in, the servants had been hard at work preparing the noon meal. However, the leek and turnip pies had been forgotten for the moment.

"He stabbed him again and again," the lad went on, relishing his tale now. "And then one of the king's attendants took a poleax to Douglas's head."

A collective gasp went up then.

"When the king was sure Douglas was dead, he and his courtiers dragged his body to the window and threw it out," the page concluded.

More murmured oaths followed. The faces surrounding Bonnie drained of color. Likewise, she was still queasy from what she'd just witnessed.

"Mother Mary," Lorna muttered, crossing herself. "Why would our king do such a thing?"

Someone in the crowd muttered something about the 'Black Dinner' then, and Bonnie swallowed hard. Few in Scotland *hadn't* heard about *that* grisly incident.

"But it happened years ago," Alba, who was standing next to her sister behind their mother, pointed out. "Surely, this wasn't revenge for that?"

"I doubt it, lass," Ainslie spoke up then. "It has more to do with the Douglases threatening James's authority. Angus has been telling me for a while how relations have been steadily worsening between the king and that clan." All gazes swiveled to the head laundress then. Of course, as her husband was chamberlain, he had access to such details. "William Douglas has been making powerful allies."

Bonnie was still feeling queasy when she took the servant's stairwell upstairs to continue her morning's work.

It was difficult to concentrate on something as mundane as changing beds when a man had been murdered within the walls of the castle.

Murdered by the *king*.

Entering a chamber, she set about ripping the old sheets off the large canopied bed within before replacing them with clean ones.

The task, which she carried out multiple times each day, was hard work this morning. She was tired, her limbs heavy, a dull ache throbbing in her lower belly.

She'd awoken at dawn to discover that her monthly courses had arrived a couple of days early. Relieved, she'd pulled on a pair of woolen leggings under her skirts and used a folded piece of linen to soak up the blood.

Straightening up from smoothing out the bottom sheet on the bed, Bonnie's hand went to her tender lower belly.

She'd taken a risk the night before but had escaped her womb quickening.

"Foolish lass," she murmured, her eyes fluttering shut. "Ye play with fire."

And she had. She'd been caught up in the excitement, and all good sense had fled. Drunk on Iver Mackay's company, she'd cast caution aside.

Heat flushed over her then as images of what they'd done up on the walls returned to her, how he'd touched her and then taken her. Even now, her breathing quickened at the toe-curling memory.

Shoving it aside, Bonnie grabbed a sheet and cast it across the wide bed. "Just be grateful ye aren't with bairn," she muttered.

Aye, she was thankful, and yet her mood all morning—before Douglas's murder—had been oddly flat.

Life would go on now as it always had. She had returned to the shadows, and there she'd stay. For the rest of her life.

Stepping away from the bed, Bonnie's hand lifted, pushing aside the neckline of her kirtle. Her fingers traced the tender spot on her shoulder where Iver had bitten her.

It was the only thing she had left of him—and soon that too would fade.

But more than the physical closeness they'd shared, she'd miss the emotional connection between them. She'd never had a conversation like the one she'd had with Iver.

She wanted to etch every word upon her mind.

Bonnie's throat tightened. Curse it, when her courses came, she was always far too emotional, and after this morning's shock, her nerves were jangled.

It wouldn't do to dwell on Iver Mackay at present, not when the memories were so fresh. Instead, she had to focus on catching up on her work.

Unfortunately though, fate was conspiring against her today, for on her next trip down to the laundry, Ainslie bustled over to her, gently took Bonnie by the arm, and steered her to a quiet corner.

Smoky the cat followed them, abandoning her sleeping kittens to greet her favorite visitor. The mouser wound her way sinuously around Bonnie's ankles while Ainslie glanced around, making sure no one was looking their way.

Her blue eyes crinkled at the corners as she smiled at Bonnie. "Well?"

Bonnie's pulse quickened. "Well, *what?*"

"Och, lass, don't keep me in suspense. I know, what with everything that's happened this morning, ye are distracted ... but curiosity is eating me up. How was the ball?"

Bonnie forced a bright, answering smile. Ainslie had been so kind to her, so generous, that she had to give her the news she was so eager to hear. "It was magical," she murmured. "Like stepping into a dream."

Ainslie's smile slid into a delighted grin. "Did ye dance with any handsome lairds then?"

Bonnie nodded, keeping her own smile plastered upon her face. "I had a few show interest in me," she lied, "and I danced until my feet felt ready to fall off."

Ainslie's expression sobered, and she stepped closer still before glancing over her shoulder. The laundry was crowded this morning, yet the slap of wet clothing and the rhythmic thud of wooden bats beating soiled washing drowned out their conversation. Nonetheless, Ainslie was being careful. "Did ye do as I advised, lass?" she whispered.

"Aye ... I introduced myself as Adair Farquharson of Braemar Castle, and no one questioned my identity."

Ainslie nodded, relief flaring in her eyes. "And ye didn't linger too long either?"

Bonnie shook her head, even as her chest constricted. She hated lying to Ainslie, and she wanted to unburden herself to her, but as kind-hearted as her friend was, Bonnie wasn't sure how Ainslie would react to hearing the truth.

"I have yer gown upstairs ... and the mask too," she murmured then. "Shall I bring them down to yer chambers after the noon meal?"

"What has the king done?" Iver paced the chamber, his long legs eating up the ground. "He'll throw us into civil war!"

"Calm down, Iver." Campbell's powerful voice rumbled across the room. "None of us should speak rashly at present."

Swiveling on his heel, Iver pinned Campbell with a hard stare. "That's rich, coming from ye, Colin," he growled. "Just yestereve, ye were muttering about the Douglas 'traitor'."

The Lord of Glenorchy shrugged, unmoved by Iver's accusation. "Aye ... a sentiment the king clearly shares."

Lennox, who was leaning against the window frame, arms folded across his chest, gave a soft snort. "There's no doubting that."

Iver muttered a curse, even as his gaze remained upon Campbell. "Do ye think James *planned* to slay Douglas today?"

Campbell shook his head. "He always carries that ceremonial dirk at his side ... and ye know the lad's got a fiery temper on him."

Iver shook his head and walked to the glowing hearth, shifting his attention to the dancing flames. "After the rage we witnessed earlier, I'd say that's an understatement."

"Aye, none of us will dare contradict him in the future ... not after this," Lennox pointed out.

Iver grimaced. Lennox wasn't wrong. Following the slaughter in the solar, James and his attendants had thrown Douglas's mutilated body out of the window before the sound of women wailing could be heard.

When the clan-chiefs and chieftains gathered had all eventually dispersed, they'd left the king, blood-splattered and panting as he emerged from his murderous rage, surrounded by his loyal courtiers.

Iver and Lennox had followed Campbell to his chamber, where they could respond to the incident in private. Even though Iver was outraged by the king's behavior, he had the wits to understand that Stirling Castle was a barrel of Greek fire right now. One spark could incinerate them all.

"I think we need some wine," Campbell announced, rising to his feet. He then crossed to a sideboard and poured three generous cups before handing them to his guests.

Iver lifted the cup to his lips and took a large gulp. It was rich grape wine, and it warmed the chill in his belly.

Campbell stood next to him, his own hands wrapped around his cup, his brow furrowed. "I know I voiced some strong opinions about Douglas last night," he said after a pause. "And I still stand by them ... however, I never expected the king to do this."

"Iver's right though," Lennox spoke up once more from where he still leaned against the window frame. "Clan Douglas won't stand for this. There *will* be reprisals."

17: THE INTERLOPER

AN ODD QUIET settled over Stirling Castle in the days following the death of William Douglas. Some of the guests departed swiftly afterward, without fanfare or drawn-out leave-taking.

However, the Mackay brothers remained.

Unfortunately for Iver, Colin Campbell hadn't forgotten that they'd accepted his invitation to visit Kilchurn. The laird had business in Stirling after the council, and so Iver and Lennox were forced to wait until he too was ready to depart.

Initially, Iver had ground his teeth at the thought of having to make a detour to Kilchurn, and to endure Campbell's clumsy attempts at matchmaking.

But these extra days in Stirling gave him the opportunity he needed.

The queen and her ladies locked themselves away for the first two days after the council, yet Iver paid them a visit on the third morning.

He hadn't wanted to disturb them earlier, for it seemed in poor taste. Nonetheless, he could delay this no longer.

He just hoped Adair hadn't already departed like so many of the other guests.

Standing in the doorway to the ladies' solar, and uncomfortably pinned by curious female stares, he asked if they knew the whereabouts of Lady Adair Farquharson.

The queen was seated by the fire, embroidering. Two of her ladies sat at her feet. One of them wound wool onto a spindle, while the other sorted through a large basket of thread. A third lady worked at a loom by the window.

This chamber was like a more richly furnished version of his mother's solar back at Dun Ugadale. Scented with dried herbs, warm, and filled with brightly-hued cushions, it was a welcoming, feminine space.

Queen Mary met his eye before shaking her head. "Apologies, Mackay," she said, her voice low and melodious. Her face was a little pale and drawn this morning. "But I know no one by the name."

Iver stiffened. "Ye don't, Yer Highness?"

As a clan-chief's daughter, Adair should have spent time with the queen and her ladies during her stay at Stirling.

Mary held his gaze for a moment longer, curiosity igniting in her blue eyes. She then shifted her attention to her companions. "Do any of ye know Adair Farquharson?"

One by one, they all shook their heads.

"Ye would remember the lady if ye had seen her," Iver said. "For she has russet hair ... of a similar shade to the king's."

"All the Farquharsons have red hair," one of the court ladies, the one at the tapestry, answered with a pert smile. "He has a large brood of sons and daughters ... but I don't recall one called Adair."

Iver's brow furrowed.

A large brood of sons and daughters? Adair had said she only had two younger sisters.

An awkward silence fell in the ladies' solar then.

Iver shifted, uncomfortable under penetrating female gazes. He hadn't meant to do so, yet he'd piqued their curiosity. No doubt, he'd be the subject of gossip the moment he left the chamber.

"I'm sorry we aren't able to help, Mackay." Mary favored Iver with a weary smile. Despite the distraction Iver had provided, a shadow lingered on her face and in her eyes. No doubt witnessing Douglas's broken body land at her feet, and discovering her husband had killed him, had shaken her.

"It is I who must apologize," he replied stiffly, taking a step back, "for intruding upon ye here."

The queen gave a delicate shrug. "Don't mind about that. However, I suggest ye speak to the seneschal as well. Duncan Stewart misses little that goes on in this keep."

Iver dipped his head and took a step backward. "Thank ye, Yer Highness. I shall seek him out."

Departing the ladies solar, Iver then climbed to the next floor of the castle, making his way to the seneschal's chambers. The atmosphere in the fortress was subdued this morning. Ever since the 'bloody council' as many of the guests were now calling it, the king had retreated from sight. He was still resident at Stirling yet hadn't socialized since.

Iver didn't expect to see him before his own departure.

As he walked, a frown furrowed his brow.

It was odd indeed that the queen and her ladies didn't know Adair. She was a clan-chief's daughter, after all. Nonetheless, there had been a large guest list for the banquet and masquerade ball—she'd obviously gotten lost in the crowd. Adair wasn't like any woman he'd ever met; he shouldn't have been surprised she'd avoided the queen and her ladies.

Iver's step quickened.

Despite the events at the council having drawn his attention over the past days, he hadn't forgotten Adair.

Whenever he had a quiet moment, memories of the words they'd shared, and what they'd done in the moonlight, stole upon him.

He hadn't said anything to Lennox about her. His brother would only ask questions he didn't wish to answer—such as, why Iver was so intent on finding the woman when he'd made it clear he'd sworn off love?

Reaching the seneschal's chambers, Iver found Duncan Stewart at his desk by the window. The big man, his greying hair tied back at the nape of his neck, was hunched over an open ledger, squinting down at the page as he scratched out numbers with a quill.

The door was open, so Iver halted in the doorway and knocked on the oaken frame.

Stewart glanced up, a welcoming smile stretching across his face when he saw who it was. "Mackay ... come in."

Iver smiled back as he stepped inside the chamber. "Apologies for the intrusion. I was looking for someone ... and thought ye might be able to help."

The seneschal replaced his quill in its pot. "Whom is it ye seek?"

"A woman by the name of Adair Farquharson of Braemar ... she's daughter to the clan-chief." The seneschal's face went blank, yet Iver pressed on. "I've just been to see the queen, and she doesn't know her."

"I don't either," Stewart replied with an apologetic shake of his head.

Iver's pulse quickened. "But ye *must* do ... she attended the queen's masquerade ball. A lass with red hair, of around five and twenty, dressed in purple. I danced with her."

The two men's gazes met and held. Stewart's brow then furrowed; it was clear he was doing a mental inventory, trying to match Iver's description to one of the guests.

"I'm sorry, Iver," he said after a lengthy pause. "But I oversaw the guest lists myself. The Farquharsons didn't attend the celebrations ... and the only red-haired lady who attended was Elspeth MacKenzie. However, she's weathered at least fifty winters, I'd guess, and was attended by her husband the whole evening."

Iver's skin prickled. It was warm inside this chamber, for a hearth crackled just a couple of feet away from where he stood; nonetheless, he suddenly felt cold. "I didn't dream her up, Duncan," he muttered. "She was a real woman, in flesh and blood. And she *did* attend the queen's ball."

The seneschal sat back in his seat and scratched his whiskery chin. His dark eyes were veiled now. "Aye, well, in that case, I'd say we have an interloper."

Iver swallowed. *An interloper. God's teeth, who was she?* "Could she have been a local woman ... from Stirling?" he croaked.

"We had clan representatives from nearby—the Grahams, the Bruces, and the Drummonds—travel in just for the evening," Stewart admitted. "Yet none of the ladies match the description ye have just given me." He paused, his ruddy face tensing. "No ... I'd guess it was one of the servants."

Iver stilled. "What?"

"Aye." The seneschal's gaze glinted as he pushed himself up from his desk. "And I can guess which one."

"Have ye finished chopping those carrots yet?"

"Not yet ... but I will have shortly."

Lorna snorted. "I swear ye are as slow as a one-handed cripple."

Bonnie's cheeks flushed. "I'm working as fast as I can."

"Well, it's not fast enough."

Dropping her gaze to the carrots she'd indeed almost finished chopping, Bonnie doggedly continued with her task. Two of the kitchen lads had come down with the flux and were confined to the tiny chamber they shared—which meant that she was on kitchen duty this morning. Her own duties were a little lighter at present; now that many of the guests had departed Stirling Castle, there weren't as many chambers upstairs to service.

If anyone else had been presiding over the kitchens, Bonnie would have been eager to assist. In the days since the ball, since Iver, she'd done her best to keep busy.

She guessed he'd have departed Stirling by now—and every time she dwelled on the possibility, her belly clenched. She knew it was idiotic to wish for such things, yet she would have liked to have caught one last glimpse of him, even from afar.

But she hadn't. Iver would likely be far from Stirling this morning, on his way back to his broch upon the Kintyre peninsula.

It was mid-morning now, and Bonnie was hot and flustered as she tried her best to keep up with the tasks her aunt threw at her.

Meanwhile, Morag and Alba worked nearby. Morag was smirking now as she listened to her mother, while Alba ignored them both.

The other servants who worked around Bonnie wisely kept their heads down, focusing on their chores.

Reaching for the last carrot, Bonnie chopped it with more vigor than was necessary. She then straightened up and glanced over at her aunt. "All done."

Lorna turned from where she was adding seasoning to a stew that bubbled over the pot. "Bring the carrots over here, and add them to the stew."

Bonnie did as bid, picking up the heavy wooden board and carrying it across the flagstones toward the hearth.

But Morag chose that exact moment to move away from the bench where she'd been rolling out pastry.

"Morag," Alba whispered, a warning in her voice. "Don't—"

Morag ignored her—and the next thing Bonnie knew, her cousin's elbow collided with hers.

The chopped carrots went flying.

"Clumsy clodhead!" Lorna lunged at Bonnie, swiping at her with an open palm. And she would have caught her around the ear if her niece hadn't ducked.

"It wasn't me!" Bonnie staggered back out of reach as her aunt tried to strike her again. "Morag deliberately bumped me."

"I did not!" Her cousin's shrill voice carried across the kitchen. "She's lying, Ma."

Bonnie turned on Morag, hands clenching around the wooden board she still held. Meanwhile, pieces of carrot lay scattered around her.

But she made no move to pick them up; instead, she glanced about the kitchen, looking for allies. As expected, everyone was avoiding her eye.

Everyone except Alba.

"Morag did do it, Ma," her cousin announced then, her voice low yet sure. "I saw her."

Morag sucked in a sharp breath and cut her twin a vicious look.

Alba avoided Morag's gaze, keeping her attention upon Bonnie. A long look passed between them, and warmth kindled under Bonnie's ribcage.

She couldn't believe it; she'd never expected assistance from Alba.

Her cousin's support bolstered her courage, and she glanced over at where Morag now glared at her. "Aye, *ye* are the liar, Morag Fraser."

"How dare ye speak to my daughter like that?" Lorna grabbed a wooden spoon then and advanced on Bonnie, two spots of color flaring upon her angular cheeks. "Misbegotten *slattern* that ye are!"

Heart pounding, Bonnie faced her aunt down, watching as Lorna's fingers tightened around the handle of the spoon. The cook's arm raised, her pale-blue eyes glinting in the light of the hearth.

Bonnie didn't flinch, even as her heart slammed against her breastbone.

This was it—she had a choice to make. If she didn't want to spend the rest of her days insulted, cowed, and miserable, she needed to make a stand.

And so, Bonnie held her aunt's gaze. "Touch me, and I shall tear that spoon off ye and break it over yer head," she replied calmly.

She wasn't making a casual threat either. She'd had enough.

No, she'd never dance among lords and ladies again or know what it was like to have the likes of Iver Mackay court her, yet she wasn't *nothing*.

Lorna's gaze widened. Although she didn't lower her arm.

Their stare drew out.

"Ye don't believe me, aunt?" Bonnie's voice carried through the hushed kitchens. "Go on then ... just try."

"Ye will not get away with such insolence," Lorna gasped. "I shall inform the seneschal of this ... he will have ye flogged."

"Advise me of *what*, Lorna?" A man's deep voice boomed through the kitchens, and all gazes—including Bonnie's—swiveled to the bottom of the stairs, where Duncan Stewart stood, arms folded across his broad chest.

However, Bonnie's gaze didn't remain on the seneschal for longer than a heartbeat. Instead, it was the tall blond man standing next to him that drew her gaze.

Bonnie's breathing hitched.

Iver Mackay was staring straight at her.

18: THIS CANNOT GO UNPUNISHED

LORNA WAS THE first to recover. "This *creature* needs reminding of her place." Her hand trembled as she pointed at Bonnie. "She has just deliberately wasted food and insulted both me and one of my daughters." The head cook drew herself up then, her chin rising. "I was about to drag her before ye, to demand she be flogged … but ye have saved me the trouble."

The seneschal didn't answer Lorna. Instead, he turned to the laird next to him. "The only red-haired lass working here is Bonnie Fraser," he said, meeting Iver's eye. "Is this her?"

Bonnie swayed on her feet before realizing she'd forgotten to breathe. *Mother Mary, no!* Dragging in a lungful of air, she stared back at Iver.

He didn't need to reply—the look on his face said it all.

The moments slid by, and then he nodded.

"So, let me get this straight," Stewart muttered, his attention flicking between them. "Ye met *this* woman at the ball, masked and dressed as a lady?"

"I did," Iver replied, his voice low and flat.

"Bonnie." The sharp edge to the seneschal's voice made her drag her gaze from Iver's. Stewart was scowling at her. "Did ye attend the queen's ball?"

Bonnie swallowed to try and loosen her throat. She liked Duncan—although the seneschal ruled the castle with a firm hand, he was known to be fair. He'd never spoken to her harshly or treated her cruelly like her aunt did. But his dark eyes were narrowed now, and his heavy jaw set.

He looked vexed, and rightfully so.

"Aye," she whispered.

"It was ye!" Bonnie glanced over her shoulder to see Morag pointing at her. Behind her, Alba's round face had paled. "We saw ye dancing with him."

Bonnie's already pounding heart bolted. Dizziness barreled into her, and she staggered, grabbing hold of the edge of the table next to her to steady herself.

"What are ye babbling about, Morag?" Lorna's harsh voice cut through the kitchens. "Ye didn't attend the ball."

"We watched from the minstrel's gallery, Ma," Alba answered softly, while Morag flushed red.

Their mother's dark-blonde brows crashed together. "What do—"

"I'm disappointed in ye, Bonnie," Stewart cut the cook off. "Stirling Castle has given ye shelter, food, and employment, and this is how ye repay us."

Bonnie stared back at him. There was little point in trying to defend herself. There was nothing she could say that could make this right.

She was up to her neck in trouble.

"How did she get that gown she was wearing ... and the mask?" Morag interrupted once more. Despite that she'd no doubt be in trouble with her mother later, she was like a dog with a bone now.

Bonnie swallowed hard. She couldn't implicate Ainslie in this. "I took them," she whispered. "One of the ladies-in-waiting dropped a mask on the day of the ball ... and I kept it for myself." She paused then, aware that Iver's gaze hadn't shifted from her face. Nonetheless, it was difficult to meet his eye now. "And the gown belongs to Ainslie Boyd. It was her wedding dress, and she showed it to me a few weeks ago. The morning of the ball, I 'borrowed' it without her knowledge."

The seneschal's dark brows knitted together at this admission, and Bonnie started to sweat.

She wanted to bolt, gather her skirts and flee from the kitchens, from Stirling Castle. She wanted to disappear into the wilds forever. But, instead, she would have to remain within these walls and face her punishment.

It took every ounce of courage she possessed to raise her chin and meet Duncan Stewart's eye. "I know I did wrong," she said huskily, "and I am sorry."

The seneschal's mouth pursed. He then stepped back and jerked his chin toward the stone steps behind him.

"We shall continue this discussion in my quarters," he muttered. "Upstairs ... *now*."

It was overly warm inside the seneschal's chamber. The fire blazed in the hearth, and despite that the air outdoors was crisp this morning, the sun poured into the room through the thin layer of glass.

Nonetheless, Iver barely noticed the heat.

The chill that had settled over him earlier still hadn't thawed.

He couldn't take his gaze off the chambermaid who stood in the center of the chamber, waiting for the seneschal to deliver his punishment.

The mask she'd worn on the night of the ball had obscured the top half of her face, her hair had been unbound, and she'd been wearing a stunning gown, yet it *was* her. Even in that drab, work-worn kirtle and apron, her hair pulled back from her face, he was looking upon the same woman.

In fact, observing the chambermaid, Iver couldn't believe he hadn't recognized her during the ball. It was obvious now that she was the shy lass he'd spotted twice in the days leading up to the event. Their gazes hadn't met on those occasions though, and apart from her gasped thanks, they hadn't spoken.

Her audacity stunned him. For a chambermaid—the lowest of the servants within a castle—to steal a mask and gown—and pretend to be one of the guests, was bold indeed.

It was also insanely reckless.

Did she really think she could get away with it?

Gaze downcast, hands clasped together, the lass didn't meet the seneschal's eye as he positioned himself in front of her. Her lovely face was drawn and pale, and she swallowed convulsively.

Earlier, in the kitchens, she'd been unable to tear her gaze away from Iver. But now, she didn't look in his direction.

"Bonnie," Duncan Stewart sighed her name. "What possessed ye, lass?"

Bonnie. The name suited her. It was earthy yet feminine, just like she was.

Iver caught himself then, his jaw tightening. *Don't fool yerself, Mackay. She pretended to be someone else. Ye don't know her at all.*

He'd been born cursed when it came to women, it seemed—he always fell for the wrong ones.

"I'm not sure," she whispered. "A madness of sorts." Her chin rose then, and she met the seneschal's gaze. Her blue-green eyes glistened. "I am grateful for the life I have ... but sometimes, I wish for more."

The seneschal's brows crashed together. "Such wishes ruin people," he muttered. A shadow rippled across his face then. "As it did yer mother."

"Did she disgrace herself that badly?" Bonnie asked huskily.

Stewart's expression saddened at her question. "Greer was lovely. Full of joy and life, and a rare beauty ... with golden hair and eyes the color of the sea in summer. Most of the lads in this keep were half in love with her." His mouth curved then. "Me included."

Bonnie's gaze widened, yet the seneschal's smile turned rueful. "I was young once too, ye know." He huffed another, weary, sigh. "But Greer wasn't interested in any of us. Instead, she flew too close to the sun and burned like Icarus."

Iver frowned at these puzzling words—as did Bonnie. "So, ye know who my father is?"

The seneschal's expression shuttered before he shook his head. "I thought yer mother's tragedy was behind us … but now I worry ye shall travel a similar road." He paused then. "This cannot go unpunished."

"I know," Bonnie whispered, her shoulders slumping.

A brittle silence rushed in, and suddenly, Iver could hear the steady 'thump' of his own pulse. He cleared his throat then. The pair seemed to have forgotten he was also present. "What kind of punishment are we talking about?"

Stewart glanced his way. His face was still carefully blank. Nonetheless, the concern in his eyes gave him away. He cared for the lass and didn't want to punish her. "A public flogging," he replied roughly. "Afterward, she shall be put in the stocks for three days."

Bonnie's face had gone ghostly now, and she trembled. But she didn't utter a word.

Even so, Iver's gut twisted. She'd made a fool of him, had stolen items that didn't belong to her, impersonated a member of the ruling class, and attended a ball she'd never been invited to.

Aye, she'd done wrong, and he was angry with her. All the same, the thought of her being whipped, of scarlet blood blooming upon her soft skin, of her humiliation and fear, made queasiness roll over him.

He didn't want this.

Iver met the seneschal's eye then. "Duncan," he murmured. "Could ye give Bonnie and me a few moments alone?"

Bonnie made a soft, choked sound at this request, her hands twisting tighter. Meanwhile, Stewart stiffened.

"Ye can leave the door open, if ye wish," Iver continued, his gaze never wavering. "Fear not, I mean the lass no harm."

Heartbeats slid by, and then the seneschal reluctantly nodded. He cast Bonnie a probing look. "I shall be waiting down the hallway," he told her. "Call if ye need me." Stewart strode from the chamber then, leaving the door ajar behind him.

They were alone—for the first time since they'd stood together on the castle walls.

Iver's pulse quickened. How different this meeting was.

Bonnie dragged her gaze to him then. She wrapped her arms around her torso to quell her trembling. But ever since Stewart's departure, her shaking was even more evident.

"God's blood, lass, don't look at me like that," Iver muttered. "I'm not going to rage at ye."

She swallowed yet didn't reply.

Iver moved over to the hearth and turned to face her, warming his back against the flames. Cold still suffused his gut, yet he was doing his best to ignore it.

Their gazes met once more. "Well, Bonnie Fraser," he said softly, testing out her name on his lips. "This a fine mess we're in."

"I'm sorry, Mackay," she whispered. "My behavior was foolish and selfish."

"Call me 'Iver'," he replied. "I think we're past formalities now, don't ye?"

She nodded, although her features tightened. She watched him like an injured sparrow might watch the castle's mouser—waiting for him to pounce.

Moments passed before Iver heaved a deep sigh. "Was any of it real?"

She blinked. "Excuse me?"

"We spent hours together, Bonnie. We danced, talked ... shared secrets. Was everything ye told me a lie?"

"No," she whispered. "Not everything."

His mouth twisted. "Adair Farquharson with a pushy father who sent her to Stirling to find herself a husband?"

Spots of color bloomed upon her pale cheeks. "Aye, I made that part up ... but some of the things I shared with ye were real. The younger 'sisters' I referred to are my cousins. I was brought up by my aunt." She broke off there, her breasts rising and falling sharply. "I don't expect ye to understand." Bonnie gasped out the words. "Ye grew up in a different world to me ... and ye are a man. Yer horizons are vast, yet mine are narrow indeed. I knew that ball was forbidden to me, yet for one night, I dared to dream." Her gaze speared his then, her chin lifting as the flush on her cheeks deepened. "Our paths had already crossed before we met at the ball, yet ye didn't recognize me. Like most of the high-born, ye are oblivious to those who serve ye. We are invisible."

Heat ignited in Iver's gut, dousing the chill. "Ye presume much about me," he ground out. He took a step toward her then. "I *do* remember ye, Bonnie ... the shy chambermaid who wouldn't look me in the eye."

A muscle flexed in her jaw. "Aye, ye have made the connection *now*, yet ye didn't at the ball. Ye saw what ye wished to." There was an edge to her voice—one that made Iver's quickening anger subside a little. As much as he didn't want to admit it, she had a point.

Iver was a chieftain. From the day he'd come squalling out into the world, he'd been treated as someone to be valued. Aye, he'd suffered disappointments and loss—even the high-born didn't escape such things—but he had no idea what it was like to have no prospects.

He had no doubt Bonnie's life was one of drudgery—and listening to the words she'd exchanged with the seneschal upon entering this chamber, she'd been born under a shadow of scandal. It sounded as if her mother had disgraced herself, and Stewart worried Bonnie would go the same way.

Silence fell between them, stretching out while the hearth crackled and the wind made the windowpane creak. And as the moments slipped by, Iver's temper cooled. Eventually, he raked a hand through his hair, murmuring an oath under his breath. "Things got ... out of hand ... on the walls that night," he admitted haltingly. "All the same, I wondered why ye fled ... although I now understand." He moved closer to her then so that they stood no more than a couple of feet apart.

Bonnie continued to hold his eye.

The directness of her gaze made his breathing quicken. It was still there—the pull between them. He'd have thought the shock of discovering her deception might have severed it, yet he was keenly aware of the woman standing close to him.

"I was careless the other night," he said, his voice roughening. "Ye could be with bairn."

She swallowed once more. "I worried about that too," she admitted, her own voice husky. "But ye need not worry ... my courses arrived the morning after."

A little of the tension that had knotted under Iver's ribs eased at this news. Surely, that was an added complication neither of them needed. Nonetheless, Bonnie was still in serious trouble. "I don't want to see ye flogged or put in the stocks," he admitted roughly.

"Why not?" she whispered. "I deceived ye."

"Ye did ... but I cannot let ye be punished because of it." His hand itched to reach up and stroke her cheek. Standing this close to her was affecting him. His heart was now pounding.

"Unfortunately, ye have no say in the matter, Mackay."

Iver's gaze cut left to see Duncan Stewart standing in the doorway. The seneschal had obviously decided they'd had enough privacy. His brow was furrowed as he viewed them.

"I disagree," Iver replied, his tone cooling. "This situation involves me, does it not?"

"Don't interfere." Stewart folded his burly arms across his chest. "Bonnie Fraser is under my guardianship, not yers."

Heat flared in Iver's belly once more, his pulse spiking. He knew he shouldn't get involved in this, yet he couldn't help it. The blood roared in his ears, instinct overriding good sense, as he replied, "Well, that can be remedied." He shifted his attention away from the seneschal. His gaze fused with Bonnie's. She was staring at him, her eyes wide, her lips parted. "If the lass will agree to be my wife."

19: THAT WAS THEN ... THIS IS NOW

BONNIE COULDN'T HELP it—she gasped.

She certainly hadn't been expecting a proposal. In truth, she hadn't expected Iver Mackay to be understanding in the least about what she'd done. When Duncan left them alone, she'd been frightened about what the laird would say to her.

She'd expected harsh words, insults even.

Yet, instead, he surprised her. She hadn't meant to blurt out what she had, but there was something about him that freed her—as he had on the night of the ball.

She'd imagined her lies would have ruined everything, would have shattered the bond they'd formed in those few hours they'd spent together.

But he didn't want to see her punished. And now, he was offering to wed her to prevent it.

"Iver," she whispered, recovering her wits. "Ye don't have to do this."

A stubborn expression settled over his handsome features. "No, I don't ... yet I wish to."

"What game are ye playing, Mackay?" Stewart demanded. He entered the room now, his expression thunderous. "This lass has erred, but how dare ye mock her?"

"This is no mockery, Duncan." Iver's own gaze narrowed as he turned to face the seneschal. "I'm serious. If Bonnie agrees to it, I wish to wed her. And I will do it as soon as we can find a priest willing to conduct the ceremony."

Bonnie's heart lurched at these words. This was indeed madness.

She barely knew Iver. Perhaps he had an unstable temperament—a man prone to extremes. Yet, even as she considered this, her gut told her otherwise. She knew Iver didn't take marriage lightly. Indeed, he'd sworn never to take a wife.

And yet, he was willing to put that all aside—to help her.

Stewart halted before him. His already high-colored face had turned a deep red now.

Panic clutched at Bonnie's throat then. Duncan was only protecting her. However, she worried the two men might start throwing punches if things went much further.

"Iver," she repeated, her tone sharpening. "Ye don't want a wife—ye told me so."

His attention cut back to her. "I didn't," he replied. "But that was then ... this is now."

"What kind of fool answer is that?" the seneschal growled. "I know a beautiful woman can addle yer wits, man, but ye aren't talking sense."

Iver's mouth kicked up into a smile. Bonnie's breathing caught. His response was unexpected. "Nothing about the past few days makes sense," he replied, with a rueful shake of his head. "But ever since I met Bonnie, it's as if I've woken up ... as if I have my old self back."

"The lass pretended to be someone she isn't," the seneschal pointed out, unnecessarily, Bonnie thought. "The woman ye were infatuated with doesn't exist."

Iver's smile widened. "Aye, she does. When ye left us alone, and we spoke together, I realized they are one and the same." Bonnie's breathing hitched at this admission, but Iver hadn't yet finished. His expression hardened as his gaze bored into Stewart's. "I'll not let ye take a stick to Bonnie ... and I'll not leave Stirling without her."

The two men stared at each other while Bonnie's pulse fluttered wildly in her throat.

Duncan's face was still as red as earlier, yet as Bonnie watched him, his gaze softened. And then, to her surprise, his hands unclenched at his sides. He glanced over at her, a muscle feathering in his jaw. "Is this what ye want, lass?"

Bonnie swallowed.

Lord, of course she did.

The man of her dreams had just proposed marriage to her. She'd be a fool to be insulted.

He's only done so out of obligation, a voice hissed in her ear then. It was as if her aunt were standing behind her, watching the scene unfold. *Mackay's a decent man who wishes to do the right thing. He doesn't really want ye. Why would he? Ye are a low-born bastard!*

Queasiness rose then, although Bonnie swallowed it down. She didn't need Lorna whispering to her. If she let it, that cruel voice would ruin everything.

The door to her prison was open—and for the first time, she could see daylight.

Suddenly, she didn't care what the reasons were for Iver's proposal, only that he'd made it.

Iver had turned back to her now. His smile had faded, and his expression was expectant. And so, she favored him with a tremulous smile. "Aye," she whispered. "I would be honored to wed ye, Iver."

It was rare Lennox Mackay was at a loss for words—but Iver felt a certain satisfaction at seeing this was one of those times.

His brother's mouth even gaped open, his dark-blue eyes widening. After a lengthy pause, Lennox found his tongue. "What?"

Iver crossed to the sideboard and poured himself a few inches of wine. He then raised the cup to his lips and drained it in two gulps. "Ye heard me. I'm getting married tomorrow morning and require a witness. Will ye do me the honor?"

Lennox swore under his breath. "And who is the lucky woman?"

"Her name is Bonnie Fraser. I danced with her at the masquerade ball."

Understanding lit in Lennox's eyes. "I *knew* it," he muttered. "Ye've been as testy as a ram in rutting season ever since that eve."

Iver scowled. He didn't appreciate the comparison and decided it was time to shock his brother into silence once more. "She's a chambermaid in this keep. The same lass ye winked at in the hallway on our first night here."

Lennox, who'd been reclining in a chair by the fire, his feet up on a settle and crossed at the ankle, bolted upright. Confusion then shadowed his gaze. "How is that possible?"

"She donned a stolen mask and gown and attended the ball pretending to be a clan-chief's daughter," Iver replied. "I went looking for the woman I thought was Adair Farquharson this morning ... and discovered she was someone else."

Lennox's brow furrowed. "This makes no sense. Ye are babbling."

"It's quite a tale, I'll admit," Iver replied, placing the empty cup on the sideboard, "but it's the truth."

Lennox pushed himself to his feet. "And why the devil would ye marry a chambermaid?" Iver didn't answer, and as their gazes fused, Lennox's expression shifted. He then gave an incredulous shake of his head. "Ye have had yer way with her, haven't ye?"

"That's none of yer business."

Lennox folded his arms across his chest. "Aye, ye have ... I know that look on yer face." He paused, taking a step closer. "What have ye gotten yerself entangled in, Iver?"

"Nothing I can't handle."

"Is she carrying yer bairn?"

Iver shook his head.

The two brothers stared at each other a moment longer before Lennox pushed past him and poured himself a cup of wine. "Satan's cods," he muttered. "I know we all rib ye about the fact ye've never married, but I never thought ye'd do something like this." He gulped down the wine and then turned to Iver. "Ma will have a fit if ye bring a low-born lass home as yer wife."

Iver's stomach hardened as he imagined Sheena Mackay's reaction.

Indeed, their mother wasn't a woman to be trifled with. She'd been on at him for years to take a wife—but a chambermaid wasn't what she had in mind.

Stubbornness straightened Iver's spine then. Aye, *no one* would be happy about his decision, yet he wouldn't be swayed. Now that he'd made up his mind, he dug his heels in.

When he'd stepped into his father's role at the age of eighteen, he'd expected his life to go a certain way. Yet it hadn't. He'd always felt as if he was waiting for something, although he had no idea exactly what.

And as he'd stood in the seneschal's chamber, staring into Bonnie's eyes, listening to her impassioned words, he'd known what it was he'd been waiting for.

Her.

She wasn't what he'd planned for his future. He couldn't rationalize his thoughts or decisions when it came to Bonnie Fraser. He was following his gut now.

Earlier he'd thought Duncan Stewart would continue to challenge him, yet he'd capitulated. The fight had gone out of the man, and when Stewart had glanced over at Bonnie, Iver saw the tenderness and concern in his eyes.

Iver knew little about the seneschal's personal life. He'd wed years earlier, but his wife had died young. He'd never remarried and didn't have any children.

Perhaps Bonnie was the daughter he'd always wanted.

Iver had also marked the relief on the man's face. He hadn't wanted to punish her, yet she'd left him with little choice.

And when Bonnie accepted Iver's proposal, his heart had kicked hard against his ribs. Joy, giddying in its intensity, had surged through him, making his limbs tingle.

That reaction confirmed that his instincts were true.

He and Bonnie Fraser hardly knew each other, and their union would likely ruffle some feathers, but they'd have the rest of their lives to remedy that.

The thought of marrying, after so many years on his own, made his chest tighten and his pulse race. But fear of being hurt wouldn't hold him back. Not any longer.

Ignoring the look of stern disapproval on his brother's face—lord, he looked like their mother when he wore that expression—Iver met his gaze squarely. "Ye didn't answer my question, Len. Will ye bear witness to my marriage tomorrow morn?"

20: OIL AND WATER

AINSLIE BOYD STARED at Bonnie for a long while, her eyes so wide that their whites gleamed in the light of the lantern hanging on the wall behind them. Wiping nervous palms on her apron, Bonnie waited for her friend to get over her shock, to offer her congratulations.

However, when the head laundress answered, it wasn't the response she'd hoped for. "Lord have mercy on ye, Bonnie Fraser ... what have ye done?"

Bonnie's pulse quickened, the dampness on her palms increasing. She'd been nervous to come down to the laundry and tell Ainslie about her impending nuptials. Yet, since the laundress had played a part in this, she'd made herself do it.

The seneschal was also likely to approach Ainslie about her dress, and Bonnie wanted to prepare her.

"Fear not," she replied, managing a smile. "I told Duncan Stewart that I 'borrowed' yer wedding dress without asking ye. No blame will be cast upon ye."

A shadow crossed Ainslie's kindly face, and she shook her head. "Och, lass ... I don't care about that." She broke off then, glancing over her shoulder at where one of the laundry maids was watching them, her expression keen. "Get back to work, Esme," Ainslie snapped, in an uncharacteristic show of bad temper. She then turned to Bonnie once more. "Ye promised me ye would be careful."

Bonnie heaved in a deep breath, her cheeks warming. "The magic of the occasion got to me," she admitted.

"Before I knew it, Iver Mackay and I were spending the evening together … and then we took a walk on the walls afterward."

Ainslie raised a hand to her bosom and murmured an oath under her breath. "Ye were alone with him?"

"Aye, but none of that matters now, Ainslie … this time tomorrow, I shall be Iver's wife."

Ainslie swallowed, and the look she gave Bonnie was a blend of pity, exasperation, incredulity, and fear. "Do ye really believe it's as simple as that?" Bonnie opened her mouth to answer, yet Ainslie cut her off. "Our worlds are like oil and water … we don't mix."

Bonnie shook her head. "They can … sometimes."

Ainslie folded her arms across her chest, her mouth pursing. "Tell me *one* occasion where a story between two people from such different ranks ended well?"

Bonnie's pulse quickened further. Curse it. She wished she'd kept her happy news to herself now. Better she said nothing to anyone and just wed in secret before leaving Stirling Castle without fanfare.

She'd thought Ainslie would be pleased for her, yet she wasn't.

Silence stretched between them before the head laundress broke it. "Ye can't think of one, can ye?"

Bonnie didn't answer. Truthfully, she couldn't. However, she wasn't going to admit such.

A sickly sensation washed over her then. Ainslie's reaction had dented her newfound confidence. Now, old insecurities rushed in, dousing her excitement.

Why the devil would Iver Mackay want to wed the likes of ye?

Heart racing, Bonnie stepped back from the head laundress. "Please don't say a word about this to anyone," she said, trying to mask her reaction. No, she shouldn't have confided in Ainslie.

A lifetime within these walls, and she had so few she could trust.

Ainslie nodded, even as her mouth thinned. "I won't."

"Thank ye."

"Och lass, don't look at me like that ... I'm only worried about ye."

"There's no need to worry," Bonnie replied, meeting Ainslie's gaze once more, even as she felt the prick of tears rising behind her eyelids. "I can look after myself ... I've had plenty of practice, after all."

Seated upon the pile of sheepskins in her attic, Bonnie did let herself weep. She didn't usually return to the loft at this time of day. She should have been lighting hearths in the bedchambers, for the weather had turned cold again, yet instead, she'd retreated to her sanctuary.

Blinking away tears, she glanced around, taking in the space she'd soon be leaving behind.

If Mackay doesn't come to his senses.

There it was again—her aunt's mean voice, tormenting her. Eroding her joy, her excitement.

Of course, it didn't help that Ainslie believed she was a fool as well.

Inhaling deeply, Bonnie wiped at the tears that streaked her cheeks. She didn't understand why, yet she'd never been accepted at Stirling. She was tired of feeling like an outsider in the very place she'd been born. A fighting spirit had erupted in her over the past days, initiated by the night of the masquerade ball. That evening had shown her a glimpse of another existence. One where she mattered.

And when Lorna and Morag had ganged up on her in the kitchens, she'd struck back.

Drawing a shaky breath, Bonnie tried to claw back her resolve, her excitement.

Ainslie's reaction had been a disappointment, but she had to rally. And she wouldn't make the mistake of telling anyone else. They'd all find out soon enough anyway, and she'd be the subject of gossip for months to come.

Not that Bonnie would be here to listen to it.

But, unfortunately, Bonnie's uncertainty didn't go away—and when she awoke in the early dawn the following morning, doubt plagued her.

Nerves cramped her belly. And as she lay there, watching pale light filter in from around the edges of the sacking upon the window, she worried that she'd somehow pushed Iver into wedding her.

He's a decent man ... he wants to do the right thing.

But what if he came to his senses afterward, and then blamed her for trapping him? What laird wanted to be saddled with a chambermaid?

Heart thumping, she pushed aside her blankets and sheepskins and wriggled into her clothing. She didn't usually rise this early, but her conscience wouldn't let her be.

Guilt clutched at her chest. She couldn't go through with this.

Climbing down the ladder from her loft, Bonnie then descended the tower and made her way through the sleeping keep to Iver Mackay's chamber.

Aye, she'd remembered where he slept.

Nausea churned within her as she approached his door.

She couldn't believe she was doing this—that she was throwing away her only chance of escaping Stirling. But she had to.

She couldn't bear it if Iver ended up hating her.

There was no other choice; she had to release him from his rash proposal.

Sucking in a deep breath, she knocked.

It took a while for him to answer the door. She was raising her hand to knock again when she heard the whisper of bare feet on the stone floor within.

Bonnie's already thundering pulse started to roar in her ears, and she froze to the spot.

The door opened then, and Iver stood before her—pale hair tussled, and blinking. He would have slept naked, as most folk did, yet he'd donned clothing to answer the door: braies, which had been hastily laced, sat low on his hips, and an untucked léine. He looked deliciously rumpled and sleepy.

Heat flushed through Bonnie, the greeting she'd been about to utter deserting her.

Gaze widening, Iver favored her with a warm, if surprised, smile. "Bonnie ... ye are up early. The ceremony isn't until mid-morning."

"I can't do this, Iver." The words tumbled out of her then. On the way down, she'd rehearsed what she'd say, and had promised herself she'd get through this with dignity.

But face to face with him, her intentions fled.

She just had to get through this so she could bolt.

His smile faded. "What?"

"Ye are wedding me out of pity," she gasped. "And ye will only grow to hate me for it."

Their gazes locked.

A moment later, Iver stepped toward her, and then, to her surprise, he lifted his hand to her face. His palm cupped her jaw as if she were made of eggshell.

"Pity isn't what motivated me, lass," he murmured. "I don't want ye to ever think that."

"But why then?" she breathed. His touch was distracting. Her fingertips tingled; how she ached to reach for him.

"There are turning points in all our lives," he replied, maintaining eye contact as his thumb caressed her flaming cheek. "And yesterday, I reached one." His mouth lifted into a rueful smile. "Meeting ye made something shift inside me. Ye parted the clouds ... and let sunlight back in. I never want to turn my back on it again."

Bonnie swallowed as the misery that had knotted itself under her ribs slowly unraveled. "Are ye really sure about this?" she whispered back. "For soon, it'll be too late for regrets."

His smile widened, the gleam in his eye causing her breathing to quicken. "I'm certain."

Bonnie Fraser wed Iver Mackay wearing the least threadbare of the two kirtles she owned. It was a dull brown, although she'd put on her newest léine underneath it. She'd also worn a blue woolen shawl around her shoulders.

It was lovely, finely woven and edged in gold ribbon, a gift from her husband-to-be.

And Bonnie was grateful for it, as without the shawl, she'd look drab indeed.

Even so, she'd done the best with what she had. She'd considered asking Ainslie to help her prepare, yet her friend's unenthusiastic response to her wedding had made her decide against it.

She'd brushed her hair till it crackled and pulled half of it back from her face in an elaborate knot. She'd then ventured into the Nether Bailey and picked a handful of snowdrops, which she'd woven into her hair. It was still too early for the rest of the spring flowers, but snowdrops, with their delicate white bonnets, had already raised their heads.

They stood on the steps of the Church of the Holy Rude. Nestled just under the rocky outcrop beneath the castle, the church's stone bulk rose above them. Father Callum, a small, portly man with apple-cheeks and a ready smile, read out the words that would unite them, while Bonnie and Iver faced each other, their hands bound by a length of Mackay plaid.

The feel of Iver's fingers wrapped around hers—for the first time since they'd coupled against the castle walls—was doing strange things to Bonnie's already racing pulse.

She couldn't believe this was actually happening.

Earlier that morning, she'd been determined to release him from his promise.

But now, here they were, standing together on these steps, before the stone archway that led into the church, while an icy wind and flutters of snow swirled around them.

Iver's prediction on the eve of the ball was right, after all. Winter wasn't releasing its hold just yet.

At the foot of the steps, two silent figures bore witness to this union. The seneschal of Stirling Castle and Iver's brother. Both wore heavy fur cloaks about their shoulders to ward off the cold.

As the priest continued to bless the couple he was binding, Bonnie glanced Duncan and Lennox's way. The former wore a resigned, weary expression, while the latter didn't bother to hide his displeasure.

Catching Bonnie's eye, Lennox's mouth pursed.

Bonnie's stomach clenched.

It seemed that *everyone* was against this union. It astounded her then that Duncan had let it go ahead. Shifting her attention to the seneschal, she was greeted by a kindly half-smile. The tension in her belly eased just a little.

As her guardian, Duncan Stewart could have forbidden her from marrying Iver. But instead, he'd let the choice be hers.

Her throat constricted. He was a good man, and she'd never forget his kindness.

Another icy gust hit them, the snow swirling more thickly now—and the priest clutched at his robes, hurrying through the rest of his blessings before declaring them wed.

Gazing down at her, Iver's mouth curved.

It was a slow, secret smile, one that made warmth spread through Bonnie's chest. It was an expression that made her trust him.

He leaned in then, his lips brushing across hers in a gentle, reverent kiss. Bonnie's eyes fluttered shut, and she leaned into it.

An instant later, it was over. Iver withdrew, and Father Callum was deftly unwrapping the plaid from around their joined hands. He then thrust the ribbon at Iver and flashed them both a wide smile before hurrying back in out of the biting wind.

Below the steps, neither of their witnesses moved.

However, Iver didn't glance at Duncan or Lennox. Instead, he favored Bonnie with another warm smile. "Welcome to the clan, *Lady* Mackay," he murmured.

21: LEAVE-TAKING

HEADS BENT AGAINST a flurry of snow, the small party passed through the heavy gates and under the raised portcullis. However, they found a commotion ensuing in the stable yard beyond.

Slowing her stride, her arm linked through Iver's, Bonnie's gaze swept the group of lathered horses and the warriors who sat astride them. They were shouting at the helmed guards who now encircled them, spears raised.

Bonnie's brow furrowed. The newcomers wore clan sashes across their chests—of black and pine-green crosshatching.

She wasn't familiar with the plaid, yet it seemed Iver was. His arm stiffened against hers. "The Douglases," he murmured.

"Aye." Beside him, the seneschal's heavy brow creased into a frown. "I was worried this would happen."

"Where is the king?" One of the warriors yelled then, his angry voice cutting through the howl of the wind. "Why does he not come out here and face us?"

Some of his companions thrust their fists into the air and shouted. "Jamais Arriere!"

"Never behind," Iver translated the French. "It's their clan motto."

The warrior who'd demanded to see the king spied the approaching party then. His gaze speared the seneschal.

"Stewart!" he boomed, swinging down from his courser. "And where is our ruler? Ashamed to come out and face those he has wronged?"

"Calm yerself, Brogan," Duncan greeted him, drawing to a halt a couple of yards back from the knot of horsemen. "I don't want any more blood spilled within these walls."

The warrior, big and broad with close-cropped black hair, scowled. "I shall not 'calm' myself." He then went to move to his horse's rear end and plucked something he'd pinned to its tail.

Crossing the remaining few yards between him and the seneschal, he then thrust what looked like a sealed roll of parchment at him.

Stewart took it, his expression shuttered. "What's this?"

"Letters of safe conduct." Brogan Douglas's mouth twisted, and he spat on the ground. He then turned on his heel, glaring up at the keep that loomed to the north. "Yer promises are worth horse shit!" he roared into the wind, clearly hoping the king was listening at one of the windows above. "Hear this, ye lowland *fazart* ... from this moment forward, clan Douglas disavows our oaths to ye and yer house!"

"Well, that was pleasant." Lennox removed his cloak inside the entrance hall to the castle and shook off the snowflakes.

Bonnie tensed. They'd left the seneschal and the Stirling Guard to deal with the angry Douglases and retreated indoors. Yet there was something in Lennox's voice that made her wonder if his sarcasm was directed at the incident they'd just witnessed or the wedding ceremony.

It could have been either—since Iver's brother hadn't smiled all morning.

She hadn't spent any time with the man, yet if her first impressions were correct, Lennox wasn't at all like his elder brother. Both were quick-witted, yet there was an edge to Lennox. Like Iver, he was tall and strongly built, with penetrating midnight-blue eyes and striking features. However, his hair was dark blond rather than pale and cut short in an aggressive style that suited his unfriendly demeanor.

Iver heaved a sigh and turned to his brother. "We all knew a reprisal was coming," he replied, his brow furrowing. "I fear this is just the beginning of things." His attention shifted to Bonnie then, and his expression softened. "I like the snowdrops in yer hair." Lennox made a strangled noise in the back of his throat, yet Iver ignored him. "The color of the shawl suits ye too ... as I knew it would." He paused, his mouth lifting at the corners. "But ye will need to dress warmly today, for the weather is turning against us." He took off his heavy woolen cloak and wrapped it about her shoulders.

"But won't ye need this?" Bonnie murmured, even as she pulled the cloak close. It smelled of pine and leather, and of him.

Iver's mouth quirked. "Fear not, I have a fur mantle upstairs." He glanced over at Lennox once more. "Tell Campbell, we're ready to leave."

His brother favored him with a curt nod and stalked off.

Iver watched him go, a crease forming between his brows.

"I don't think he's happy about all of this," Bonnie murmured when Lennox was out of earshot.

Iver gave a soft snort. "No, he isn't. But don't worry about Len. He just has to get used to the idea, that's all." He shifted his focus back to her, his brow smoothing. He then gave her the same slow, sensual smile he had after their wedding ceremony before he reached out and brushed a lock of hair off her face. "Gather yer things, Bonnie ... soon Stirling will be behind us."

And so it was that Bonnie left Stirling Castle.

The fortress—where she'd been born, where she'd spent five and twenty years—was no longer her home.

Over the years, she'd ventured outside its walls to visit the riverside market in Stirling town or to celebrate one of the fire festivals. But she'd never ridden through the gates on horseback before. Indeed, she'd never ridden a horse.

Perched in front of her husband, her back nestled against the warm strength of his chest, Bonnie felt like pinching herself. Was this real?

It was as if she were looking down on herself from above, as if she were living a scene from one of the tales she'd heard as a bairn—of a dashing laird sweeping a maid off her feet and carrying her away to his castle.

The snow fell heavily now, fat flakes from a pewter-colored sky, and worry fluttered up within Bonnie. Should they have delayed their departure?

However, Iver was set upon leaving this morning—and she knew why, for she too felt the same urgency.

His proposal and their marriage had both been swift, and so would her leaving be. In the wake of William Douglas's murder, tension lingered within Stirling Castle. The king likely didn't know about Iver's hasty marriage yet. Iver would want to leave before James started asking any awkward questions.

Nonetheless, she couldn't imagine the king cared, especially at present.

Bonnie glanced over her shoulder then, her gaze traveling to the crowd of servants who'd come out to see them go. Huddled against the cold, they watched the party of twelve—the Campbell and the Mackay lairds and their escorts—ride out of the stable yard toward the gates.

Duncan Stewart stood near the front. Catching her eye, he raised his hand in farewell. However, unlike after the wedding ceremony, the seneschal didn't smile. Instead, his expression was somber.

Bonnie's throat constricted. She hoped Duncan didn't regret helping her.

Her gaze then flicked to where Ainslie stood a few feet back from the seneschal.

The two women's gazes met, and the ache in Bonnie's throat intensified. After their conversation in the laundry, she'd avoided Ainslie. She'd thought she wouldn't wish her well, and yet—to her surprise—the head laundress smiled at her.

Bonnie swallowed before returning the smile. Maybe she was wrong. Perhaps Ainslie was happy for her, after all.

Her attention shifted from Ainslie—and her smile faded when she spied her aunt and cousins amongst the crowd. Bonnie swept her gaze over the three women one last time. Her kin.

Jaw clenched, her faded straw-colored hair whipping in the wind, Bonnie's aunt stood tall and stiff, clutching a woolen shawl about her shoulders. The resentment in Lorna's stare was palpable.

Likewise, Morag glowered at Bonnie, as if hoping that the force of her glare would strike her from her horse.

Bonnie was relieved to be beyond both their reach.

Drawing in a deep breath, she finally glanced over at Alba.

As expected, there was no hostility in Alba's gaze. All the same, she didn't look happy. The lass's brow was furrowed, her face flushed, and she was blinking as if she was close to tears.

Maybe her relationship with her cousin might have been different over the years if Alba wasn't so influenced by her mother and sister.

Even so, Bonnie wouldn't forget how Alba had stood up for her in the kitchens.

Their gazes fused, and Bonnie smiled. A moment later, she mouthed the words, *Find yer fortune.*

She hoped that Alba would break away from her mother and sister's oppressive influence.

Nodding to her cousin, Bonnie turned from the watching crowd and focused on the gate that loomed before her.

Alba Fraser's gaze tracked Bonnie through the fluttering snow as she neared the archway that led out of the castle. Seated before that handsome laird, her cousin looked like a princess.

She had snowdrops woven through her fiery hair.

A short while earlier, as they sat around the table in the kitchens, Alba had learned the laird's name was Iver Mackay, and that he ruled a large tract of land on the Kintyre peninsula.

And Mackay was a sight indeed. Alba had never seen a man so striking, with his pale-blond hair cascading over the heavy wolfskin cloak he wore.

She remembered watching them dance together at the ball and seeing how taken Mackay had been with the fire-haired woman who twirled around him.

Alba's heart started to kick painfully against her ribs then.

Even now, she still reeled at her cousin's audacity.

Bonnie had done what none of them would have dared to, and after the seneschal had escorted the disgraced chambermaid from the kitchens the day before, Lorna had crowed. "Finally, that wee bastard will get her due." She'd flashed her daughters a wide smile then. "We shall make sure we're at the front of the crowd when she receives her flogging."

Her mother's viciousness had upset Alba, yet Morag had laughed.

Neither of them noted that the rest of the kitchen had gone silent—that the other servants viewed them with a jaundiced eye.

But Lorna's jubilation had ended this morning.

Her mother had made strange choking sounds after hearing the news. Meanwhile, Morag had fallen silent, her features pinching.

However, Alba hadn't quite believed it was true.

It was only when she witnessed Mackay lift Bonnie into the saddle before him that she realized it was actually happening.

Her cousin was leaving them all behind. She was a laird's wife. She would soon preside over her own household, command her own servants.

Longing reared up in Alba's chest then, so strong and swift that she stifled a gasp. How she wished Bonnie was taking her with her.

An instant later, her vision blurred as tears stung her eyelids.

Find yer fortune.

Aye, it was fine advice indeed, yet Alba had no idea where to start looking.

22: YE SHALL APOLOGIZE

"HOW ARE YE faring?"

Iver's breath tickled Bonnie's ear as he leaned in to talk to her.

"Well," Bonnie replied, "although this wind is cold enough to freeze Satan's balls."

He huffed a laugh, and embarrassment prickled across her skin. She'd forgotten herself just then, replying as if she were in the company of a fellow servant in Stirling keep. Now, she was suddenly, painfully, aware of their differing ranks. Ladies didn't speak like that.

"Aye ... the weather's worse than I'd thought," Iver replied, a smile in his voice. "Fear not, we've almost reached Doune. I'd hoped to go farther today, yet it's best we don't."

Relief feathered through Bonnie, both at this declaration and at the realization he wasn't ridiculing her. She didn't want to complain, yet after hours in the saddle, in the teeth of the wind, her hands, feet, and backside had gone numb.

As if sensing her discomfort, Iver leaned forward and wrapped his fur cloak around them both.

Bonnie leaned back into him, her breathing quickening at their closeness.

Despite the cold and the snow that blew in their faces, forming a white mantle over the company of horses and riders around them, the intimacy of riding with Iver had affected her ever since they'd set out from Stirling.

The last of her embarrassment faded then. Instead, she was acutely aware of the warmth of his body and the strength of his thighs pressed against hers. She glanced down at where one arm wrapped protectively around her. He held the reins loosely with the other hand, and Bonnie found herself studying the strong yet elegant lines of his wrist and fingers.

Memories of what it had felt like to have those fingers sliding across her skin, caressing her until she unraveled in his arms, made excitement curl tight in her loins.

It was still their wedding day, although they hadn't yet consummated their union.

However, they *would*—and it would likely happen tonight.

Nervousness fluttered up then, tempering the delicious anticipation.

Their first encounter had been unplanned, wild—and she'd been pretending to be someone else. But the next time she coupled with Iver, it would be as Bonnie Mackay, his wife.

There would be no mask to hide behind.

And for some reason, that scared Bonnie a little; she wondered if she was ready for it. Their relationship was already intense, but once they consummated their vows, there really would be no going back.

"I must say ye impress me, Bonnie," Iver said then, his deep voice intruding on her thoughts. "This is a huge change for ye, but ye are taking it all in yer stride."

Bonnie gave a soft snort. "Do ye think so? I turned up at yer door at dawn this morning babbling like an idiot."

Another laugh rumbled against her back. "Ye were understandably nervous."

"I still am," she admitted huskily. "We come from different worlds, Iver ... I hope ye will be patient with me."

He gave her waist a gentle squeeze, his breath feathering against her ear once more as he answered, "Always."

Trying to ignore the fluttering in her belly, for his responses were both reassuring and disarming, Bonnie let her gaze travel forward to where Lennox rode alongside Colin Campbell.

Earlier, Iver had told her they'd be stopping off at Campbell's castle on the way home. The journey back to Dun Ugadale from Stirling was seven days, at least—likely more in bad weather—and the Lord of Glenorchy had invited the Mackays to stay as his guests.

Unfortunately, she hadn't warmed to Campbell. Neither had she missed the glint in the laird's eyes when they'd been introduced in the stable yard of Stirling Castle.

Lennox's thinly veiled disapproval just simmered beneath the surface when they'd met, and continued to do so, but Bonnie found that preferable to Campbell's insolence. Iver's brother hadn't dragged his gaze over her as the Lord of Glenorchy had. Campbell had then glanced across at Iver before drawling, "Congratulations are in order, I hear?"

"Aye, Colin," Iver had replied, his expression veiled. "May I introduce ye to my wife, Bonnie?"

Campbell had screwed up his face then before turning away and striding over to where one of his men had readied his horse.

Once they were away from Stirling, the journey, and the poor weather, had come as a relief to Bonnie. Campbell was too intent on getting to their destination, and finding a fire to warm himself before, to bother focusing on Iver's new wife.

Eight warriors rode with them—four Campbells and four Mackays—their escort home.

Campbell and Lennox rode a few yards ahead, and, as the day drew out, the two men eventually shared a few words. However, when the Lord of Glenorchy barked a laugh at something Lennox had said, Bonnie's skin prickled.

Her earlier insecurity resurfaced then, heat rising to her cheeks.

Is he laughing at me?

The day was darkening when they finally rode into Doune.

A castle rose on the banks of the River Teith, its towers outlined against the smoky sky. The snow still fell in silent flurries, although the biting wind had eased a little. Around them, a glittering blanket had settled over the world.

Bonnie's breath grew shallow with wonder at the sight of the great keep frosted in white. It was magnificent. She imagined they'd find shelter there, yet the party stopped at a tavern instead.

"Doune is one of the king's residences," Iver explained as they drew up in the stable yard behind the Glenardoch Inn. "He stays here when he goes hunting." Her husband paused then, glancing over at where Campbell had just swung down from his heavy-set bay stallion. "Colin wants to avail himself of the Stewarts' hospitality, but I'd rather not."

Bonnie tensed. She wondered if she was the cause for his reluctance.

Was he embarrassed to introduce her?

Banishing the thought, for it did her no good to worry about such things, she replied, "But the king isn't in residence."

"No, and I've had enough of politics. A tavern will suit *all* of us better tonight."

Iver dismounted then, his booted feet sinking up to the ankle in fresh, powdery snow, before helping Bonnie down from the saddle.

Face to face, for the first time in hours, their gazes met.

Iver's nose and cheeks were flushed with cold, yet he was smiling down at her.

The worries that had been building within Bonnie as the day progressed eased just a little. How could she doubt him or worry about the future when he looked at her like that?

A wall of warm, smoky heat hit them as they stepped inside Glenardoch Inn's common room. Moving across the sawdust-covered floor at Iver's side, Bonnie inhaled the smell of woodsmoke and savory cooking smells, blended with the less savory odors of sweat and damp wool.

The inn was busy at this hour, with warmly dressed figures huddled at trestle tables, their hands wrapped around tankards of ale.

Serving lasses wended their way between the tightly packed tables, jugs of ale and platters of food in hand.

Campbell moved ahead to talk to the innkeeper. After a brief exchange, he returned to them with a grin. "I've got their last three chambers," he announced. His gaze then shifted to the warriors who'd followed them inside. "It looks like ye lads will be sleeping with the horses tonight."

Muttering ensued, although it settled soon enough when the men escorting the lairds seated themselves at a nearby table. With a cup of ale in hand, as they flirted with the serving lasses, the Campbell and Mackay warriors soon forgot about where they'd be bedding down later.

Seated at a table with Iver, Lennox, and Campbell, Bonnie said little as the three men discussed the trip ahead, and which route they'd take.

In truth, she was still awed by the fact she was traveling with her *husband*. She found herself stealing glances at Iver.

He was so handsome, his face burnished in the light of the nearby hearth.

Her breathing caught. *Is he really mine?*

With the snow, they decided to avoid the high road, which was usually faster—for it would take them through the Trossachs, the mountains that shadowed the sky to the northwest. Instead, they'd take the lower, slower road that cut due north toward Loch Tay.

Bonnie thought that idea sounded sensible.

Dishes of hearty vegetable stew and heavy loaves of coarse bread arrived shortly after, and they abandoned their conversation, falling upon their meals instead.

"Ye have a hearty appetite, eh, lass?" Campbell winked at Bonnie as he ripped off a chunk of bread.

Bonnie, who'd just swallowed a mouthful of mutton, stilled. The sense of wonderment at her new situation and the deliciousness of her meal ebbing.

That was no compliment.

Campbell shifted his gaze to Iver then, raising an eyebrow. "I must admit, I was sore ye refused my daughter, only to take up with a chambermaid." "But maybe ye did right, finding yerself a sturdy lowborn lassie to wed." He picked up his tankard and favored Iver with a mocking toast. "My wife, God bless her soul, was a pale, sickly creature who picked at her food ... not like this one. She'll bear ye plenty of strapping sons, I'll wager."

Bonnie flushed hot, while next to her, Iver's thigh tensed against hers. "Bonnie isn't a sow at market," he growled. "Kindly refrain from speaking of her as such."

Campbell snorted. Nonetheless, he minded Iver's warning. Next to Iver, Lennox remained silent, his expression shuttered as he observed the exchange between his companions.

The meal resumed, yet Bonnie no longer had any appetite for it. Her stomach closed, and she abandoned her half-eaten dish, picking up her cup of ale instead and taking a sip.

Once again, she felt like an imposter among these people. Iver told her their differing classes didn't matter. Yet he was the only one who thought so.

A blast of chill air gusted across the interior of the Glenardoch Inn then, drawing all their attention.

A big man wearing a plush fur cloak around his broad shoulders strode inside. His face was flushed with cold. Recognition tickled at Bonnie. Had she seen him before? He was clearly someone of importance, and might have been considered handsome too—if not for the hard set of his jaw and the deep line between his dark eyebrows.

The man's cool grey gaze swept across the busy common room before his attention fastened on the party seated by the hearth.

And then his frown slid into a scowl.

"Great ... just what we need," Iver muttered under his breath. "Sutherland."

Bonnie tensed, recalling the masked man, dressed as a wolf, who'd scuffled with Lennox during the ball. Aye, she *had* seen him before.

Across the table, Lennox murmured a salty curse.

"Leave it, Len," Iver replied, his voice tight. "Let's not cause any trouble."

Meanwhile, the innkeeper approached Malcolm Sutherland. His face was apologetic as he explained that the last chambers had been taken, and that he didn't have any more space inside the inn. Sutherland and his men were welcome to eat and drink here, but they'd have to sleep with their horses in the stables.

Sutherland's frown slid into a fierce scowl at this news.

"What?" he boomed, his voice cutting through the rumble of conversation inside the crowded common room. "Ye'd let a lowly Mackay chieftain and his chambermaid slut wife take one of yer rooms, yet deny the Sutherland *clan-chief's* son?"

The talking around them stopped with shocking abruptness, while the innkeeper blanched at the slur.

A chill washed over Bonnie. Suddenly, she no longer noticed the warmth of the nearby fire; it was as if she'd just been turfed outside into a swirling blizzard.

Moments passed, and then Iver rose to his feet. "Ye shall apologize to my wife, Sutherland," he growled.

The clan-chief's son gave a rude snort in reply. He then grinned and looked around him, catching the eye of one or two of the grizzled local men seated at nearby tables. "Listen to that, lads. Mackay thinks I should beg forgiveness from the woman who likely scrubbed my piss pot at Stirling Castle." He paused then. "I'm sure she'd have sucked my rod too, if I'd asked her."

This comment brought sniggers and guffaws of laughter from the surrounding patrons.

Bonnie's skin started to prickle. And despite that it felt as if bricks of ice had settled within her chest and belly, heat flamed across her cheeks. Suddenly, Campbell's earlier comments seemed trifling. Indeed, the Lord of Glenorchy had the manners of a prince compared to Sutherland.

To make his point even more clearly, Sutherland then spat on the sawdust-covered floor. "I'll not apologize, Mackay," he said, holding Iver's gaze. "What do ye say to that, eh?"

23: PANDEMONIUM

IVER EXHALED SLOWLY. It was so quiet in the common room that Bonnie could hear the rasp of his breath, along with the rapid thud of her own pulse.

She'd expected her husband to reply, to throw an insult Malcolm Sutherland's way. But he didn't.

Instead, he stepped over the bench seat and strode toward the clan-chief's son, his long legs carrying him swiftly across the common room.

"No fighting in here!" the innkeeper cried, inserting himself between the two men. "Take it outside!"

However, Sutherland merely shoved the lanky fellow aside and launched himself at Iver.

And just like that, pandemonium erupted.

Bonnie cringed against the table as cups and dishes flew. Lennox and Campbell leaped to their feet and rushed forward. Likewise, the Mackay and Campbell warriors abandoned their meals, meeting Sutherland's men head-on as they surged inside.

Moments later, Glenardoch Inn's common room was filled with brawling men.

Heart pounding in her ears, Bonnie got up and moved over to the wall, pressing up against it. Wisely, the other patrons scrambled out of the way, many of them narrowly avoiding the swing of a heavy fist or the kick of a booted foot.

The innkeeper was shouting at Iver and Sutherland to stop, but both men ignored him. They were slugging at each other, oblivious to anything else. Meanwhile,

Lennox had one of Sutherland's men in a headlock and Campbell head-butted his opponent, breaking his nose. The Lord of Glenorchy was grinning as he turned to face the next man. Colin loved a good brawl, it seemed.

Bonnie didn't share his delight. Instead, queasiness rolled over her as the brawl continued. How could anyone enjoy pummeling someone else with their fists?

Her attention shifted to her husband then—and there it stayed. Iver was holding his own easily against Sutherland, yet when the clan-chief's son kneed him in the stomach—he'd been aiming for Iver's groin but missed—she clamped a hand over her mouth to stop herself from crying out.

God's blood, can't anyone stop them?

Unfortunately for the Sutherlands, the Mackay and Campbell party was larger than theirs. It didn't take Iver and Colin's warriors long to overpower their opponents—and a short while later, Sutherland's men lay groaning on the floor.

Meanwhile, Iver and Sutherland fought on. Recovering from a blow to the jaw, Iver punched Sutherland in the mouth, sending the man crashing into the table behind him. The sound of splintering wood rose above the grunts and curses.

Pressing his advantage before Sutherland could rally, Iver straddled the prone man and delivered two more hard punches to his face.

"My wife will have that apology now, Malcolm," he grunted.

Sutherland glared up at Iver, blood trickling out of his nostrils. However, instead of complying, he mumbled a further insult through split, bloodied lips.

And in response, Iver drew the dirk from his hip and leaned forward, placing the thin, wickedly-sharp blade to the clan-chief son's throat. "Ask. Her. Forgiveness," he said, enunciating each word carefully.

A pregnant silence fell in the common room.

Bonnie's breathing hitched, her stomach churning once more. Sutherland had grossly insulted them both, yet she didn't want Iver to kill anyone. What had started out as a rambunctious brawl had just slid into something far more dangerous.

The edge to Iver's voice warned he was just a moment away from slitting Malcolm Sutherland's throat.

She knew it, and so did everyone else in the room.

As did Sutherland, for his big body stiffened and the arrogance drained from his bloodied face.

"I'm sorry," he rasped finally.

"My wife's name is 'Bonnie'," Iver replied. "Address her when ye ask her forgiveness."

"I'm sorry ... Bonnie," Sutherland repeated, each word tearing from his throat. He didn't look like a man used to being bested. This would be a bitter gall to swallow indeed. He didn't glance her way as he apologized—didn't dare move lest the dirk blade cut into his throat.

Bonnie watched Sutherland, her brow furrowing. No, she didn't like violence—and yet something within her sang at seeing this bully submit.

Satisfied, Iver withdrew the blade from Sutherland's throat. "Good," he murmured. "Now get out of here, Sutherland. Ye heard the innkeeper; this establishment is full. Find somewhere else to bed down tonight."

"Ye've made an enemy for life there," Lennox murmured as they watched the battered, bloodied, and bruised Sutherland party depart the Glenardoch Inn. The clan-chief's son was the last to leave. Limping heavily, Malcolm cast a baleful look over his shoulder at Iver.

A moment later, the man was gone, swallowed up by the swirling snow and the darkness outdoors.

Iver pulled a face before reaching up and rubbing his bruised jaw. "Aye ... yet it couldn't be helped."

"Ye'll get no quarrel from me," his brother replied. "Sutherland's been owed an arse-kicking for a while."

"That may be the case, lad," Campbell agreed from behind them. "However, when his Da hears ye pulled a dirk on him, he'll want reckoning."

"Let him take it up with Niel," Iver snapped, resheathing his dirk. He turned then to where the innkeeper was standing in the middle of the common room, looking around in dismay at the broken furniture and shattered crockery.

Frowning, Iver retrieved his coin purse from his belt. He then emptied a handful of pennies onto his palm and approached the man. "Sorry about that, Murdo," he said, holding out the coins to him. "This should help pay for the damage."

The innkeeper nodded, although his mouth compressed into a thin line as he took the pennies. "Aye, well, at least ye didn't kill him," he muttered. "I don't need any trouble with the local bailiff."

Iver didn't answer. In truth, he'd come closer than any of them likely realized to slitting Sutherland's throat.

Ever since he'd made his decision to marry Bonnie, the lass had weathered censure. Colin's snide remarks toward her during supper had caused Iver's temper to quicken. But Sutherland's vile insults had severed his self-restraint.

And in the aftermath, Iver felt as if he'd awoken from a long sleep. His blood was up. Every sense was blade sharp. Only a fool would dare cross him right now.

His attention shifted then, across the common room to the wall near the hearth, where his wife stood. Bonnie had watched the whole fight. She'd seen him come close to killing a man. Her face was pale and strained, her gaze wide, yet she watched him steadily. One hand rested upon her chest as if to calm a racing heart.

Iver favored her with a reassuring smile, and she returned it with a tremulous one of her own.

Relief filtered through him then. Aye, she'd had a shock, but there was no fear in her eyes.

"I'm sorry ye had to witness all that, lass," Iver said as they mounted the stairs, arm in arm, to the rooms upstairs a short while later. They'd left Lennox and Campbell by the fireside. The mess had been cleaned up, and the common room was quiet once more.

Bonnie cut Iver a sidelong glance. "Sutherland gave ye little choice in the matter," she replied softly. "He didn't just insult my honor ... but yers."

In truth, the incident had shaken her.

Chambermaid slut wife. Sutherland's goading voice still rang in her ears. Was that how others saw her?

Ainslie had tried to warn her that being accepted by the high-born wouldn't be easy. Nonetheless, Bonnie had never expected to be so grossly insulted. The sneers and laughter that had followed Sutherland's words had been an added humiliation. Of course, Iver's reaction wiped the smirks off their faces, but she wouldn't forget their disdain. She and Iver had broken the rules of society with their union, and people had noticed.

"Aye, but I tire of others voicing their opinions about ye, Bonnie," Iver replied, gently rubbing his jaw. She wouldn't be surprised if he had a bruise there by morning. "Sutherland might have the manners of a goat, yet *Campbell* also offended ye this eve."

Bonnie pulled a face. He was right, although Campbell's comment paled into insignificance compared to Sutherland's. She remembered then, something else the Lord of Glenorchy had mentioned during supper. "What was Campbell saying about his daughter?"

Iver's mouth pursed. "He offered her to me on the eve of the ball ... and I refused. His sour attitude is likely because he's taken offense that I chose another."

"And a chambermaid with a hearty appetite at that," she replied tartly.

"Aye, well ... he'll know now to mind his tongue in the future." Iver squeezed her arm gently then, even as his voice hardened. "I shall not stand for it."

They reached the top of the stairs and made their way down a narrow hallway to their chamber. Murdo, the innkeeper, had told them it was the last one on the left.

"I've asked for a bathtub to be filled for us," Iver said then, meeting Bonnie's eye once more. His lips lifted at the corners. "I don't know about ye, but after all that excitement, I could do with soaking up to the neck in hot water."

Bonnie smiled back, the unpleasantness in the common room fading just a little. She'd never had a bath before, although she was shy to admit such to Iver. Aye, she'd filled plenty for guests at Stirling, hauling steaming pails of hot water up and down the flights of stairs from the kitchens—but when she washed herself, it was before a basin of cold water in her loft.

They let themselves into their chamber. It was the best one the inn had to offer—spacious and clean with scrubbed wooden floors, a large canopied bed, and a roaring hearth. A huge empty iron tub sat before the fire.

Bonnie's gaze traveled around the space, a sigh gusting out of her.

"Does the room please ye, wife?" Iver murmured.

She turned to find him standing before the closed door, his gaze upon her.

Their gazes fused, and Bonnie's pulse fluttered. "Aye," she replied softly. "I've never stayed anywhere like this, Iver." Her cheeks warmed then. After the awful incident downstairs, she was painfully aware of their differing ranks. Suddenly, she wondered if he'd laugh at her. After all, this chamber was likely humble compared to his broch.

She tore her gaze from his, lowering it to the floorboards between them, wishing she didn't feel so uncomfortable. Her belly twisted then. *What have I done?* She'd been overjoyed to wed this man—and they seemed to be getting on so well—yet her new situation was much harder to deal with than she'd expected.

She'd hoped to take her new life in her stride, but now she was struggling.

Iver's boots whispered on the floor as he approached her. A moment later, his fingers gently took hold of her chin, raising her face so that she met his eye once more. His expression was searching, tender, as he looked down at her. "I know what just happened was upsetting, Bonnie ... but ye need not worry. I shall always defend yer honor."

Bonnie's throat constricted at this vow, and she swallowed to loosen it. "Thank ye."

His mouth lifted at the corners in that sensual half-smile that he saved just for her. His fingers left her chin then, sliding up so that his hand cupped her cheek. "I've been looking forward to being alone with ye again," he admitted, his voice lowering. "God's bones, how this day has dragged."

Bonnie let out a soft laugh, even as nerves and excitement danced in her belly. "It has?"

A knock intruded then, splintering the moment.

Iver stepped back, letting his hand fall away from her face. His mouth then quirked once more. "That'll be the water for our bath."

24: I COULD LOVE HIM

STANDING BY THE hearth, Bonnie watched as three husky lads, Murdo's sons, entered the chamber. The young men hauled heavy pails of steaming water. The two serving lasses who worked downstairs followed them inside, with more water—and soon the iron tub was filled.

Alone with Iver once more, Bonnie glanced down at where steam rose from the bath. Another sigh escaped her. The hot water looked delicious.

Despite that she'd been seated by the fire in the common room, her toes and fingers were still chilled.

"Go on." The smile in Iver's voice made her glance up. He'd seen the longing on her face. "Ye take yer turn first ... I'll bathe once ye are done."

Bonnie tensed as realization dawned. She was a married woman now and was about to strip naked in front of her husband.

Of course, they'd already been intimate—yet on the night of the masquerade ball, she'd been in disguise. There was an intimacy about this situation that made the nerves in her stomach twist tighter.

Sensing her anxiety, Iver's smile softened. "Don't worry, I shall turn away while ye undress and get into the tub."

Bonnie flashed him a relieved smile in reply. She felt a trifle foolish, especially after what they'd done just a few nights earlier. Nonetheless, she appreciated his gesture; it put her at ease.

Aye, she was Iver Mackay's wife now, but she didn't feel any different on the inside. All day, an odd lingering guilt had dogged her steps—she'd even found herself worrying about who was going to service the chambers she usually took care of.

It shouldn't have come as a surprise to Bonnie that she couldn't change a lifetime of habits in just one day—yet she found it discomforting, nonetheless. And after Sutherland's disgusting insults, she still felt like an imposter—a chambermaid playing at being a lady.

Iver turned away then, hanging their cloaks up behind the door before seating himself on the bed with his back to her.

Seizing the moment, for she didn't want the bath water to cool, Bonnie quickly disrobed, wriggling out of her kirtle and léine.

And when she stepped into the bath, her breathing caught.

Hades, it was hot—almost scalding. Biting down on her bottom lip, she lowered herself into it, careful not to slosh water over the sides. The tub was deep, and the water completely covered her, rising to just under her armpits.

For a moment, Bonnie just sat there, letting the heat seep into her chilled limbs. She wasn't used to spending all day in the saddle either, and the hot water soothed the aching muscles in her back, backside, and thighs.

What luxury it was to immerse herself into steaming water like this—she'd always envied those who got to enjoy the baths she helped prepare at Stirling Castle, and her first experience of one didn't disappoint.

A cake of soap sat on a chair next to the tub, and she picked it up, holding it to her nose and sniffing.

Her mouth curved. *Lavender.*

The only soap she'd had access to over the years was a coarse block of lye soap she borrowed from the laundry. However, this was something else. When she ran the soap over her arm, she found it smooth, and as she began to bathe, the scent of lavender rose up, enveloping her.

Bonnie's smile widened, a little of the wretchedness that twisted her inside loosening. *I could get used to this.*

Her courses had just ended the day before, and although she'd done her best to clean herself with a bowl of lukewarm water and a linen cloth, it was wonderful to be able to wash properly.

She quickly cleaned her body before ducking her head under and lathering up her hair.

"Are ye enjoying yer bath?" Iver asked then.

"Aye," Bonnie sighed. "It's my first."

"I thought it might be."

Her cheeks warmed then. Of course, he'd realized a humble chambermaid wouldn't have access to such luxury. Sliding forward in the tub, she leaned back into the water and rinsed off her hair.

Straightening up, her gaze went to Iver once more. He still had his back to her. Admiring the breadth of his shoulders under the thin léine he wore, Bonnie murmured, "It's all right … ye can turn around."

Her modesty was protected by the water, after all.

He did as bid, his gaze traveling directly to her, and the melting look he gave her made Bonnie's breathing hitch. "What a sight ye are," he said, his voice roughening slightly. "So lovely it hurts me to breathe when I look upon ye."

His words disarmed her.

Swallowing, Bonnie's fingers tightened around the block of soap she still gripped. She didn't doubt his sincerity; yet, once again, shyness prickled her skin.

"I can't wait to get ye home," he continued.

The sensual promise in his tone tightened Bonnie's chest; suddenly, she felt short of breath. "Who's looking after yer broch, while ye are away?" she asked, eager to steer the conversation onto an easier, and safer, topic.

"Kerr," Iver replied, his mouth lifting into another half-smile. "He heads my Guard … and if any issues arise, Brodie is there to assist him."

"Do ye have many problems at Dun Ugadale?"

He shrugged. "Some crop up from time to time. A handful of my tenants have long-standing feuds … and there's been an increase in sheep and cattle rustling of late." His expression sobered then as he paused, a hush drawing out between them. "I've let all three of my brothers take too much responsibility in recent years … while I cut myself off from everyone to brood on my lot in life." Iver's dark-blue eyes glinted then. "But when I return home, with ye by my side, that will change."

"I'm sure yer brothers don't mind helping out."

He pulled a face. "Perhaps not, yet I worry they will eventually become resentful. My brothers are too important to me." He paused then, his gaze shadowing. "And Lennox is already vexed."

Bonnie tensed at the mention of Lennox. Silence fell between them before she asked, "And what are Kerr and Brodie like?"

"They are both fair-minded men, and loyal ones too." Iver met her eye then. "Do ye fear that they will respond to ye in the same manner as Lennox has?"

"Aye," she admitted softly.

He sighed. "They will be shocked … but give them *all* time, lass, and they will fall under yer spell." His mouth twitched then. "As I have."

Her lips curved into an answering smile, her mood lightening once more. "So soon?" she asked, her tone teasing.

"Aye, it feels as if we've known each other for longer than just a few days, does it not?"

Bonnie slowly nodded. He was right, it did. "I'm nervous this eve," she admitted then. "Yet I feel safe with ye. I did from the moment we first met."

"There's no need to feel anxious around me," he rumbled. "I'll not take anything ye don't wish to give."

Her pulse quickened. "But it's our wedding night."

"It is … but there's no rush."

Bonnie placed the soap on the chair once more and rinsed the suds off her fingers. To her surprise, she found her hands were shaking. "Ye had better take yer turn in the bath," she said shyly. "Before the water cools."

Iver nodded and rose from the bed. He then picked up one of the large drying cloths and shook it out, holding it up like a curtain before him as he approached the tub.

He then averted his gaze. "Come on, lass ... I'm not looking."

Bonnie gripped the sides of the tub and pulled herself up. Stepping out onto the sheepskin rug before the fire, she took the cloth from him and wrapped herself in it. Flashing him another shy smile, she then padded barefoot over to the bed. "It's all yers."

She settled down on the edge of the bed, deliberately keeping her back turned.

Behind her, she heard the rustle of fabric as Iver undressed, followed by splashing as he climbed into the tub and lowered himself down.

And when he let out a contented sigh, Bonnie smiled. "It's blissful, isn't it?"

"Aye," he murmured.

More splashing ensued, and when Bonnie imagined him running the soap over his wet, naked body, heat flushed over her.

Biting down on her bottom lip, she reached for another drying cloth and began toweling off her hair.

The moments stretched out, and the splashing eventually ceased.

Bonnie couldn't help it; she glanced over her shoulder at Iver—and her heart jolted against her ribs when she found him watching her, his gaze hooded.

He was much taller and broader than Bonnie, and so the water didn't cover him as well as it had her. His muscular arms were braced on the sides of the tub, and his knees protruded from the water. The firelight gleamed on his wet skin and broad chest.

Bonnie noted the silvery scars that traced his chest and arms—marks of a warrior. His hair was wet and slicked back from his face, highlighting his proud bone-structure: an aquiline nose, strong jaw, and high cheekbones.

Their stare drew out before Bonnie eventually cleared her throat. "I hope the water is warm enough for ye."

"It is." His gaze glinted then. "Ye'll be pleased to hear I have a tub in my bedchamber in my broch ... and when we return home, ye can bathe in it as often as ye wish."

The warmth in his voice made heat curl in Bonnie's lower belly. "I look forward to that," she replied.

It was difficult to hold his eye and not let her greedy gaze trail over the glistening expanse of naked male just a few feet from her.

Did he have any idea what a sight he was? Aye, she was still nervous, yet the urge to move over to the bathtub, to reach out and trace the lines of his chest with her fingertips, to tangle her hands in his wet hair, was almost overwhelming.

Throttling the impulse, she glanced away. A brief pause followed before she shifted her attention back to him once more. "Are any of yer brothers married?"

Iver shook his head. "Not yet." His mouth curved. "Maybe I have broken the curse upon us."

"So, there are no other women besides servants residing within yer broch?"

"No ... there's my mother."

Something about the way he said that made Bonnie tense. "Will she need to be won over too?"

"I fear so."

Bonnie stiffened at this admission. The men in Iver's family would need to get used to the fact their laird had wed a woman far beneath his rank—yet Bonnie instinctively knew his brothers wouldn't be her biggest challenge. She knew first-hand how vicious women could be. And there was nothing certain women hated more than seeing another forget her place.

"Ye don't believe she'll welcome me then?"

Iver sighed. "Not initially, no." He leaned back against the rim of the bathtub, his gaze lifting to the rafters above. "My mother is ... a force of nature. She's a good woman, and tougher than any man I've ever met, yet certain events have embittered her. She and my father had a difficult marriage. They fought like pit dogs while I was growing up … and when Da found solace in the cook's bed, their relationship worsened further still." His features tensed then. "Of course, when the lass bore Da a son, Ma was incensed. She wanted the woman and her bairn banished from the broch, but Da refused. And to her ire, he raised Brodie as his son."

Bonnie's gaze widened. "Yer youngest brother is …" Her voice trailed off then. She didn't want to say 'a bastard', for she'd had the name flung at her often enough over the years.

Iver's gaze dropped to her face, his expression serious now. "My *half-brother*, aye … although I've never seen him as such. He's kin, and that's all that matters."

"And yer mother accepts him?"

Iver pulled a face. "Barely." He sighed then. "Brodie's Ma died … around six months before my father's hunting accident. He took her death badly too, which made my mother even angrier."

"And yet she didn't cast yer brother out?"

"She couldn't. The decision was mine, not hers. I'd never banish him … just as I wouldn't Lennox or Kerr." He paused then. "When we arrive at Dun Ugadale, I shall ensure that my mother takes ye through yer new role with patience and goodwill." He smiled then, his eyes crinkling at the corners. "Thanks to ye, I no longer want to shut myself away. Instead, I wish to be involved in all aspects of daily life in my broch and on my lands."

Their gazes fused, and the warmth that had flickered to life in the pit of Bonnie's belly during their conversation spread over her abdomen. They still had so much to learn about each other, and yet every time they'd spoken over the past couple of days, she found herself increasingly drawn to him.

Iver was proud. He had a warrior's arrogance, but he also possessed a sensitivity he tried hard to mask from the world—a vulnerability that meant he carried emotional wounds longer than did him any good. And there was strength and decency in him. He was a man who appeared to care deeply about his kin.

I could love him.

Her initial instinct about this man had been right. Bonnie hadn't had much good fortune during her life, but she was lucky indeed that her path had crossed with Iver's.

Silence fell between them once more, although Bonnie was the one to finally break it. "I appreciate what ye said earlier," she murmured. "About ye being willing to wait." She flashed him a half-smile, even as her heart started to race. "But ... I just wanted ye to know that I *am* ready. I wish to lie with ye, Iver ... tonight."

25: MAKE ME YERS AGAIN

BONNIE'S ADMISSION MADE Iver's breathing catch.

He'd meant it when he'd told her he didn't want to rush her. He'd seen how on edge she was when she entered their bedchamber. Despite the intimacy they'd already shared, this was different.

Tonight, there were no masks, no swirling crowd and music. On the eve of the masquerade ball, they'd both drunk enough wine to rob them of inhibition, and standing there in the moonlight, a kind of madness had caught them up.

But things had changed now.

This was no romantic dream. He'd discovered who she really was, and then they'd gotten married. They'd spend the remainder of their lives together.

And she was right: the path ahead of them wouldn't be easy.

Lennox had been in a sour mood ever since the wedding, and Campbell had been disrespectful—while Sutherland had slighted Bonnie outrageously. Of course, his insults had been a deliberate provocation. The man wanted to get even with Iver after the incident at the masquerade ball.

Instead, Iver had humiliated him.

Today's unpleasantness was a warning about what lay ahead.

Kerr and Brodie weren't likely to be any more impressed by his behavior than Lennox, and his mother would flay him with her tongue for his reckless decision. Yet there would be wide-reaching repercussions too. He'd just tossed a stone into the still waters of a loch, and the ripples would reach the Mackay clan-chief and chieftains. Several chieftains from allied clans would think he'd lost his mind. Others, like Campbell, would be vexed that he'd refused to wed their daughters while taking a chambermaid as his wife.

But Iver was ready to confront them all.

For Bonnie.

And the way she was looking at him now, those sea-green eyes limpid in the ruddy glow of the firelight, made his pulse take off.

Sitting there on the edge of the bed, her small, curvaceous form swathed in a linen drying cloth, her wet hair tumbling in dark-red curls down her back, she was breathtaking.

Still not quite believing he'd heard right, Iver wet his lips. "Are ye sure?"

Her gaze never wavered. "Aye … I wish to be close to ye."

Holding her gaze, Iver nodded. He then rose to his feet, water cascading off him, and stepped from the tub, retrieving the large drying cloth he'd hung over the back of the chair next to him.

Bonnie didn't look away.

Her cheeks flushed, and when her gaze left his and traveled down over his naked torso, to his groin, and her full lips parted, the sensuality of her reaction made hunger spike through him.

He glanced down, to find his rod standing to full attention. He'd been at half-mast already while they'd been talking—for her nearness was heady.

But now, the boldness of her gaze inflamed him further. Excitement tightened his gut, and his chest started to rise and fall sharply.

"Do ye like what ye see, lass?" he asked huskily.

"Aye," she breathed. "Very much."

"Come here then."

Bonnie's gaze returned to his. And then, wordlessly, she rose from the bed and let the drying cloth fall. The linen rippled to the floor, revealing her to him.

And Iver devoured the sight of her.

That night on the wall, he'd only seen her naked breasts—and not much else.

Of course, while she'd been bathing, he'd admired her creamy shoulders and the swell of her deep cleavage, although the rest of her had been submerged under the water.

But he was unprepared for just how comely she was.

She was small, at just over five feet tall, and yet her body was strong—all delicious curves. Her waist was narrow, accentuating the fullness of her hips and breasts. And as if feeling the weight of his stare, her rose-colored nipples pebbled.

Like him, she was breathing fast, which only made her lush breasts even more enticing.

"Bonnie," he murmured, holding out a hand.

A moment later, her fingers curled around his, and he drew her into the cage of his arms.

His mouth found hers, and he kissed her hungrily.

He'd been wanting to do this all day—to mate his mouth with hers, to taste the woman he'd married. Their kiss after the ceremony had been deliberately chaste, for his brother and Stirling's seneschal were looking on.

But Iver didn't hold back now.

Tunneling his fingers through her wet hair with one hand, he cupped the back of her head and deepened the kiss further.

A soft groan escaped Bonnie, and her small hands fluttered up, splaying across his naked chest. A moment later, they started to roam, exploring his chest and shoulders.

The smell of her—lavender and the sweet, musky scent of woman—enveloped him, and Iver dragged it into his lungs.

His heart was galloping now, and when he pulled her closer still, so that their damp bodies pressed flush, need crashed into him with dizzying intensity.

Still cupping the back of her head with his hand, holding her fast as he ravaged her mouth, he allowed his free hand to slide down the indentation of her spine. Her back curved as she pressed herself hard against him, and when his hand closed around the plump swell of her backside, she groaned again.

Tearing his mouth from hers, the blood roaring in his ears, Iver guided her over to the chair that sat between the bathtub and the hearth, and gently pushed her down onto it.

And then he fell to his knees on the sheepskin before her, moving between her thighs and scooping her breasts up in his hands. Iver lifted them to his mouth, devouring each swollen tip. He sucked gently at first, slowly working himself up into a frenzy.

Bonnie writhed on the chair, hands clenched around the edge of the seat. She was making soft mewing sounds, yet her gaze was trained on him.

Her focus made his already throbbing groin tighten further.

The effect this woman had on him was dizzying.

Leaving her breasts, he kissed his way down between them to her quivering belly and the soft russet hair below it. He then spread her legs wider still and lowered himself so he was sitting on the sheepskin—kissing his way up the smooth skin of her thigh to her sex.

And when he tasted her there, she shuddered delightfully against him. Sliding his hands under her buttocks, Iver pulled her hips up to meet his questing mouth. He devoured her like he had her mouth and her breasts, while Bonnie bucked and twisted in his grip.

She was making choked, breathy sounds—and Iver stopped pleasuring her a moment to glance up at her face.

Her cheeks were flushed, sweat beading across her brow. She was also biting down on her bottom lip, to prevent herself from crying out.

"It's all right, lass," he murmured, letting his breath feather across the sensitive flesh between her thighs. "Ye can make a noise … the walls are thick … and no one will care."

Indeed, this was a busy travelers' inn on a main highway heading into the Highlands. The proprietor and his family likely heard all kinds of noises coming from the chambers.

Her eyes flickered open, glazed with a need that made his stomach clench.

Christ's blood, she was beautiful.

Slowly, she released her plump lower lip from her top teeth, staring down at him as he started to caress her between her thighs with his fingertips, as he had that eve under the silver glow of the moon.

Her eyes snapped wide, and she started to tremble.

"That's right," he crooned, continuing to stroke her. "Now, let me hear how much ye like this."

Bonnie let out a soft whimper, rolling her hips against him.

"Aye, that's a start," he murmured. "But I think ye can do better."

He slid a finger deep inside her then, curling it upward.

Bonnie gasped.

Iver lowered his head once more, continuing to slide his finger in and out, while his mouth found her.

"Iver!" she gasped.

He didn't reply—he was too busy flicking his tongue over her sensitive flesh.

Moments later, Bonnie bucked against him, her high, keening crying echoing through the chamber. He held her fast, pleasuring her as her groans, cries, and pleas tumbled forth.

Only when he'd reduced his wife to a panting, whimpering wreck, did he finally release her. He pulled back then and rose to his feet, drawing her with him.

A moment later, Iver settled himself onto the chair and pulled Bonnie astride him.

Breathing hard, as she recovered her breath, she reached between them, her small hand wrapping around his engorged shaft.

Iver glanced down to see that it was leaking from the tip.

Bonnie's lips parted as she stared down at him. And then she slid her fingers up his length, her palm gliding across the slick head of his rod.

A groan rumbled up from Iver's chest, and he leaned back against the chair, letting his head fall back as she stroked him with both hands now.

His bollocks tightened, excitement quickening in his gut.

If she continued touching him like this, he'd spill all over himself.

Taking hold of her hips, his fingers digging in, he lifted her up and over him, letting her guide his rod into position.

And then, he settled her down upon him.

He'd wanted to inch into Bonnie slowly, yet the feel of her tight heat enveloping him was too much.

Greedily, he pushed down on her hips, driving her upon his shaft.

Bonnie cried out. Her back arched, and her thighs widened further still to accommodate him. An instant later, their bodies were flush, and Iver was buried to the hilt deep inside her.

Bonnie stilled then, her breathing fast and shallow now.

"Bonnie," he rasped. "Are ye all right?"

She nodded. However, her body had gone as taut as a drawn longbow. "It's just … a lot," she whispered.

Reaching between them, Iver found the spot that made her unravel against his mouth earlier. Gently, he rubbed it with the pad of his thumb.

And as he did so, Bonnie let out a long, shuddering sigh and relaxed against him.

"Sorry, lass," he murmured, continuing to stroke her. "I got overeager." He brushed aside the curtain of damp hair that cascaded over her shoulder then, his gaze alighting on the fading bruise he knew he'd find there. His fingertips traced the mark, his chest tightening. "As I did that night on the wall."

"Don't apologize," she gasped, rolling her hips against him as he rubbed harder, her body quivering now. "I liked it. Ye made me … yers." Her gaze speared his then, her eyes glistening with pleasure. "Make me yers again, husband."

His breathing hitched. He leaned toward her then, as she bent her head to him, and their mouths collided. And as their tongues entwined, he grabbed hold of her hips once more and started to slide her, slowly, up and down the length of his rod.

And it was almost too much for him.

She was so hot, so wet, so tight he couldn't think straight.

Their kisses grew frenzied, while he continued to move her in lazy, languorous strokes, down to the root of his shaft and then up to the tip, till she almost slipped free of him.

And all it took was a few strokes to turn Bonnie into quicksilver in his arms.

She writhed on his rod, sweat gleaming over her pale curves as she cried out against his mouth.

He knew this position would be intense for her, and it was. Iver felt the flutter of muscles inside her against his shaft and sensed she was close.

Bonnie tore her lips from his then, arching back as she peaked, a cry ripping from her throat. Her core clamped against his length, wet heat flooding around him.

Iver lost control.

He rolled forward off the chair, bringing her with him. An instant later, Bonnie was on her back on the sheepskin, her legs pinned wide, while he plowed her in frenzied thrusts.

Iver was dimly aware then of his own hoarse cries filling the room—and of someone banging on the wall, shouting at them to shut up—and then his release barreled into him, and he was lost.

26: THIS IS REAL, LASS

BONNIE LAY UPON the sheepskin, limp and boneless—her pulse beating in her ears.

She couldn't move. She couldn't speak.

It surprised her that Iver was able to move either. However, he pushed himself off her, rolled to his feet, and scooped Bonnie up into his arms, carrying her to the bed.

There, the ropes creaked as they settled onto the straw-filled mattress.

Iver pulled a blanket over them, for it was drafty away from the fire. Inside this snug room, it was easy to forget that snow covered the land outdoors; the innkeeper had predicted a blizzard was on its way, so it was likely they'd be making a late start the following morning.

Not that Bonnie cared about any of that—all that mattered was the man she now snuggled into.

Iver's body was strong and warm, and when she placed her palm upon his chest, she felt the thunder of his heart. Like her, he hadn't recovered from their coupling.

Wriggling closer still and placing her head in the hollow of his shoulder, Bonnie's mouth curved. The man next door had sounded irate indeed. "I thought ye said no one would hear us?" she murmured.

A laugh rumbled through Iver's chest. "Aye ... but I think it was my bellowing he objected to."

Bonnie's smile widened. Indeed, he'd let go—although she'd loved listening to it.

Once Iver had found his release, they'd both quietened down—and so had the guest in the next chamber.

A thought occurred to her then, and her smile faded. Raising her head, Bonnie looked up at him. Indeed, a bruise was forming on his jaw. "Yer brother or Campbell didn't take the room next door, did they?" Embarrassment prickled her skin. Neither of them liked her—how would she face them in the morning after this?

However, Iver shook his head. "I made sure our chamber was at the opposite end of the inn to theirs," he assured her. His hand rose then, and he brushed the back of his fingers down her cheek. "I wanted to give us both some privacy."

Their gazes fused, and Bonnie's breathing caught. She could drown in this man's gaze, and despite what they'd just done, her body still ached for him.

As if reading her thoughts, his mouth lifted into a sensual smile. "The night is still young," he murmured. "I'm afraid our neighbor is going to have a rough sleep." His fingers now trailed up and down her spine under the blanket.

Sighing, Bonnie curled against him, her own fingertips stroking the muscular planes of his chest.

She supposed she ought to feel embarrassed about the noise they had made, and would continue to make, this evening, yet she couldn't bring herself to care.

As she caressed Iver's chest, her fingers traced the lines of rough silver scars. "Ye handle yerself well in a fight," she said softly. "Have ye seen many battles?"

He huffed a dry laugh. "Aye … too many."

"How old were ye when ye fought in yer first one?"

He paused then, deep in thought, before replying, "Around fifteen, I believe. My father took me along with him to deal with cattle raiders. I killed my first man that day … and puked my guts out afterward."

Bonnie winced. She didn't blame him. She imagined a warrior never forgot the first life he took.

"After that, there were a few battles against the Gunns," Iver continued. "Not long after I took my father's seat, I fought alongside Niel Mackay at Sandside Chase. And then, once relations improved with our old enemies, we went into battle against the Sutherlands." His mouth twisted at that last name, his gaze glinting. "For a few years there, all I seemed to do was fight."

Bonnie propped herself up onto one elbow, gazing down into his face once more. "But no longer?"

He smiled up at her. "Not for a while. I've had the odd skirmish against cattle and sheep rustlers over the years, but it's been good to enjoy a period of peace."

"I'm glad," she replied, and she was. "I don't wish to see my husband ride off to battle ... and worry if he shall return."

His mouth quirked once more. "At least this time, there would be someone waiting for me afterward," he murmured. "I remember seeing my friend Breac Mackay, the laird of Balnakeil, greet his wife after our last battle against the Sutherlands. The joy of their reunion was so poignant that I had to look away." He gave a soft snort then. "I was so bitter in those days, Bonnie."

Her chest tightened at this admission. She'd deliberately not questioned him about his disappointments with women. She didn't want to pry into a history that had nothing to do with her.

But all the same, she was curious to learn of what had made him swear off love and marriage.

"Folk can be cruel," she murmured, memories of her brief liaison with Harris Murdoch resurfacing then. When he'd left her without a word of goodbye, she'd been bereft. However, she now felt nothing but relief that things had gone the way they had—Harris didn't hold a candle to Iver.

"Aye," he replied. "Although, I was bull-headed and impulsive in my youth." He gave a rueful shake of his head then. "And as I've already admitted to ye, I had a habit of developing infatuations with women who didn't want me."

"Will ye tell me what happened?" she asked softly.

He sighed before nodding. "The first I fell for was a lass named Eilidh. But it turned out she'd been in love with someone else." His mouth kicked up into a wry smile then. "Looking back, she was reluctant from the beginning ... but I was willfully blind to it."

Bonnie winced in sympathy.

"After Eilidh, I was cautious," Iver went on. "Nonetheless, I was willfully blind *again* three years later when I met a lass called Flora." He pulled a face. "She too had already lost her heart to another."

Bonnie's brow furrowed. "Who?"

"The local priest. They'd been meeting in secret." Iver's features tightened then. "Flora's father was furious when he discovered what she'd been up to. He tried to force our union, but I refused to go through with it ... as much as I was taken by Flora, I didn't want an unwilling wife." He paused there, shaking his head once more. "Her father, the MacPherson clan-chief, hasn't spoken to me since."

"And what happened to Flora?" Bonnie asked. Something in Iver's voice warned her that this tale didn't have a happy ending.

"I heard she took the veil," Iver replied, meeting her gaze once more. "If she couldn't be with her priest, she would have no one. She resides at Iona now, in seclusion."

Silence followed these words, and a little of the well-being that had wrapped itself around Bonnie following their coupling, like the blanket that covered them, slipped away.

"I'm sorry to hear that," she murmured.

"As was I." Iver huffed a sigh before reaching up and brushing a strand of hair from her eyes. "Fate is a cruel mistress." He paused then. "So, there ye have it ... the embarrassing tales of my past entanglements. There were other disappointments too, but those two were the most galling. I made a right fool of myself on both occasions ... and after the mess with Flora, I swore I'd had enough of being the laughingstock of the Highlands. I decided I was better off alone."

Bonnie held his gaze. "And yet here we are."

His smile widened. "Here we are." His fingertips traced the line of her jaw and chin before he brushed the pad of his thumb along her lower lip. "Meeting ye changed my life," he admitted softly. "Ye released me from self-imposed exile."

"I'm glad," she whispered back. "Ye are a good man, Iver … and I swear yer heart is in safe hands with me." She broke off there, suddenly embarrassed.

Neither of them had shared deep feelings yet, and she wondered if she'd said too much. After all, he wasn't in love with her. All the excitement of the day—the wedding, their departure from Stirling, the journey, the brawl, and then their coupling—had clearly addled her wits. Aye, they were husband and wife now, and there was no denying they shared a strong connection, yet it was still early days between them.

She was worried about ruining things—for she clearly remembered that Harris had departed the day after she'd admitted she was in love with him.

Averting her gaze, Bonnie tried to stem the blush that crept up her neck.

Iver gently caught her under the chin and lifted her face so she met his eye once again. "That was a fine thing to say, lass," he murmured. "Yet ye now appear mortified. What's wrong?"

Bonnie cleared her throat. "I'm not used to speaking so candidly with anyone," she admitted, wishing her cheeks weren't starting to burn. "Sometimes I feel that if I say the wrong thing all of this will disappear … that I'll wake up to discover meeting ye was nothing more than a dream."

He held her gaze. "This is real," he assured her. "And ye can't say the wrong thing to me. All I ask is that ye are honest. Tell me yer worries, yer hopes, yer fears, and I shall share mine."

Butterflies tumbled through Bonnie's stomach at these words. His voice had turned husky now; his response was sincere.

She had to remember that Iver wasn't Harris Murdoch.

He'd wed her, and he was taking her home.

27: RESPONSIBILITIES

MALE LAUGHTER REVERBERATED in the stillness, traveling over the icy waters of Loch Awe.

Glancing ahead at where Colin Campbell rode next to Lennox at the head of the company, Bonnie frowned. "Campbell gets on well with yer brother," she noted.

Iver huffed a sigh. "Aye ... the pair have been as thick as thieves ever since we left Stirling."

Bonnie's frown deepened. Both men had barely acknowledged her presence during the journey from Doune to Kilchurn. The past four days had been cold and tiring, and not just because of the weather.

Her attention shifted then from Iver's brother and the Lord of Glenorchy, to where a castle, its dove-grey curtain walls gleaming in the pale glow of the winter sun, perched upon a rocky islet.

The waters of Loch Awe, which they'd been riding alongside for the past few hours, were still this afternoon, reflecting Kilchurn's bulk.

Her breathing caught, her brow smoothing. "It's beautiful."

"Aye," Iver murmured. "Last time I passed this way, there was little to see. Campbell has done much work in the past years."

Bonnie didn't answer. She was too busy taking in the view. Snow-clad mountains encircled the fortress, the largest of them etched looming against the afternoon sky, and she tilted up her chin to view it properly.

"That's Ben Cruachan," Iver said, noting the direction of her gaze. "Dramatic, isn't it?"

Bonnie's mouth curved. It was, indeed.

Up ahead, Campbell and Lennox drew up their horses and waited for Iver to approach. And as they neared, Campbell flashed Iver a grin. "Just look at that, eh, Mackay. I bet ye haven't seen much to compare to Kilchurn."

"No," Iver admitted. "I haven't."

Campbell turned then, his arm sweeping to the castle rising against the western sky. "I wanted curtain walls to rival any castle in Scotland," he boasted. "This fortress is impenetrable."

They urged their horses forward, continuing on their way. It was a bone-chillingly cold afternoon. Their breaths steamed in the gelid air, and they rode along an icy road with mounds of frozen snow on either side.

Meanwhile, Kilchurn Castle gradually marched closer. And as they approached, Bonnie spied a low-lying causeway, visible just above the still waters of the loch, leading between the mainland and the islet.

It was a perilous crossing, for the causeway was slippery, and blocks of ice gently nudged at its edges in the freezing water.

Before them, the gates rumbled open and the portcullis rolled up, welcoming the laird home.

"Don't worry, lass," Iver murmured into Bonnie's ear as they crossed. "I'll try to keep our stay here as brief as possible."

The thunder of shod hooves on ice echoed against the high curtain wall before them, and then they were riding up the slope into the castle itself.

Moments later, Bonnie found herself inside an internal courtyard. A tall tower house loomed on the eastern side of the cobbled space, while lofty walls, lined with what looked like stables and guard barracks, encircled them. Stable hands were waiting for the party, and they swiftly relieved the laird and his guests of their horses.

Iver lowered Bonnie to the ground, and then he handed his courser over to the young man waiting to take the animal. As her husband gave the lad some instructions on how to handle his spirited gelding, Bonnie drew her woolen cloak close.

It was a tranquil afternoon, yet the damp cold drilled to the marrow of her bones. She wriggled her tingling toes in her boots before reaching up to rub the tip of her nose. It was numb.

Meanwhile, an older man with a bald head and a careworn face approached. "Welcome back, Campbell," he greeted the laird.

"It's good to be home," Campbell grunted back, turning to him. He then motioned to his companions. "Athol, this is Iver Mackay ... laird of Dun Ugadale and his brother. Iver and Lennox, meet my steward, Athol MacNab."

Bonnie tensed, while next to her, Iver scowled. It hadn't gone unnoticed that Campbell didn't introduce her.

Jaw clenched, Iver shifted his attention to the steward. "May I present my wife, Bonnie?"

"Pleased to meet ye, My Lady," MacNab replied, offering her a smile.

Bonnie smiled back, instantly warming to the man.

Meanwhile, Campbell's gaze had shifted, searching the steps to the keep behind MacNab. "Where's Davina?"

The steward's face tensed. "She has a headache ... and has taken to her bower."

The laird scowled. "Aye, well, make sure she's well enough to attend supper this eve." His heavy jaw tightened. "We have guests, and she shall be hosting them."

MacNab nodded. "I shall see it done."

"Good." Campbell then turned back to Iver and Lennox. "Right lads, my steward will have servants take yer things up to yer chambers ... in the meantime, take a closer look at what I've built." He motioned to the tower house. "It's five floors high ... what do ye think about that?"

Lennox flashed him a grin. "Impressive."

"Aye," Iver replied with a little less enthusiasm. "It's fine indeed, Colin."

Campbell turned then, gesturing to the stone steps leading into the tower house. "Come, lads ... let us warm ourselves by the fire in my hall."

"Wine?" A serving lass appeared at Iver's elbow, a ewer in hand.

"Aye, thanks." He held his cup up for her to fill. Opposite him, Lennox did the same.

The two brothers sat before the roaring hearth. As asked, they'd joined Campbell in his hall. Meanwhile, Bonnie had retired to the chamber she and Iver would share upstairs. Nearby, Campbell and his steward were standing together, discussing something a few yards away.

Iver ignored the Lord of Glenorchy. In truth, he was still simmering over the man's rudeness in the courtyard earlier. The incident with Sutherland in Doune also remained fresh in his mind. He wouldn't tolerate any slur, implied or otherwise, against his wife.

Taking a sip of wine, Iver's gaze settled upon his brother's face. He noted Lennox's surly expression. They'd spoken little during the journey north, and it appeared Lennox wasn't in a talkative mood now either.

He'd been laughing and chatting with Campbell earlier, yet his manner had changed.

Iver exhaled sharply. It was time to clear the air. "Things have been strained between us over the past days, Len," he said, breaking the heavy silence between them. "Are we going to continue like this?"

Lennox's mouth pursed. He then lifted his cup to his lips and took a gulp before shrugging. "Maybe."

Iver's spine stiffened. "Out with it then," he muttered. "If something weighs upon ye, get it off yer chest."

"Don't pretend ye don't know," Lennox shot back, his fingers tightening around his cup of wine.

Their gazes fused before Iver asked, "Why does my choice of wife bother ye so much?"

A nerve flickered on Lennox's cheek. "Ye are a *chieftain*, Iver," he ground out. "And such a role comes with responsibilities." He paused then, his eyes narrowing. "Ye seem to have forgotten that these days. Instead, ye leave the running of yer broch and the management of yer lands to others."

Iver stilled. He shouldn't have been surprised that Lennox's bitterness wasn't just to do with his hasty marriage to a low-born woman. It was much deeper rooted. "Do ye not wish to be my bailiff then?"

Lennox's mouth thinned. "I'm the second-born son," he replied, his voice clipped now. "And yet ye put Kerr in charge of yer Guard ... while my role has made me the most unpopular man on the Kintyre peninsula."

Iver snorted, even as his pulse started to thud in his ears. Indeed, he had chosen Kerr over Lennox to lead the Dun Ugadale Guard—and in truth hadn't thought much about his decision ever since. It had been the right one, for although Kerr was younger, he had a steadiness, a seriousness, that Lennox lacked.

Iver's dismissive response made Lennox scowl. "Of course, ye wouldn't have noticed." His mouth twisted. "For yer head has been too far up yer arse of late."

Iver clenched his jaw. Lennox's sharp tongue would get him into trouble if he didn't leash it.

Nonetheless, his brother wasn't yet done. He leaned forward, his face hardening. "And now, ye have gone and made a great fool of yerself."

"Excuse me?" Iver's voice lowered to a growl.

"Are ye so besotted that ye fail to see what's around ye?" Lennox leaned forward, his gaze never leaving his brothers. "All of Stirling Castle was whispering about ye before we departed."

Iver stared back at him. His heart now kicked against his ribs, his anger quickening like a flame on dry tinder.

However, oblivious to his rising temper—or perhaps wishing to goad him further—Lennox pressed on, "And everywhere we've stopped en route, folk speak of the laird who allowed himself to be led around by his prick. If ye—"

Lennox never finished his sentence.

Iver's patience snapped, a red curtain falling over his gaze. He'd had enough of the unasked-for opinions of others. He was sick of being slighted—especially by a member of his own family.

Wine sprayed everywhere as he launched himself from his seat. His right fist flew, and he punched his brother hard in the mouth, knocking Lennox backward in his chair.

His brother recovered swiftly, rolling to his feet with a roar, even as blood poured from his split lip. He launched himself at Iver, and suddenly the pair of them were at each other's throats.

The tension of the past days—if not months—exploded. They both lashed out, each seeking to punish the other.

Lennox's fist connected with Iver's gut, knocking the air from his lungs.

"Shitweasel," Iver wheezed as he struck once more. Fury pulsed through him now—he'd teach his brother to mind his tongue. This time, his knuckles collided with Lennox's cheek.

His brother snarled an answering insult and slugged him in the jaw.

"That's enough, lads," Campbell's voice boomed in Iver's ear. Strong hands then grabbed him by the shoulders and hauled him back.

Meanwhile, Athol MacNab gripped Lennox by the arm. Although he was getting on in years, and thin, the steward was stronger than he looked.

Rubbing his throbbing jaw and panting to recover his breath, Iver twisted free of Campbell's hold. He then cast a baleful look in his brother's direction.

Lennox wiped his bloody mouth with the back of his arm, his own gaze smoldering.

"I don't care what ye were quarreling over." Campbell was scowling as he met Iver's eye. "But there will be no brawling in my hall, Mackay ... is that clear?"

"Aye, Campbell," Iver grunted, even as rage still pulsed in his gut like a stoked ember. "Very."

28: A FINE MESS

"I BRING FINE news from Stirling, daughter," Colin Campbell announced, his mouth curving. "I have secured *ye* a husband."

The hall of Kilchurn Castle fell silent.

Like everyone else seated at the laird's table upon the dais, Bonnie's gaze settled upon Davina Campbell.

In truth, she hadn't paid much attention to Campbell's daughter during supper. Instead, she'd been wondering what had passed between Iver and Lennox. The brothers glowered at each other across the table. And judging from the red welt on her husband's set jaw, just above the fading bruise Sutherland had given him, and Lennox's split lip and swollen cheekbone—they'd been fighting.

She'd wondered earlier why Iver hadn't come upstairs to fetch her for supper—and now she knew.

Nonetheless, Colin Campbell's statement made her shift focus, to the slender figure seated opposite. Clad in a lovely grey kirtle trimmed with fur, Davina's elfin face was pale, bordering on ashen. She also bore dark shadows under her eyes. The steward had said the laird's daughter had been abed with a headache earlier; indeed, she didn't look that well.

Like her father, the lass had raven-colored hair and blue-grey eyes. Yet the physical similarity between father and daughter ended there. She didn't have her father's pugnacious jaw or aggressive bearing—and Bonnie guessed she'd favored her mother in looks. Colin was onto his third bowl of stew, while his daughter picked at her meal like a sparrow.

Davina's slender jaw flexed now, her shoulders tensing. "What?" she asked huskily.

"Take the wool out yer ears, lass," Campbell replied with a snort. "Murray MacPherson is prepared to overlook yer past … it's a fine offer indeed."

Beside Bonnie, Iver inclined his head. "The MacPherson clan-chief?"

Campbell flashed him a broad smile. "Aye … like me, he's a widower … and wishes to father a few more sons while he still has the strength in him to do so." The Lord of Glenorchy paused then, his gaze glinting. "That's why I lingered in Stirling for a few days after the council. I was husband hunting for dear Davina."

A brittle hush fell over the table once more. Meanwhile, the warriors seated at the tables beneath the dais had stopped eating and drinking and were observing the exchange between the laird and his daughter.

"MacPherson must be nearly thrice her age," Iver pointed out after a lengthy pause.

"Aye." Campbell's smile faded, irritation flaring in his eyes. "What of it?"

"I shall not wed him." Davina's voice, high now, intruded.

All gazes shifted back to her.

Campbell's dark brows crashed together, his thick fingers clenching around the stem of his goblet. "His age matters not, lass. He's a clan-chief … an influential one."

"I don't care who he is," she replied, a nerve jumping in her cheek. "I shall not wed Murray MacPherson … I shall not wed *anyone*."

Campbell slammed his goblet down. "Enough of this nonsense, Davina. Ye aren't going to remain unmarried, and that's final."

She swallowed. "Send me to Iona, father. I wish to take the veil."

"Not this again," he muttered. "I've already told ye, I'll not hand ye over to those nuns. Yer fair face will make me a strong alliance with one of my neighbors."

"Then ye shall be waiting forever for that day."
Davina pushed aside her bowl of stew and rose to her feet. Her slender body vibrated. "For I shall not take a husband. Ye robbed me of the only man I will ever love."

A weighty silence fell after these words, rippling across the hall.

Bonnie's gaze roamed over Davina's taut features. Surprise and curiosity rippled through her at such a bold declaration. What was this about?

Campbell was the first to recover. "Sit. Down," he bit out.

However, his daughter was hell-bent on defying him this eve, it seemed, for she merely turned and walked away.

Bonnie watched her descend the steps from the dais to the main floor, her long, graceful back rigid as she made for the door.

"Davina!" Campbell roared. "I didn't give ye permission to leave!"

But she ignored him—and moments later, Davina exited the hall.

Breathing hard, the laird glared after her. His face had turned red, and a vein pulsed in his temple.

Bonnie tensed, waiting for him to yell to one of his men—to instruct them to haul his errant daughter back to the table—but to her surprise, he didn't.

Instead, he grabbed his goblet of wine and sculled it in one long draft. "Infuriating wench," he muttered under his breath. "She gives me no end of trouble."

"Perhaps ye should heed Davina's wishes, Campbell," the steward murmured, meeting his eye across the table. "Why don't yet let her take the veil?"

Campbell scowled at MacNab, his grey-blue eyes narrowing. "No," he growled. "And the last thing I need is ye to take her side." Sitting back in his seat, he heaved in a deep breath, clearly seeking to settle his temper. The laird cast a glance in Iver's direction. "Apologies for my ill-mannered daughter, Mackay."

Iver nodded. "The lass seemed upset," he replied. "What happened to the man she spoke of?"

Campbell's heavy jaw tensed. "He overstepped … and paid the price."

The warning in his voice was clear, and Iver heeded it, dropping the subject. They'd clearly borne witness to a delicate family matter.

After a moment, Campbell poured himself another goblet of wine and sat back in his chair. "We shall not let my daughter's outburst ruin our evening," he muttered. "How about a game of Ard-ri after supper? I'll then take ye lads out boar hunting in the morning."

"I take it Lennox and ye had a fight?" Bonnie put down the hog bristle brush she'd been using to comb out her hair, her gaze fixing on where her husband stood by the fire, watching her.

She'd spoken gently, yet Iver stiffened, giving Bonnie her answer.

"Was it about me?" she asked softly.

He shrugged. "It doesn't matter."

Her brow furrowed. "Aye, it does." She paused then, tensing. "I don't want to come between ye."

"Ye won't," he replied, a crease appearing between his eyebrows. "Lennox and I needed to be honest with each other … and now we have been." Iver huffed a sigh, dragging his hand through his hair in a gesture she'd come to recognize as frustration. "It wasn't *just* about ye, lass … Lennox had some grievances he wished to share about some of my other decisions."

Silence fell between them, tension replacing the easy atmosphere that usually filled the room when they were alone.

Eventually, Bonnie shattered it. "Such as?"

Iver's mouth pursed. "I've known for a while that Lennox doesn't enjoy his work as bailiff … yet I hadn't realized he was angry I made Kerr the Captain of the Dun Ugadale Guard and not him."

"And why didn't ye?"

Her husband huffed out an irritated breath. She could tell he didn't want to talk about this, yet *she* did. If they were to be happy together, he couldn't just sweep uncomfortable subjects aside. Iver had told her that he planned to make some changes upon his return home—and it sounded as if his relationship with his brother sorely needed addressing.

"Kerr is younger than Lennox by two and a half years," Iver replied after a heavy pause, "but he's always had a sensible head on his shoulders. Lennox can be impulsive and reckless … not great qualities for a captain."

Bonnie considered his words. "Sometimes people don't show us what they're capable of … unless we give them a chance," she pointed out, with a small smile.

A stubborn expression settled upon Iver's face then. "Aye, well, Len is going to have to accept the way of things," he muttered. "Brodie's our broch's blacksmith and doesn't complain about it."

"If Lennox dislikes being bailiff, maybe ye could appoint someone else to the role," she suggested. "Perhaps he'd be better suited to another position."

Iver's brow furrowed. "Lennox and I shall work out our differences, Bonnie … we always do, in the end." There was an edge to his voice now, a gentle warning not to push any further.

Bonnie heeded it. Even so, her chest tightened. This was a side of her husband she hadn't seen before—Iver Mackay could be bull-headed, it seemed. He didn't like compromise.

"So, ye are going hunting tomorrow?" she asked, forcing a lightness she didn't feel into her voice.

Iver nodded. His expression was shuttered now.

Bonnie looked down at where she'd draped her new shawl over her lap and stroked its fine weave with her palm. "What do ye think about the situation with his daughter?"

He gave a soft snort. "It sounds like a fine mess."

"Campbell won't force Davina to wed anyone, will he?"

"I doubt it ... he's more of a blusterer than a brute. Nonetheless, the battle of wills will continue for a while yet, I'd wager."

She glanced up, her attention settling upon Iver once more. "I wonder what happened to make her so sad."

"So do I ... although I doubt anyone will tell us." He pushed himself off the mantelpiece then and crossed to the bed, lowering himself down next to Bonnie. Iver then caught her hands in his and squeezed gently. "Don't fash yerself, lass," he murmured, his mouth curving into a soft smile. "Everything will get sorted between Len and me."

29: HOW DO I BE A LADY?

THE MEN DEPARTED on their hunt shortly after dawn.

Clad in his fur cloak, Iver left Bonnie with a kiss. Still abed, she listened to the baying of the hounds in the courtyard below. She'd wanted to go down and see her husband off, but Iver had insisted she didn't get up.

"It's freezing out there, lass," he'd said with a boyish smile, his eyes still sleepy. "Stay here, where it's warm."

So, she remained under the covers, listening to the excited yipping below. Presently, the rumble of male voices filtered up, joined by the impatient snort of horses. And then, with a clatter of shod hooves on icy cobbles, they were off.

A short while later, silence settled over Kilchurn once more.

Bonnie lay there still, her gaze traveling to where the hearth glowed on the far side of the bedchamber. Iver had put on a fresh log before leaving, ensuring that the room was cozy for her.

A smile tugged at the corners of her mouth.

Aye, yestereve, Iver had revealed he had a stubborn streak, yet he was also considerate.

But as Bonnie snuggled under the blankets, worries about the future crept in, stealing her peace. Whatever Iver said, it was clear that Lennox disapproved of her. The brothers' relationship might have been strained, but *she* had worsened things. And soon she'd have to deal with the rest of his family—with his mother.

Bonnie's smile faded. God's blood, she wasn't ready.

Iver did his best to reassure her, yet his words weren't enough. She needed a woman's advice on the best way to handle herself when she arrived at Dun Ugadale.

Davina.

Aye, Campbell's daughter had problems of her own—but surely, she'd talk to Bonnie? In truth, Davina intimidated her a little. Nonetheless, she must have felt lonely here, without any women of her own age to spend time with.

Decision made, Bonnie threw aside the heavy blankets and sat up.

She wouldn't lie abed—not when she had a visit to make.

To Bonnie's chagrin, Davina Campbell didn't look pleased to have a visitor.

Turning from her loom, her grey-blue gaze narrowed as a maid ushered Bonnie inside the solar.

Bonnie flashed Davina a warm smile. "It's a beautiful morning outdoors." The woman's frown deepened, and Bonnie's smile faltered. She'd felt bold earlier when she'd made her decision to intrude upon Davina's privacy. But now that they were face to face, nervousness fluttered up. "And I was wondering if ye would join me for a walk."

Davina's jaw tensed. "I'm occupied at present," she replied, motioning to the loom. It sat before the window, where silvery light filtered in. Beyond, Bonnie caught a glimpse of cornflower-blue sky.

Bonnie moved forward, her gaze resting upon the jumble of greens and blues upon the tapestry.

Her own brow furrowed then. Over the years, she'd seen several detailed tapestries that hung from the walls within the chambers of Stirling Castle. They usually depicted battles, festivals, or pastoral scenes. But this one didn't seem to depict anything.

Seeing her reaction, Davina tensed. "I've never been an able weaver," she muttered. "But it passes the time."

Their gazes met, and Bonnie smiled once more. And this time, her nerves settled. She could tell Davina wasn't enjoying her work. "Well, let us pass the time by taking a walk upon the shore of the loch. Will ye not come with me?"

"It's been a long while since I did this."

Bonnie cast a sidelong glance at her companion. "Why is that, My Lady?"

Davina heaved a deep sigh. "It doesn't matter." She paused then, arching an eyebrow as she met Bonnie's eye. "We're of equal ranks … ye shouldn't address me as 'My Lady'."

Bonnie's cheeks warmed. Of course, Davina was right. Nonetheless, it was difficult to change the habit of a lifetime. She was used to keeping her gaze averted around her betters—and never would she have dreamed of addressing any of them by their first name.

Even so, she was pleased Campbell's daughter had agreed to venture outdoors with her.

Like Bonnie, Davina was bundled up against the cold. The fresh air had brought some color to her pale cheeks, although there remained a fragility about her.

Despite the sun, it was still cold. The women's breaths steamed in front of them. The ground was slippery too, as the morning's frost started to melt, and Bonnie and Davina picked their way gingerly along the shore.

They walked in silence for a while.

Bonnie had been tempted to make light conversation about the beauty of their surroundings or to compliment Davina on the fine weave of her cloak—yet she sensed the young woman wouldn't welcome such talk.

Instead, she decided to be candid with her. "I was wondering," she began hesitantly, "if I could ask yer advice."

Davina glanced her way and inclined her head. "On what?"

"Ye will have heard of who I am … and how Iver and I met?"

The ghost of a smile graced Davina's lips and then disappeared. "Aye," she replied, glancing away. "The servants' gossip has reached me."

Bonnie's cheeks warmed further. "I know how they chatter only too well," she murmured. "For I was once one of them. We watched the lives of those above us as if it were mummery put on for our amusement."

Davina shot her another look, her dark, finely arched brows knotting together. "Ye did?"

Bonnie nodded. "It made our lives a little more interesting."

Her companion's sharp gaze roved over her face. "What did ye wish to ask of me?"

Bonnie drew in a deep, steadying breath. "How do I *be* a lady?" Davina's gaze widened, yet Bonnie rushed on. "I want to bridge the gulf between Iver's world and mine ... I want to make him proud of me."

"And ye think acting the part will make that so?" The edge to Davina's voice nearly made Bonnie wince.

"I don't want to 'act the part'," she admonished her gently. "I want to embody whatever it is a high-born woman has that I don't."

Davina's gaze widened. After a beat, she glanced away, staring out across the glittering surface of the loch. "That is yer mistake right there," she said softly. "In thinking that there is any difference between those of high and low birth. If ye cut me, I still bleed as ye do. In childbirth, I have no lesser risk of dying. And when it comes to happiness, I have no greater right to it than ye do." She paused before glancing Bonnie's way again. "True nobility comes from yer heart, Bonnie. If ye want others to treat ye with respect, ye must walk with yer head held high ... *ye* must believe ye are worthy of admiration."

Bonnie was so taken aback by Davina's response that she stumbled and nearly pitched forward onto the icy shore. Recovering, she shot her companion an incredulous look. "Is it really that simple?"

Davina's mouth curved. However, the smile didn't reach her grey-blue eyes. "Aye, it's simple," she replied. "But I never said it was easy."

Breathing hard, Iver watched his brother drive his spear into the neck of the large boar. The animal's black bristled bulk jerked, and then it slumped upon the ground, unmoving.

Colin Campbell whistled to his dogs then, and they removed themselves from where they'd been clinging to various parts of the boar's body. It had been a long and arduous hunt, and they'd chased their quarry far through copses of skeleton trees, where the undergrowth of brambles was silvered with frost.

The boar was a mature one with huge yellowed tusks, and in the end, it had turned on its hunters and charged, its squeals of outrage echoing through the frozen woods.

But now the stout-hearted beast was dead.

Around them, Campbell's men looked on. Once the boar had been bailed up, they'd all dismounted and grabbed their spears. Meanwhile, their horses stamped impatiently and tossed their heads, their bits jangling, behind them.

Lennox's bruised face was flushed as he straightened up. He'd taken a risk, getting in as close as he had, for even injured and bailed up by the hounds, the boar was dangerous.

Many a hunter had died after being gored by one of those wickedly sharp tusks.

Yet Lennox enjoyed the thrill of such a risk.

"Well done, Len!" Campbell huffed. "A fine kill indeed."

Lennox's expression softened as he glanced back down at the dead boar. "He was a worthy adversary."

"It was a clean kill," Iver said then. He and Lennox had barely spoken all morning—tension bristling between them—yet it seemed churlish not to congratulate his brother.

Lennox's gaze swung his way, and his smile faded. He then favored his brother with a curt nod.

"There will be much boar stew served over the coming moon, I'll wager," one of Campbell's men quipped.

"Aye." Another warrior grinned. "And some blood sausage once Lent is over."

Congratulating each other on the successful hunt, the two men who'd spoken made their way through the milling pack of panting dogs, to where Lennox still stood next to the boar.

Together, they helped him drag it over to the stocky garron they'd brought with them. They then heaved the beast over its back.

Returning to where his courser stood next to Lennox's, Iver strapped the long spear he'd been carrying onto its back before mounting. He then glanced up at the sky.

It had been a fine morning for a hunt. They left Kilchurn in the early dawn, yet judging from the sun—a bright silver orb in a pale-blue sky—it was past noon now.

They'd ridden far in pursuit of the boar, and now it was time to begin the ride back to Loch Awe.

The warriors were in high spirits during the journey home.

Campbell rode at the front of the party, flanked on either side by Lennox and Iver. And although the two brothers did not speak to each other, the Lord of Glenorchy didn't appear to mind. It seemed the man had plenty to say. Hunting was his favorite pastime, and so he talked at length about the morning they'd just passed, and the tactics they'd employed.

"Ye wield a spear well, Len," Campbell said, grinning at him. "Ye'd be a formidable foe on the battlefield."

Lennox grunted at the compliment, although his mouth curved.

"He is," Iver replied. "We have fought shoulder-to-shoulder many a time. Ye should see him wield a claidheamh-mòr. The last time we fought against the

Sutherlands, those remaining at the end of the skirmish ran from him."

Iver's words weren't empty flattery. Indeed, although all four of the Mackay brothers were highly skilled in combat, Lennox had a slight edge over them all.

His brother's expression sobered. "Aye, well that seems like years ago now." He met Campbell's eye then, his mouth twisting. "These days, my brother prefers to use my aggression to collect rent from his reluctant tenants."

Campbell snorted. "What a waste of talent."

Iver clenched his jaw, heat flaring in his stomach. He couldn't believe Lennox had complained about his lot in front of Campbell. It appeared that, since he'd already voiced his bitterness about being Iver's bailiff the evening before, he wouldn't suppress it going forward.

Campbell wore a smirk now, and Iver's temper smoldered.

Some things didn't need to be shared. As soon as they departed Kilchurn, he and Lennox were going to have words—again.

Iver wouldn't tolerate his brother's malcontent, or his disloyalty.

"Well lads," Campbell said after a heavy pause. "Today's hunt was so successful, let's have another tomorrow ... what say ye?"

Hearing their laird, the warriors following close behind gave shouts of encouragement.

However, Iver frowned. Aye, he'd promised Campbell he'd stay at Kilchurn a few days—but his mood was soured now, and his patience had reached its limits. He didn't want to spend days in the company of this coarse-mannered man, neglecting his lovely wife in the meantime.

He wanted to take her home.

"Thank ye, Colin," he replied, "but I must decline. Several overdue tasks await me at Dun Ugadale ... and I have an important missive to pen to my clan-chief." He met Campbell's gaze then, favoring him with a thin smile. "We shall depart tomorrow morning."

30: THE OFFER

LENNOX MACKAY WAS seated in front of the hearth in the hall of Kilchurn Castle, staring moodily into the dancing flames, when the heavy tread of approaching footsteps warned him his solitude was about to be shattered.

He tensed, anticipating that his brother had come downstairs to speak to him.

Iver was the last person he wanted to see right now. Every time their gazes had met today, Lennox's temper flared hot. He wanted to finish the fight his brother started, but they hadn't had the opportunity.

Yet when Lennox glanced over his shoulder, he spied Colin Campbell, not Iver, approaching.

"Ye are up late, Len," Campbell greeted him.

The laird had wrapped himself up in a cloak of his clan plaid, green and blue—it was of a similar hue but without the emerald and deep blues of the Mackay plaid.

"I don't feel like sleeping just yet," Lennox replied.

"Aye, I know the feeling," Campbell replied. "Usually, a good hunt relaxes me, yet I'm restless this eve." He motioned to the ewer of blackberry wine and cups on a shelf above the hearth. "Will ye share a cup of wine with me before we retire?"

Lennox nodded.

Wordlessly, the laird poured them two cups, handed his companion one, and then settled into a chair opposite him.

Wrapping his fingers around the cup, Lennox raised it to his lips and took a cautious sip. His split lip still stung whenever he drank anything, and now was no exception. Nonetheless, the wine was welcome. It was the same one they'd drunk at supper—deep and fruity, it tasted like summer.

"It's a shame ye are leaving so soon," Campbell said then. "I've enjoyed yer company ... and was hoping for another rousing boar hunt."

Lennox grimaced. "Aye, well ... the choice wasn't mine, Colin," he replied. "Iver made his decision without consulting me."

Like he always does.

Their gazes met briefly, and they shared a moment of understanding.

Iver hadn't warmed to Campbell over the past few days, but Lennox got on with the man well enough. He enjoyed his plain speech and bawdy sense of humor. Nonetheless, the scene the night before with the laird's daughter had been awkward; Campbell had handled it badly.

"Aye, well, he is infatuated, lad," the Lord of Glenorchy murmured. "That's what happens when a woman bewitches a man."

Lennox snorted. Indeed, Iver was besotted by his chambermaid.

His jaw clenched then. He had nothing against the lass personally. Bonnie appeared sweet-natured. But his brother had no business marrying her. What was the point of swearing off marriage all these years, if he ended up wedding a woman this far beneath him?

It was just another sign that his brother didn't take his role seriously.

Silence drew out between the two men before Campbell eventually cleared his throat. "Ye don't strike me as rivals," he observed, his gaze glinting. "Do ye wish *ye* were the chieftain of Dun Ugadale then?"

Lennox shook his head. He heaved a sigh, considering his words carefully. Although he'd made a deliberate jibe on the ride home—aye, he'd seen the ire spark in his brother's eyes—he was wary of criticizing Iver behind his back.

His brother didn't deserve that.

"I don't want to be laird," he replied. And that was the truth—he didn't. "I just want to be allowed to choose my own path in life."

Campbell nodded, his brow furrowing. He then took a sip of wine, savoring it as he glanced over at the flickering fire. The logs were burning down low now to glowing golden embers.

"Ye don't have to return to Dun Ugadale, ye know?" he said after a long pause.

Lennox raised an eyebrow before drinking from his cup once more. "I don't?"

"It sounds to me as if ye are a man craving a challenge." Their gazes met then, and Campbell's mouth curved into a rueful smile. "What if I offered ye a position here?"

Lennox inclined his head. "What sort of position?"

"Captain of the Kilchurn Guard."

Lennox's breathing grew shallow. He wondered if the laird had overheard his and Iver's argument the evening before. Did he know that Lennox had wanted to lead the Dun Ugadale Guard, yet had been passed over in favor of Kerr?

"That's a generous offer, Colin," he replied cautiously, viewing Campbell over the rim of his cup. "But won't the current captain object to being demoted?"

Campbell pulled a face. "There is no captain of the Guard at present. I killed him."

Lennox's gaze widened. Yet he remained silent, waiting for Campbell to explain himself.

"My daughter formed an inappropriate ... relationship ... with my previous captain," Campbell admitted, his mouth twisting. "When I discovered it, we fought, and I did indeed slay him." He paused then, his gaze shadowing. "I felt vindicated at the time, for the man was far beneath her in rank, and had committed a grave insult ... yet it seems that Davina will never forgive me."

"She might," Lennox murmured. "With time."

Nonetheless, he'd seen the glint in the young woman's eye the day before. Davina Campbell possessed a waifish beauty and was too fragile looking to appeal to Lennox, who preferred his women buxom. However, she was a stubborn lass—not so different from her sire, it seemed.

The older man sighed then and dragged a hand down his face, revealing that the situation was weighing on him even more heavily than he'd let on. "I don't choose a captain lightly," he said after a lengthy pause, "but over the past days, I've seen that ye are a man with a character I admire." Their gazes fused then. "I'd be honored if ye'd stay on at Kilchurn."

"I'm remaining here."

Iver halted. "What?" He'd been on his way across the courtyard outside the tower house, to retrieve his horse, when Lennox called his name.

His brother now stood before him, jaw set and shoulders tense, as if he was readying himself for another fight.

"Colin has offered me a position at Kilchurn ... and I have taken it."

Iver's breathing grew shallow, while beside him, Bonnie was silent. Meanwhile, the party of four warriors who'd accompany them home stopped saddling their horses and swiveled to watch them.

Lennox ignored his audience. "I'm to captain his guard," he added, his eyes glinting.

Recovering, Iver scowled. "But ye are needed at Dun Ugadale."

A taut silence followed these words before Lennox growled back, "Ye can find yerself *another* bailiff."

Iver's pulse started to hammer in his ears. He couldn't believe Lennox was doing this. Attempting to leash his rising anger, he folded his arms across his chest. "Is this revenge?"

Lennox snorted. "No."

"Why then?"

His brother's expression shuttered. "I need a change."

They stared at each other then, and Iver's mouth thinned. Lennox wasn't being honest with him; nonetheless, Iver didn't want to brawl with him again, especially in front of Bonnie. "So, ye are set on this?"

Lennox nodded.

"And there's nothing I can say to change yer mind?"

Their gazes met once more. Lennox looked as if he hadn't slept the night before: a dark-blond stubble covered his strong jaw, and his short hair was mussed. "No," he replied gruffly.

Lennox's attention then shifted from Iver to where Bonnie still stood at her husband's side. Wrapped up in a woolen cloak, her red hair braided in a long plait down her back, she watched her brother-by-marriage warily. Iver didn't blame her. Lennox hadn't given her much reason to like him.

"I owe ye an apology, Bonnie," Lennox muttered. "I've been an arse."

Bonnie's gaze widened, while Iver's mouth thinned. He appreciated the gesture, yet his brother's lack of grace vexed him.

Lennox huffed a sigh, revealing that his inarticulate words frustrated him as well. His gaze then flicked between Iver and his wife. "I wish ye both happiness," he added. "I *mean* that."

"Thank ye," Bonnie murmured.

Lennox favored her with a tight smile. He then glanced Iver's way once more. "Explain my decision to Kerr and Brodie, will ye?" he asked. "They will understand."

31: MUCH UNSAID

RIDING FROM KILCHURN Castle, wrapped in Iver's arms, Bonnie glanced over her shoulder at the heavy curtain wall etched against the pale-blue morning sky. The sun had just risen behind them, glittering over the frozen landscape.

The fortress was majestic, perched on the rocky islet with the sparkling waters of Loch Awe around it.

Bonnie had mixed feelings about leaving Kilchurn.

She wasn't comfortable around Colin Campbell, and yet her talk with his daughter the day before had caused a shift within her.

Davina's voice still echoed in her ears. *If ye want others to treat ye with respect, ye must walk with yer head held high ... ye must believe ye are worthy of admiration.*

And in the wake of that conversation, she'd tried to walk a little taller, to look servants in the eye when she talked to them. Davina was right. Bonnie needed to stop looking at those above her as if they were superior to her. They weren't.

She was still nervous about meeting Iver's family, yet she wouldn't let them cow her. When she rode into Dun Ugadale, she wouldn't hang her head in shame.

Bonnie's mouth curved then, and she leaned into Iver. However, she noted just how rigid his body was.

Her smile faded.

Lennox's decision had upset him. None of them had seen it coming, although perhaps they should have.

Things between the two brothers had been strained. The tension had reached boiling point, and something clearly had to change.

And the position Campbell had offered Lennox was an honor indeed.

Even so, they'd left Kilchurn with much unsaid.

In the aftermath of Lennox's announcement, both the brothers had each retreated behind their shields. Lennox had looked on silently while Iver went to retrieve his courser. And when Iver had re-emerged from the stables, his expression had been inscrutable.

Yet the tension in his muscles now betrayed him.

Lennox's apology earlier had surprised Bonnie. It was unpolished, yet sincere—and when their gazes met, she'd warmed to Iver's brother for the first time. His choice, to go against his elder brother and strike out on his own, had taken bravery, and she respected his decision.

She too knew just how hard it was to break free of the expectations of others.

But now Lennox was behind them, and Iver hadn't spoken since they rode out of the castle.

Sensing that he wasn't in a talkative mood, Bonnie didn't break the silence between them. Instead, she looked away from Kilchurn, lifting her chin and squaring her shoulders as her gaze traveled over the hills that unfolded to the west.

And despite her newfound confidence and resolve, her belly fluttered once more.

Soon they'd strike onto the Kintyre peninsula and complete the last leg of their journey toward their destination—toward her new home.

Iver pulled up his courser before the large standing stone. And for the first time since they'd departed from Kilchurn Castle three days earlier, his mood lightened.

"Ye know ye aren't far from my broch when ye spy the *Crois Mhic Aoidh*," he announced.

"Mackay's Cross," Bonnie murmured, leaning forward to get a better look.

"Aye," Iver replied before touching the brooch that pinned his cloak to his gambeson. "This is the spot where the Bruce gave my great grandfather the 'Ugadale brooch' after he transported him safely to Arran."

"Really?" Bonnie twisted in the saddle, flashing him a smile. "Yer family helped Robert the Bruce?"

He smiled back, pride tightening his chest. "Aye, lass. The Mackays have long played an important part in Scottish history."

Their party had just drawn up on open moorland, upon the southern slopes of Doire na h-Earbaige. Like the standing stone, the sight of the hill's tawny bulk rising above him gave Iver a sense of homecoming. And he saw the same warmth on the faces of the four warriors who'd accompanied them. The eldest of them, Ian, appeared misty-eyed this morning.

All of them, Iver included, had a deep love for these lands.

Iver's gut clenched then. He'd thought Lennox felt the same way about their home on the Kintyre peninsula, yet his brother had accepted Colin Campbell's offer without hesitation. It seemed Iver had badly misjudged the situation with his brother.

Pushing aside the regret that had dogged his steps every furlong south, Iver focused once more on Mackay's Cross.

The ancient stone before them had a pointed top and stood just over five feet, listing slightly.

"Do ye know who put it here?" Bonnie asked then.

"No," he admitted, "only that it has stood here long before the Mackays settled these lands." He paused then, pointing to the letter engraved on the weathered stone. "My grandfather etched out an 'M' on each side."

Bonnie shifted to view the stone once more. "How close are we to Dun Ugadale?"

Iver noted the change in her voice—the subdued edge that crept into it. In contrast to his own brooding mood, Bonnie had been in good spirits since leaving Kilchurn— had even seemed excited about seeing her new home— yet she was quiet this morning.

"Aye." He gave her waist a gentle squeeze. "Just a few more hours, lass." Leaning in, he brushed his lips across her cheek before whispering in her ear. "Don't worry, Bonnie, it'll go fine."

She gave a shaky laugh in response. "Of course, it will."

"Remember, I'll be right there at yer side," he reassured her.

Bonnie's small hand covered his, their fingers entwining. "I know," she murmured.

Iver straightened up then, glancing over his shoulder at his warriors. "Ready to go, lads?"

Ian flashed him a grin. "Aye ... my wife awaits."

They turned their horses southeast and urged them into a brisk canter, traveling over windswept moorland framed by bare hills. They were three-quarters of the way down the Kintyre peninsula here, not far from the largest town on the headland, Ceann Locha.

It was an isolated spot, out on a limb from the rest of Scotland—but Iver liked its remote position. When he'd been younger, he'd always wanted to be in the thick of the action, yet these days, his soul yearned for the peace of his broch.

And when he caught sight of the sparkle of sunlight on the water, his pulse quickened. The ache under his breastbone, at the rift between him and Lennox, eased just a little. Kilbrannan Sound, the body of water that stretched between the peninsula and the Isle of Arran, lay before them—which meant Dun Ugadale lay not far away.

And when he returned home, things would be different. No longer would he hide away from the world. No longer would he leave his brothers to make the hard decisions. Instead, he'd be the laird they all deserved.

32: SCANDAL

BONNIE HAD TOLD herself she wouldn't let nerves get to her. Nonetheless, as their destination approached, it felt as if someone had just released a sack of moths in her belly.

Drawing a slow, deep breath, she kept telling herself she *was* worthy of being Iver's wife. She *wouldn't* embarrass him with her rough manners and unpolished speech. However, with each furlong they rode southeast, it grew harder to cling to her newfound confidence.

And when the bulk of Iver's broch hove into view, her heart started to pound like a Beltaine drum.

Dun Ugadale was exactly as Iver had described it—an ancient roundhouse, perched upon a rocky promontory, with a tower looking out to sea. High walls wrapped around the base of the stronghold, protecting it from the elements and attack.

The broch really did have a windswept setting. Green hills surrounded the broch, without a tree in sight. A scattering of bothies, squat stone houses with turf roofs, crouched before the fortress. Surveying the settlement, Bonnie saw a woman hanging out flapping washing on a line outside her cottage, while another scattered grain for fowl. Meanwhile, children played knucklebones in the dirt.

The men guided their horses onto a muddy track that led down to the promontory, between carefully tilled fields, where cottars hoed around the first of the spring cabbages and kale. And on the hills behind, black-faced sheep grazed placidly while tiny lambs tottered around. Despite her fluttering stomach, Bonnie smiled at the sight.

Snowdrops, crocuses, and daffodils waved their greeting in the brisk sea breeze, at the roadside—another reminder that despite the chill in the air, spring was upon them now.

A new beginning, she reminded herself, her spine straightening. *For us all.*

Her gaze traveled to the grey walls of Dun Ugadale. The stronghold looked as if it truly belonged here, as if it had grown out of the moss and lichen-covered rocks rather than being constructed by the hand of man.

Iver urged his courser up the causeway that led toward a high stone arch. The gelding's hooves clattered on cobblestones, the sound echoing off the surrounding stone.

Moments later, they were inside the walls of Dun Ugadale, and Iver was drawing up his horse in the barmkin before his broch.

And as Bonnie expected, a welcome party had emerged from the roundhouse to greet him. Her gaze alighted on a handsome woman wrapped in a thick green shawl standing in the midst of the group. She looked to be in her sixth decade, yet still stood tall and strong. Her silver hair caught in the breeze, while her penetrating gaze scanned the newcomers.

There was no doubt this was Sheena Mackay, the former Lady of Dun Ugadale.

Two men flanked the woman. The one standing to her left was tall and lean with pale-blond hair like Iver. He wore a quilted gambeson over a léine, and chamois braies. A heavy woolen cloak hung from his shoulders, and he carried a dirk at his hip. In contrast, the man to Sheena's right was of a stockier build with curly walnut-brown hair, a strong jaw, and a furrowed brow. He was clad in a heavy woolen tunic over soot-stained braies and a long leather blacksmith's apron.

"Greetings!" Iver called out, swinging down from his horse. He then turned and helped Bonnie down from the saddle, placing a protective arm about her shoulder as he steered her toward the three figures.

"Welcome home, brother," the blond man called back. His gaze alighted then upon Bonnie for a moment before it shifted to the riders behind her. "Where's Lennox?"

"He's at Kilchurn," Iver replied, his tone veiled. "Colin Campbell asked him to captain his Guard ... and he agreed."

All three of his kin tensed at this news, even as their gazes now rested upon Bonnie. Swallowing her nervousness, she smiled back at them.

Both men then frowned at their elder brother, and Bonnie sensed their disapproval. From the look on their faces, they believed Iver had done something to chase Lennox away.

"But Len is needed here," Sheena replied, her voice clipped.

"Aye, he is," Iver agreed, his own brow furrowing, "but this was what *he* wanted ... and I'm not his warden." He paused then, an uncomfortable silence settling over the windy barmkin, before clearing his throat. "Ma, Kerr, and Brodie ... may I present Bonnie ... my wife."

"Good day." Bonnie flashed Iver's kin another smile.

None of them smiled back.

Instead, Kerr and Brodie's faces went slack, while Sheena's lips parted. However, she was the first to recover. "Well, Iver ... this is a surprise indeed." Her gaze, midnight-blue and filled with sharp intelligence, drilled into Bonnie. Her expression turned speculative as she scrutinized her. "And what clan do ye hail from, lass?"

Bonnie kept her smile firmly in place as she replied, "Fraser."

Iver's mother inclined her head, a crease forming between her finely arched brows. "Fraser?" She glanced then over at her eldest son, confusion clouding her gaze. "Don't mistake me, Iver ... I'm delighted ye have finally come to yer senses ... but I'm surprised. We have little to do with that clan." Her attention flicked Bonnie's way once more. "What branch of the Frasers do ye belong to? Are ye a lowlander or a Lovat?"

"A lowlander," Bonnie replied, even as her pulse quickened.

In truth, she knew little about her mother's clan. If Iver's mother asked her anything else, she feared she wouldn't be able to answer.

"Bonnie grew up at Stirling Castle" —Iver's hold on her shoulders tightened just a fraction, a warning that he was about to reveal the truth— "where she worked as a chambermaid."

The stunned look on his family members' faces was almost comical.

Nonetheless, despite that she'd told herself she wouldn't let herself feel intimidated, Bonnie's pulse started to race.

"How did ye meet?" The blond man asked after a long pause, incredulity in his voice.

"At the queen's masquerade ball," Iver replied. "It's quite a tale, Kerr ... one I will recount later."

Bonnie's breathing grew shallow. She hoped he wouldn't. Surely, they could leave out all the details.

The brown-haired man, Brodie, remained silent, his expression bewildered. Meanwhile, Sheena Mackay's face had gone the color of milk. Moments later, two high spots of color appeared upon the older woman's cheeks. Drawing herself up, she viewed her firstborn with a narrowed gaze. "A *chambermaid*, Iver?"

The laird held his mother's eye steadily. "Aye, Ma ... but let's not dwell on that. Bonnie is the woman I have chosen to spend my life with ... and I expect ye to give her a warm Mackay welcome."

It wasn't a mild afternoon, and a cold, damp salt-laced wind barreled across the barmkin. All the same, Bonnie had started to sweat.

She'd expected their arrival to ruffle some feathers, yet Sheena Mackay was even more intimidating than she'd anticipated.

Standing just a few feet from the woman, it was clear to see that she'd been a rare beauty in her youth. Her high cheekbones and proud bearing spoke to a Norse heritage, and her thick silver-white hair would have once been the same shade as Kerr and Iver's. But there was a hardness to her face that hinted at bitterness, and the way she'd said 'chambermaid' made queasiness churn within Bonnie.

Don't let her frighten ye, Bonnie told herself firmly. *Ye are this woman's equal.*

Sheena shifted her gaze from Iver, and then she looked her daughter-in-law up and down, taking in her plain kirtle visible under the woolen cloak. "Who were yer parents?" she asked, her voice clipped, as if she were addressing a servant and not the new Lady of Dun Ugadale.

"Ma." Iver's voice held a warning edge. "I—"

"My mother was a cook at Stirling Castle," Bonnie replied, cutting him off. It was best she spoke for herself. Her spine straightened as she met Sheena's eye. "I don't know who my father was ... and my mother died birthing me."

Silence followed these words—and Sheena Mackay looked her over once more, this time her lip curling.

Bonnie sucked in a deep breath and pushed down her frustration. Of course, many people—her aunt had been one—believed that the character of someone born outside of wedlock was morally inferior to other folk. Indeed, the chaplain at Stirling had preached that illegitimate children carried a stain upon them and could never be trusted.

It was a stigma Bonnie had fought against her entire life—and she was ready to face it down now.

Next to Sheena, Kerr shifted uncomfortably, his gaze flicking from Bonnie to Iver's face. However, Brodie didn't move. Instead, he watched his sister-by-marriage, his handsome face taut.

But Bonnie wasn't focused on Iver's brothers—but on his mother.

And as she watched Sheena's face, the woman's expression changed. She'd been disgusted just moments earlier, yet now it was as if something had just dawned upon her. "How old are ye?" she demanded, her voice clipped.

Bonnie lifted her chin. "Five and twenty ... why?"

Sheena snorted.

"Mother!" Iver snapped. "That's enough. Ye have—"

"God's troth, son, have ye wool between yer ears?" Sheena interrupted him. A heavy silence fell then, and Iver's expression darkened. A muscle flexed in his jaw, betraying his simmering anger. Meanwhile, his mother stared back at him, gaze gleaming. "Do ye have any idea who this woman is?"

Queasiness rolled over Bonnie. All the way here, she'd told herself she'd win over Iver's mother. But now she saw that wasn't going to happen.

"What kind of foolish question is that?" Iver bit out, tightening his grip around Bonnie's shoulders. "Of course, I do ... and I love her."

Bonnie's breathing caught. *He loves me.*

That was the first time she'd heard the words, and the announcement nearly made her forget the awkwardness of this situation.

She glanced up at him, and their gazes fused.

Iver's mouth then quirked, and warmth wrapped itself around her.

There was no denying it—she loved him too. Wholeheartedly.

Bonnie's lips parted as she readied to tell him so. However, Sheena made a frustrated sound in the back of her throat.

Bonnie jerked her gaze from Iver's to see that Sheena was glowering at him. "Did I really give birth to such a fool?" she muttered. "Have ye paid no attention to court gossip over the years?"

"No, Ma," Iver snapped. "I leave such base matters to ye."

Sheena drew herself up. "Well, that's a pity indeed." She bit out the words. "For if ye had, ye'd have realized yer mistake." She paused then, her gaze narrowing. "Ye have shackled yerself to the bastard daughter of James the First."

In an instant, the warmth that had wrapped itself around Bonnie after her husband's declaration sloughed away. In a heartbeat, her elation changed to confusion. "What?" she whispered.

"I'd know that flame-red hair anywhere." Sheena continued, her blue eyes glinting. "But it was only when ye told me about yer birth and yer age that I solved the riddle." Her gaze swept to Iver's stunned face. "I remember the scandal of her birth well. I was at Stirling Castle five and twenty years ago ... visiting my sister who was a lady-in-waiting to Queen Joan at the time." Sheena's attention shifted back to Bonnie's face, and there it stayed. "I recall how jealous the queen was at the discovery that the king had been dallying with one of the cooks ... and had gotten her with bairn." She paused, her mouth pursing. No doubt this tale reminded her of her own husband's infidelity. After a moment, Sheena continued, "Joan wanted the lass cast out, yet James refused. Their shouting echoed off the walls of Stirling Castle for days."

A lump formed in Bonnie's throat, and she swallowed hard.

She wanted to throw Sheena's words back in her face, to call her a liar.

But her gut told her it was the truth.

Somehow, deep down, she'd always known there was a reason why no one at Stirling would speak about her father.

How many of them knew?

Surely, not everyone—for all it would have taken was a loose-lipped laundress or stable lad to let the scandal slip. However, Bonnie sensed that some of them—Ainslie and Angus Boyd, Duncan Stewart, and Lorna Fraser—*did* know. Suddenly, the glint she'd often witnessed in her aunt's eyes when she'd called her a 'bastard' made sense. She'd always sensed there was something else, something deeper, that Lorna never spoke about.

And now she'd discovered who her father really was.

Nausea rolled over Bonnie then as she recalled the times she'd caught a glimpse of the current king. Her half-brother. His distinctive fiery hair was the exact same hue as her own. They had the same shaped face too, the same pale, lightly freckled skin.

Why hadn't she made the connection herself?

Her belly cramped. Why would she? It sounded ludicrous, even now, that royal blood flowed through her veins.

Suddenly, it felt as if her whole world was unraveling before her eyes.

Over the years, she'd imagined her father had been some visiting nobleman—a lesser chieftain or laird perhaps. Her mother's tragic end had cast a shadow over Bonnie's life, and the sting of knowing she'd been born in such circumstances had never left her.

But this was something else.

Does the king know?

Likely not. She guessed his parents had never told him. His father—*their* father—was assassinated when he was but a bairn, and Queen Joan had died around eight years earlier.

Sometimes kings acknowledged their bastards—even the illegitimate daughters—but James the First hadn't.

He'd never had the chance to.

Yet the fact he'd refused to send her mother away, hinted that he'd had feelings for Greer Fraser. Had he lived, Bonnie's life might have been very different.

Grief twisted in her chest. *I could have known him.* For years, she'd imagined her father was alive, just living elsewhere, but in fact, she was an orphan. Both her parents were long gone.

Meanwhile, now that she'd made her declaration, Sheena had pursed her lips, as if she were looking upon something foul.

Something innately flawed.

A sob rose within Bonnie, clawing its way up from her chest to her throat. Suddenly, she felt lost and utterly alone in the world.

An instant later, she twisted out of Iver's grip.

"Bonnie!" He made a grab for her, his handsome face drawn and pale, yet she ducked out of his reach, darted around his courser, and ran for the gates of Dun Ugadale.

Shouts followed her, but she barely heard them above the roaring in her ears.

Her feet flew over slippery cobbles, and she nearly tumbled down the causeway outside the gates. However, she managed to right herself just in time. She then picked up her skirts and sprinted like a hare pursued by wolves.

She wasn't sure why she was running, or where she intended to go—only that she had to get away.

Maybe if she fled far and fast enough, she might outrun who she was.

33: NOTHING TO APOLOGIZE FOR

IVER REMAINED LONG enough in the barmkin to lock gazes with his mother.

Sheena stood as tall and proud as ever, her dark-blue eyes gleaming with victory.

"Ready yerself to kneel before my wife and beg her forgiveness," he ground out, enunciating each word. "For when I find her, that is exactly what ye shall do."

Not waiting to see his mother's reaction—for frankly, he didn't care—Iver swiveled on his heel and followed Bonnie out of the barmkin.

Out on the causeway, he broke into a run, glancing around as he searched for his wife.

Moments later, he spied her.

She hadn't followed the road west, but instead had scrambled down the rocks to the pebbly shore and was sprinting north.

Her footing was uneven, and she often stumbled, yet Bonnie ran with surprising speed.

She was already some distance ahead of him.

Cursing, Iver slid down the rocks and pursued her along the shore.

It took a while to catch up. Bonnie's work at Stirling Castle had kept her fit and strong. She had considerable endurance.

Sweat slid down Iver's back between his shoulder blades, and his lungs started to burn as the chase went on. Nonetheless, yard by yard, he slowly closed the gap between them. And finally, with his last burst of speed, he reached his wife.

Catching Bonnie by the arm, he pulled her up.

But to his surprise, she fought him, struggling in his grip, her small fists pummeling him as she tried to free herself.

"Bonnie!" he gasped. "Stop this!"

His chest constricted as she shook her head frantically, tears streaming down her face. The devil take his mother. If she'd taken a dirk to Bonnie's chest, it would have hurt less.

Pulling his wife hard against him, Iver wrapped his arms around her, pinning her arms to her sides, and letting her collapse against his chest.

"It's all right, sweetheart," he murmured as sobs wracked her. "Let it out. I have ye."

They stood like that for a while, their bodies pressed close while Bonnie wept into his gambeson. A cold, damp wind that smelled of brine and seaweed snagged at them, yet Iver paid it no mind. All he focused on, all he cared about right now, was the upset woman in his arms.

"There, my love," he whispered, his throat tight. "None of this matters. I don't care who yer father is. Ye will always have a home with me, I promise ... and ye will always be loved and cherished." And as he spoke, he stroked her back. He wasn't sure if she heard any of it, so deep was her upset.

She'd had a shock. He couldn't imagine what it would feel like to discover his father was a past king of Scotland.

He sensed her grief too—for a past she couldn't change, and parents she'd never known. It was as if a lifetime of tears had been storing themselves up—and finally, today, his mother's revelation had broken the dyke holding them back.

Iver wanted to be able to soothe his wife's hurts, to be able to change things so that she didn't have to suffer, but he couldn't.

He could only hold her while the storm passed.

Bonnie wept for a long while, until she was too tired to continue.

Slumped against Iver's broad chest, held tight in the cage of his arms, she gradually became aware of her surroundings once more—of the cry of gulls and the crash of the waves against the pebbly shore where they stood.

She also realized her husband was gently stroking her hair and murmuring endearments to her.

Swallowing, Bonnie raised her face from his gambeson, where she'd left a large soaking patch upon the quilted material, blinking up at Iver through wet lashes.

"I'm sorry," she croaked, her throat raw from weeping.

His midnight-blue eyes guttered. "Och, lass ... ye have nothing to apologize for." He shifted his hand from where it now rested on her shoulder, to her wet cheek, cupping it gently. "Instead, it is I who must ask yer forgiveness. My mother was insufferably rude."

Bonnie swallowed once again. "And yet she spoke the truth."

"Aye ... but there are ways of saying things."

She nodded, drawing in a shaky breath, as the wind buffeted them. "I can't believe I'm half-sister to the king," she murmured finally. Indeed, even saying those words aloud made her skin prickle.

Iver's mouth lifted at the corners. "Aye ... ye are a Stewart of royal blood. Something that no doubt both vexes and intimidates my mother."

Bonnie gave a soft snort. "I think she's more concerned about the fact I'm a bastard."

A muscle tightened in her husband's jaw, and Bonnie felt a pang of pity for Sheena. Her first born son wasn't a man lightly crossed, even by his own mother. "I won't let anyone shame ye," he said, his voice roughening. "Ye know that, don't ye?"

Reaching up a trembling hand, Bonnie stroked his cheek, feeling the rasp of stubble against her fingertips. "I love ye, Iver," she whispered. "I wanted to tell ye so, back there in the barmkin ... before yer mother interrupted me."

Iver's eyes gleamed, a wide smile creasing his face. Staring up at him, it dawned on Bonnie that he'd been waiting to hear her say those words.

Iver Mackay appeared outwardly confident—and he *was* strong, determined, and protective—yet insecurities had plagued him over the years. He'd loved and lost before and had learned to guard his heart. Deep down, he worried that she too might not return his feelings.

Revealing his love for her had taken more than she realized.

And his relief that she felt the same way was palpable.

Cupping her face with both hands now, he leaned in, brushing his lips over hers in a tender kiss. And when he drew back, his eyes glittered with unshed tears. "I told ye that ye would never stand alone here ... and I meant it," he murmured. "I know ye don't want to see my mother again ... and I can't say I blame ye ... but she owes ye a heartfelt apology. Shall we return to the broch and get this over with?" He paused then, his mouth quirking. "Don't worry, I'll be gentler with her than I was with Sutherland."

Standing in Dun Ugadale's hall at Iver's side, Bonnie surveyed the tall woman before the roaring hearth. Sheena looked as proud as ever, even if her gaze was narrowed now, her mouth compressed.

A large brick of peat burned upon the fire behind her, the smoke creating a blue fug that hung beneath the heavy beams crisscrossing the rectangular space. They weren't alone with Iver's mother. His two younger brothers were also present. Kerr and Brodie sat upon chairs flanking the fire, tankards of ale on their knees.

And judging from the way they were both looking at their elder brother, neither were impressed with him.

Did they believe Iver's decision to wed a lowly chambermaid had shamed them all?

Meanwhile, Iver was staring his mother down as if she were his foe. Arms folded over his chest, legs braced, he watched her silently for a few moments before inclining his head. "Remember what I said to ye earlier, Ma?" he said eventually.

Sheena stiffened, and Bonnie wondered what words had passed between mother and son before Iver had followed her.

"It's now time," the laird continued. "Go on … we're waiting."

Silence fell, drawing out while all gazes rested upon Sheena.

The crackle of the hearth filled the void, accompanied by the muffled sounds of voices and clanging pots from the kitchen next door.

And when it was clear that Sheena was content to let the silence continue, Iver's jaw tightened.

However, before he could speak, Bonnie stepped forward, lifting her chin to meet the taller woman's eye. "Can ye not see past the circumstances of my birth?"

Sheena's mouth pursed. "I only want what's best for my son."

"No, ye don't," Iver replied. "If ye did, ye wouldn't have taken such vindictive pleasure at humiliating my wife earlier."

Sheena's face flushed at this rebuke.

"I should really thank ye," Bonnie said after a pause. She meant it too; in the aftermath of her upset earlier, she felt oddly calm, at peace. "Ye have solved a mystery that has long eluded me. I've always wanted to know who my father is … and now I do."

Sheena's eyes widened; she hadn't expected such a response.

But Bonnie hadn't yet finished. "Aye, I'm the bastard daughter of James the First … but does that make me unworthy of yer son?"

"No," a gruff male voice interrupted them. Bonnie glanced over at where Brodie still sat by the fire. His expression was veiled, yet his hazel eyes were fierce. "Ye are welcome here, Bonnie." He set down his tankard and rose to his feet, crossing to where she stood.

And then, to her surprise, he reached out and took hold of her hand, squeezing it gently. Brodie had strong hands, calloused and scarred from his work in the forge. "I too know what it's like to be born with a stain upon my name," he said, while a few feet away, Sheena winced. Ignoring her, Brodie continued, "Iver has weathered much over the years ... and we've had our differences ... but it brings me joy to see him smile again. Ye are welcome here, *sister*."

"Aye." Kerr also rose smoothly to his feet and crossed to them, taking Bonnie's free hand. "Brodie speaks for me too. If Iver is happy, then so am I." He cast a veiled gaze over his shoulder at his mother. "And I'm sorry for the poor welcome ye received earlier."

Warmth suffused Bonnie's chest at Brodie and Kerr's words. She'd feared they'd resent her as Sheena did.

"Yer apology is appreciated, Kerr," Iver rumbled, "but unnecessary. *Ye* weren't the one to insult my wife."

Brodie and Kerr released Bonnie's hands and stepped back, allowing their brother and his wife to face Sheena once more.

Bonnie's breathing quickened. Iver's mother was bristling now; she chafed at being cornered like this.

"We can wait here all night, Ma," Iver murmured after a pause. "As long as it takes till ye admit ye wronged Bonnie ... till ye ask for her forgiveness."

Mother and son locked gazes then, a battle waging between them, before Sheena finally dropped her gaze.

"I was rude," she said finally, her voice barely above a whisper, "and I apologize."

"Ye can do better, Ma," Iver replied, anger creeping into his voice.

Bonnie's stomach twisted. Her husband was relentless; he wasn't giving up until his mother showed real remorse.

Pity constricted her chest then; she could see what this was costing Sheena. Tension was vibrating off her body. She was a proud woman, unused to humbling herself. It struck Bonnie then that, even if she'd been a wealthy laird's daughter, of respectable birth, they still would have locked horns.

Eventually, Sheena raised her gaze and met Bonnie's. A nerve flickered in her cheek. "I'm sorry, lass," she said huskily. "I was cruel."

Bonnie went to her then and took one of the hands that was still curled into a fist at her side. Lifting it, she cupped Sheena's hand between her own. To her surprise, her mother-by-marriage's palm was damp. The woman did a fine job of appearing to have nerves of iron, yet this confrontation had gotten to her.

Sheena's eyes widened then. She hadn't expected Bonnie to do something so bold.

Nonetheless, Bonnie held her eye, holding her hand firmly in her grip. "I accept your apology, Sheena," she said, her voice carrying in the silent hall. "I don't wish for us to be enemies."

34: MY BEATING HEART

"WE NEED A new bailiff."

"Well, ye could try Kyle MacAllister."

"Aye, I hear he tires of sheep farming these days. He doesn't want to follow in his old man's footsteps."

The three Mackay brothers walked the wall that ran around the broch. It was a windy evening, and all of them had slung heavy cloaks about their shoulders.

Iver had only been back at Dun Ugadale a few hours, yet restlessness churned within him.

Usually, whenever he returned home, he'd retire as soon as he could to his solar—alone. But he'd promised himself things would change—and they would.

He would.

"Right," Iver murmured, nodding to his brothers. "I shall ride out tomorrow to talk to him."

Kerr cocked an eyebrow. "Ye don't want me to do it?"

Iver shook his head. He intended to take the reins again, and that meant interviewing any potential bailiff to make sure he got the right man for the job.

"What happened with Lennox?" Brodie asked then. As usual, his youngest brother's voice was gruff, yet there was concern in his eyes.

Iver huffed a sigh. He'd been waiting for this question and had known Kerr and Brodie would wait until they got him alone before the interrogation began. "Did either of ye know just how miserable he was here?"

Kerr pulled a face, while Brodie cut his gaze away.

Neither of them needed to say a word. Iver had his answer.

Breathing a curse under his breath, he walked ahead of his brothers along the wall, his gaze sweeping south, in the direction of Ceann Locha. "How could I have been so blind?" he muttered.

"Lennox is proud … he didn't want to say anything," Kerr replied after a beat.

"Aye, he's as pig-headed as ye are," Brodie added.

Raking a hand through his hair, Iver turned back to them. "Do me a favor, will ye?" he asked roughly. "In the future, if ye see me taking a wrong turn, tell me so."

They both nodded, although Kerr's mouth thinned. "Ye weren't in the mood to be questioned, if I recall," he murmured. "When melancholy grips a person like that, it's difficult to make them care."

Iver swallowed. Had he really been in such a grim place? "Aye, well … ye can still speak the truth to me." He paused then, searching their faces for a glimmer of resentment. "Ye'd both tell me if ye were unhappy here, wouldn't ye?"

Kerr snorted. "Of course, ye idiot."

Meanwhile, Brodie's mouth lifted at the corners. "Ye aren't getting rid of either of us that easily."

Relief gusted through Iver, loosening the tightness in his chest. "I didn't want to get rid of Lennox either," he admitted, his voice roughening.

"Don't worry about him." Kerr stepped up next to Iver and slapped him across the back. "Len has always been a bit wild … he should have stretched his wings years ago."

"Kerr's right," Brodie said, his mouth quirking. "If he ever makes Dun Ugadale his home again, the choice has to be his." He inclined his head then. "The men are talking about treason and murder in Stirling, Iver … when are ye going to tell us about what happened between the king and William Douglas?"

Iver huffed a sigh. With the upheaval of their arrival, he'd almost forgotten. Now though, everything rushed back. "It was a brutal scene, lads," he muttered. "Douglas refused to break with MacDonald and Lindsay, and

James flew into a rage. He stabbed the man until he bled out all over the floor of his solar before one of his courtiers clove his skull apart with a poleax. They then threw Douglas's body out the window."

Both of his brothers murmured oaths at this description. However, Iver hadn't finished. "Douglas's kin have already broken with the crown," he continued. "The relationship between the Highlands and the Lowlands balances on a knife edge once more." He grimaced then. "Tomorrow morning, I must send a missive to Niel, informing him of what has transpired ... the king has also insisted our clan-chief send him a signed declaration, pledging his loyalty. James doesn't trust Niel either, it seems."

Kerr made a disgusted sound in the back of his throat at this. "Really?"

Iver shifted his attention to Kerr to see that his brother's expression was understandably grim. "Aye ... we need to prepare ourselves for trouble."

Kerr's gaze narrowed. "Do ye want me to recruit more men for the Guard?"

"Aye ... it pays not to be complacent."

The three of them drew to a halt, and Iver's gaze shifted west, to where the wall snaked around the back of the broch. He then frowned. "The western wall looks as if it's crumbling."

"It has been like that for a while," Brodie replied, his tone wry.

Ye just never noticed. The criticism was unspoken, yet it filled the air between them, nonetheless. It made Iver wonder what else he'd failed to see of late.

A gust of biting wind buffeted the wall, and Iver yanked his cloak close. He then glanced over at the broch. He'd shown Bonnie around her new home before leaving her in their bedchamber.

She was currently soaking in the bath. He'd wanted to join her, yet he hadn't let himself. Instead, he'd walked out with his brothers, and was glad he had.

Some things had to be faced.

"Well, once I've got a new bailiff organized, I shall see about starting repairs," he announced then. "I also need to walk out to the fields and see what the cottars are planting."

Iver glanced Kerr's way then to see his usually serious brother smiling. He stiffened. "What?"

However, there was no derision in Kerr's blue eyes, just warmth. "It's good to have ye back, Iver," he murmured.

Later, as night settled over Dun Ugadale, Iver sat with his wife and kin in his hall.

Mead and ale flowed, and two of his dogs curled in front of the great hearth next to the dais.

Cory, the cook, had served up good, hearty food. It was the taste of home.

Well-being stole over Iver as he sat there in the carven wooden chair that had once belonged to his great-grandfather. His warriors sat at the tables below, and the rumble of laughter filled the smoky air.

This was another thing he'd steered clear of over the past years.

Iver had taken to consuming all his meals in his solar, avoiding the companionable chaos of his hall.

But no longer.

Glancing across the table, he noted his mother's stiff posture.

Unlike everyone else, Sheena ate her supper as if each mouthful cost her. She'd tried to avoid joining them in the hall this evening, complaining of a headache, but Iver had escorted her downstairs himself.

Just like after his father had died, when his mother had tried to cast Brodie from the broch, he had to keep an eye on her.

Of course, his reclusiveness in the past years had allowed Sheena to exert her influence more strongly. That wasn't entirely a bad thing, as she was highly capable and enjoyed being chatelaine. But those duties would fall to Bonnie now, and Iver would ensure his mother handed over the reins to her daughter-by-marriage with grace.

Feeling his gaze upon her, Sheena glanced up. Their gazes fused, and his mother's mouth thinned. Ire simmered in her eyes. Aye, she'd apologized earlier, but she was still choking on it.

"Yer mother looks vexed enough to turn me to stone with her gaze," Bonnie murmured then, drawing his attention.

Iver met his wife's eye and favored her with a rueful smile. "Aye, she's a stubborn one," he replied. "Where do ye think I get it from?"

Bonnie laughed, while Iver greedily took her in. He would never tire of looking upon his wife.

Her hair, still damp from her bath, hung in dark curls down her back, and her cheeks had a pretty blush after consuming a cup of mead. She'd donned her old kirtle over a clean léine. The garment was indeed shabby, yet it didn't dim her loveliness. Much to his mother's chagrin, he'd instructed her to adjust one of her old kirtles for Bonnie the following day, so she'd have something prettier to wear until she had new clothing made.

Iver would make good on his promise too. The seamstress in Ceann Locha had once dressed noblewomen in Edinburgh, and he would order his wife as many gowns as she wished. He couldn't wait to see the joy in her eyes when she saw all her pretty new kirtles and surcotes.

"Ye are happy to be home," Bonnie observed then.

"I am," he replied. "Is it that obvious?"

Her lips curved. "Aye, ye haven't stopped smiling since ye sat down at this table."

"This broch is as much a part of me as my beating heart," he admitted. "Although I let bitterness blind me to its value. I shut myself away so I could lick my wounds and neglected the things that mattered the most." He paused then, his mood shadowing at the memory of the time he'd wasted. "And I lost one of my brothers as a result."

"Ye haven't lost Lennox," Bonnie replied. She reached out then, placing a hand over his, squeezing gently.

"Haven't I?" Iver pulled a face. "I'd wager he resents me still."

She cocked an eyebrow. "Just wait … six months of working for Colin Campbell and he'll realize yer worth."

Iver snorted. "I'm not surprised ye never warmed to Colin."

She pulled a face, removed her hand from his, and reached for her cup. "I pity his daughter. I might have grown up fatherless, but at least no one tried to marry me to someone against my will."

"That's not unusual amongst lairds," Iver pointed out, inclining his head. "Daughters help make useful alliances."

A groove appeared between Bonnie's brows as she took a sip of mead. Swallowing, she fixed him with a level gaze. "Promise me that if we have a daughter one day, ye shall not inflict such an expectation on her," she said softly. "Swear that ye shall let her wed for love, not to suit yer own purposes."

Iver's eyes widened. "That's quite a request."

"Aye … but I don't make it lightly."

Her words surprised Iver; he couldn't imagine most lairds agreeing to such a stipulation from their wives. All the same, he'd grown up with a strong-willed mother who wasn't afraid to voice her wishes. And he was relieved that his wife wasn't only sweet-natured but knew her own mind as well. She'd need it to hold her own with Sheena.

"Very well, mo chridhe," he replied, holding her gaze. "Ye have my word."

35: WELL MATCHED

"IF YE WANT my opinion ... ye should choose the green," Sheena Mackay sniffed.

Bonnie glanced up from where she was running her fingers over a bolt of cloth and met her mother-by-marriage's eye. "Really?"

Sheena gave a stiff nod.

"Aye." The seamstress stepped close then and flashed Bonnie a wide smile. "An excellent choice, lass ... green is *definitely* yer color ... it's the hue of Kilbrannan Sound on a summer's day. And it matches yer eyes."

Bonnie's cheeks warmed at the flattery. However, she smiled back at Elsie MacDonell. The seamstress—whose shop was tucked in behind the waterfront at Ceann Locha, the nearest town to Dun Ugadale—gazed back at her expectantly.

Ever since Bonnie had set foot in her shop, Elsie showered her with compliments.

Something that was no doubt irking Sheena.

Two days had passed since Bonnie's arrival at Dun Ugadale, and her mother-by-marriage had accompanied her into Ceann Locha to organize the making of a selection of kirtles and surcotes.

Sheena had been reluctant to join her, but Bonnie had insisted.

In truth, despite that they'd made a truce of sorts, her mother-by-marriage's attitude toward her hadn't thawed.

Sheena sat in brooding silence at mealtimes, and all her interactions with Bonnie seemed to be done under sufferance. It was going to take a while for relations between them to thaw, for a rapport to be established—but such things couldn't be forced.

"Very well," Bonnie replied, excitement fluttering up under her ribcage. She couldn't believe she would soon have a collection of lovely new dresses. Sometimes, she felt like pinching herself. "I shall have a kirtle made of this fabric ... and one of the sky-blue material too." She paused then. "Can ye please make two more in the blue and dark-gold I picked out earlier."

Elsie nodded, delight sparkling in her eyes.

Theirs was an isolated spot on the Kintyre peninsula—and the folk who could afford pretty gowns made of such fine cloth were few and far between.

"We shall be back on Friday next week to collect the dresses, Elsie," Sheena said crisply while Bonnie dug into the purse that Iver had given her and extracted the silver pennies to pay for the clothing.

Lord, it felt odd to carry this much coin—indeed, to carry any at all.

Bonnie was still getting used to her new existence, and many aspects of it intimidated her. She'd met all the servants within the broch—servants she now commanded—and Sheena had reluctantly started taking her through the various tasks she was now in charge of, as chatelaine.

Bonnie wasn't used to issuing orders, although those servants she'd met—Cory, the cook, and the lads who helped him, and Maggie, the lass who kept the chambers—had welcomed her warmly.

"Aye, Lady Mackay," Elsie replied, flashing Sheena a smile. "With my sister and my two nimble-fingered daughters assisting me, I should have them all ready for ye then."

Emerging from the seamstress's shop, Bonnie and Sheena found Kerr and two of the Dun Ugadale Guard waiting for them.

"Ye were a while," Kerr greeted them, pushing himself off the wall of the building opposite. "I was beginning to wonder if ye were making the gowns yerselves."

Sheena frowned. "The choosing of fabrics can't be rushed."

"Thank ye for waiting, Kerr." Bonnie flashed him an embarrassed smile.

"Don't worry about it," he murmured, his mouth lifting at the corners. "Come on, let's get ye home."

Together, the small party made their way up the alleyway, walking out onto Ceann Locha's busy waterfront a short while later. Breathing in the briny air, Bonnie glanced around at where fishermen were selling bass, flounder, and plaice off their boats to locals.

While the men were readying the horses, she wandered across to get a closer look—and a short while later, she returned with a basket full of fish.

Sheena wrinkled her nose at the sight. "What the devil have ye bought?"

"Flounders for tomorrow's noon meal," Bonnie replied with a bright smile. "Yesterday Cory lamented the lack of fresh fish of late." She paused then, suddenly uncertain. "I thought he'd be delighted with these ... they were caught this morning."

"Flounder is Iver's favorite fish," Kerr commented as he took the basket from Bonnie and tied it to the back of his saddle. "This will please him too."

There was little Sheena could say to this, although her mouth thinned.

A short while later, the small party rode out of Ceann Locha. As Bonnie hadn't yet learned how to ride, she perched behind Kerr. They traveled alongside Sheena, while the two guards followed close behind.

It was a beautiful afternoon—and the sun that warmed their faces had some heat in it for the first time in months.

A brisk breeze whipped in from Kilbrannan Sound, and gulls circled, screeching overhead.

Bonnie, Kerr, and Sheena spoke little during the journey home. Kerr wasn't a man to indulge in idle chatter, it seemed, and Sheena didn't engage in conversation unless Bonnie initiated it.

Nonetheless, Bonnie welcomed the silence. Life had thrown a bit at her recently, and the ride gave her a little time to sort through her thoughts.

She still reeled at the discovery of the truth of her parentage.

And every time she dwelled on it, sadness tugged at her. She sometimes wondered how her father had reacted to the news of her mother's death. Had he cared for her? Had he grieved?

However, she would never know.

The tragedy of his death, and of her mother's, lay far behind her now. All she could do now was look forward.

Nonetheless, she would never forget.

It was late afternoon when the party of four horses clattered up the causeway and into the barmkin of Dun Ugadale. The sound of hammering, which echoed out from Brodie's forge, greeted them. Kerr and his men took care of the horses, while Bonnie took the fish into the kitchen.

And as she'd anticipated, Cory's rugged face lit up at the sight of the flounders. "It shall be fried fish tomorrow at noon, Lady Bonnie," he said, taking the basket.

Lady Bonnie. Warmth suffused her chest as she smiled back at Cory.

It would take her a while to get used to being called that.

To Bonnie's surprise, Sheena had followed her into the kitchen, waiting in the doorway while the Lady of Dun Ugadale talked to the cook, and when Bonnie rejoined her, she asked, "Would ye like to take a cup of wine with me in the ladies solar?"

Surprised by the invitation, Bonnie nodded warily. In truth, she wanted to go looking for her husband, who was overseeing repair work on the western walls this afternoon, but since Sheena was making an effort, she didn't want to refuse her.

A short while later, the two women sat in the ladies' solar—a small, cozy chamber on the second floor of the broch—before the glowing hearth.

With few trees to use as fuel, the residents of Dun Ugadale burned bricks of peat. It threw out a lot of heat, although Bonnie was still getting used to the pungent smoke.

The gloaming was gathering outdoors, and so they'd lowered the sacking over the small window before settling into high-backed chairs with cups of apple wine.

However, even though she'd been the one to suggest taking some wine together, Sheena seemed to have little to say.

Silence stretched out between the two women before Bonnie eventually broke it. "Thank ye for accompanying me to Ceann Locha today," she said awkwardly. "I appreciated yer advice on the fabrics."

Sheena's mouth pursed. "Aye, well, Elsie is a fine seamstress ... yet she can be pushy. If I hadn't come with ye, I fear ye might have ended up with ten surcotes of her most expensive cloth."

Bonnie nodded. Aye, she'd noticed the seamstress's keenness to show her the fine, and ludicrously expensive, damask she'd just had delivered from Edinburgh.

"I look forward to wearing the dresses," Bonnie admitted, glancing down at the faded blue kirtle she wore. "And thank ye for altering one of yers in the meantime." This was an old one of Sheena's, one she'd worn years earlier, during her last pregnancy. It had been too long for Bonnie, and she'd taken it up, but the bodice was full enough to accommodate her bosom, which was a lot bigger than her mother-by-marriage's.

"Aye, well ... yer old one had to go," Sheena replied. "I've seen scarecrow rags that were prettier."

Bonnie grimaced and took a sip of wine. Sheena wasn't wrong, although she didn't have to be so acerbic.

Another silence fell between them, this one awkward, before Sheena sighed. "Apologies, lass. That was unnecessary."

It had been, yet Bonnie managed a tight smile. "Aye, well ... the kirtle *was* a bit ragged."

Sheena made a dismissive gesture with her hand. She then settled back in her chair, her gaze roaming over Bonnie's face. "I have never seen my son so taken with anyone," she admitted then. Her voice was stilted, as if she was forcing the words out. "He's had his disappointments and is more sensitive than folk realize."

That was quite an admission, and Bonnie didn't know how to respond.

But Sheena hadn't finished. "Ever since he's returned home, it's as if a decade has lifted from his face." She paused then, her grip tightening on her cup. "It gladdens me to see him so happy."

Bonnie's throat constricted. "He brings me joy too," she whispered.

Their gazes met and held, and then Sheena favored her with an expression that looked halfway between a grimace and a smile. "I do believe ye are well matched."

A knock sounded on the door then. An instant later, it opened, revealing the laird himself.

Bonnie's belly flip-flopped at the sight of Iver standing there. He was dressed simply in braies and a dirt-stained léine, his blond hair pulled back from his face, yet to her, he'd never looked so handsome.

"Ah," he greeted them. "There ye both are." A groove appeared between his eyebrows then as his gaze flicked between his mother and his wife. "Was the trip to the seamstress successful?"

"Aye," Sheena replied, her expression sobering. "Yer wife spent a small fortune."

"Aye ... my kirtles and surcotes will be ready to pick up next Friday," Bonnie added. "We also picked up some flounder from Ceann Locha."

His mouth curved. "I know ... Cory just intercepted me on my way in."

His blue eyes were warm as their gazes fused.

Sheena cleared her throat then, set aside her wine, and rose to her feet. "Maggie will have prepared me a bath," she announced briskly, "and these old bones could do with a soak. I shall see ye both at supper."

With a nod at them both, Sheena walked from the ladies' solar, shutting the door behind her.

When she had gone, Bonnie stood up and went to her husband.

He drew her into his arms, his mouth slanting over hers for a long, lingering kiss. Bonnie sank into his embrace, her hands sliding over his chest. She felt the heat of his skin beneath the thin material of his léine and longed to slide her fingers under it.

Sensing her hunger, Iver's kiss deepened, and when they finally broke apart, they were both breathless.

"So, it went well today?" he asked huskily, brushing a curl of hair off her cheek. "My mother wasn't too caustic?"

Bonnie's mouth quirked. "She gives out compliments grudgingly ... yet, she's warming toward me, I believe."

He grinned down at her. "Good."

His hand slid down her cheek, to her jaw and neck, before moving to the neckline of her kirtle, where he brushed his fingertips over her cleavage. Bonnie's breathing grew shallow. His touch never failed to set her alight.

"I know this is one of Ma's cast-offs," he murmured. "But ye are radiant in it, all the same."

"Ye like this kirtle then?" she asked, breathless now.

His lips curved into a wicked smile, and he slid the dress off her shoulders, pushing it down so that her breasts were exposed to him. The air feathered against her naked skin, and her nipples hardened. "Aye." Iver's gaze slid down to her breasts before he grazed his knuckles across their swollen tips. "However, ye are even lovelier out of it."

EPILOGUE: THE BONNIEST WOMAN IN SCOTLAND

Four months later ...

"STRAIGHTEN YER BACK a little ... that's it ... now let yerself sink into the saddle."

Jaw tight, Bonnie did as bid. A moment later, her balance improved, and she no longer felt as if she was going to topple off the back of Ionmhas, the sturdy dun mare Iver had gifted her.

Ionmhas—*Treasure*—was a pretty garron with a dark-gold coat and black mane, forelock, and tail. Iver bought her from the horse market in Ceann Locha two months earlier. In the time since, Bonnie had discovered that she wasn't a natural horsewoman.

She seemed to have little control over the mare, and Ionmhas often stopped to graze at grass during their rides, oblivious as Bonnie tried to get her to move on.

"Ye are holding her on too tight a rein," Iver went on, from where he rode next to her on his bay courser.

"I have to, or she'll go her own way," Bonnie replied.

"No, she won't. Loosen them a bit."

She did as bid, relaxing her grip, creating some slack.

Ionmhas tossed her head, as if thanking her, and Iver huffed a laugh. "Use yer thighs as I showed ye, to guide and halt her." He paused then, still smiling. "And remember, ye are *her* mistress ... not the other way around."

"I know," Bonnie muttered.

"Come, we shall let them stretch their legs," Iver said, flashing her a grin. Before Bonnie could answer, he urged his gelding into a smooth canter. One hand gripping the pommel of her saddle—so she didn't topple off—Bonnie kicked Ionmhas into a jolting trot and then a bumpy canter.

The garron didn't have the long stride of the courser. However, she was a lot closer to the ground should Bonnie tumble from her back.

As she already had, twice now.

The track they rode upon wended its way north above where waves rolled into a rocky shore. Hills clad in heather, thistle, and wildflowers rolled out to the west, and woolly clouds scudded across a cerulean sky. It was a fine summer's morning, and a warm breeze feathered in from the south.

And despite that she was clinging on for dear life, Bonnie couldn't fail to take in the stark beauty of the surrounding landscape.

In the four moons she'd lived here, she'd quickly come to love it, and to understand why Iver was so fond of this peninsula. The rest of Scotland, and its unrest— for King James was now locked in conflict with the Douglases—seemed a world away.

It was a bumpy ride up the coast, and despite that Bonnie did her best to relax into the saddle and go with the mare's stride, as Iver had taught her, her backside was sore by the time they pulled up at the spot he'd chosen for them to take their noon meal.

Sliding to the ground and looping Ionmhas's reins over her head, she glanced over at the large flat rock that sat above the cliffs and the glittering water. Her mouth curved then. Aye, it was a lovely spot indeed.

A short while later, once their horse and pony had been hobbled—to ensure they didn't wander off—Iver and Bonnie sat upon the sun-warmed rock and unwrapped the parcel of food Cory had packed for them.

Inside the oiled leather, they found pork pies, baked with boiled eggs in them, and fresh cakes studded with small tart blaeberries.

There, they sat and ate their fill, washing the meal down with a skin of ale they'd brought. It was good to sit in peace together. The past months had been busy, and they rarely stole time alone in the middle of the day like this.

"Have ye heard from Lennox of late?" Bonnie asked eventually as she finished off her last cake.

Iver shook his head. "I wrote to him shortly after our arrival home ... but received no response." His gaze shadowed at this admission. "It's as I feared ... there's a rift between us now."

"He'll get in touch when he's ready," Bonnie assured him.

"Aye," Iver murmured, although he didn't appear convinced.

Brushing crumbs off her skirts, Bonnie glanced east at where the outline of the neighboring isle rose against the sky.

"What's Arran like?" she asked, deliberately changing the subject. Speaking of Lennox saddened Iver, and she didn't want to dampen his mood.

"Beautiful," Iver replied with a wistful smile. "It has a rugged coastline, steep mountains, and dark forests." He paused then. "My mother's family hail from the isle ... if ye wish it, we could take a trip there before summer's end?"

Bonnie grinned back, excitement fluttering up under her ribcage. "I do wish it," she assured him before shifting her attention once more to the isle's misty silhouette. Arran had intrigued her ever since her arrival at Dun Ugadale. She sighed then. "Before meeting ye, my world was so small. Yet now that I have seen what lies beyond Stirling, I find myself curious to discover more."

"That's fine news indeed, for I received a missive from our clan-chief yesterday. He is holding a gathering in September and has bid me to attend." Bonnie glanced back at her husband to see he'd raised an eyebrow. "He also made it clear that I'm to bring ye ... it seems that the rest of the Mackays want to meet my wife."

Bonnie stiffened. "Niel Mackay wants to meet *me*?"

"Indeed."

Their gazes held, and then Iver's mouth twitched. "He's a nosy bastard ... and probably wants to confirm for himself that the rumor is true."

Bonnie's pulse quickened. "What rumor?"

She'd dearly hoped that after her arrival here and the passing of the months, folk would have forgotten that the laird of Dun Ugadale had wed a simple chambermaid. The thought that gossip might have been circulating the Highlands all this while made her feel a little queasy.

However, Iver didn't look the slightest bit concerned. "Why ... the rumor that Iver Mackay wed the bonniest woman in Scotland, of course," he replied blithely.

Relief gusted out of Bonnie. She then snorted before swatting a hand at him playfully. "That's an outrageous claim," she admonished him.

He caught her hand and raised it to his lips, kissing her knuckles. "Aye, but it's true." His expression grew serious then, his blue eyes intense. "Will ye join me when I travel to Castle Varrich?"

She inclined her head. "It doesn't sound like I've been given a choice."

"Ye always have a choice. If ye'd rather not go ... for ye *will* be the center of attention ... I can make an excuse."

Bonnie considered his words before shaking her head. "I will join ye," she assured him. "I wouldn't want to be apart from ye for so long, and" —she smiled then— "if I can win yer mother over, I'm sure I can weather Niel Mackay's scrutiny."

It was true. Sheena had thawed considerably of late. She still had a tongue sharper than a whetted ax, yet it had become clear that she'd been starved of female company too. The two women often worked together on needlework and weaving in the ladies' solar.

Iver laughed and pulled her close so she perched on his lap. "Aye, lass," he murmured into her ear, causing pleasure to shiver through her. "Ye'd charm the devil himself."

The End

HISTORICAL NOTES

I did quite a bit of research for this book ... into murder, mayhem, and masquerade balls!

This series is set around the reign of James II of Scotland. James ruled from 1430 to 1460. He was the eldest surviving son of James I of Scotland, succeeding to the throne at the age of six, after his father was assassinated. When he was eighteen, James married Mary of Guelders, and they had seven children. His reign was characterized by struggles to maintain control of his kingdom, especially against the Douglases. James was killed by an exploding cannon at Roxburgh Castle in 1460.

He had a distinctive vermillion birthmark on his left cheek, which earned him the nickname, 'fiery face'. However, the moniker also referred to his hot temper. At the time of this novel, James would have been twenty-two years old.

During the story, I allude to some real historical events, including the infamous 'Black Dinner'. In 1440, the young earl of Douglas, just sixteen at the time, and his young brother were dining with James at Edinburgh Castle.

The tale went that the king, who'd only been ten, was enjoying the dinner until someone brought a platter containing a black bull's head—an omen of death—to the table and placed it before the young earl. Despite the boy king's protests, the earl and his brother were dragged from the hall, given a mock trial, and then beheaded. James Douglas, the father of William (the 8th Earl of Douglas), was rumored to have been behind the murders—for he coveted the title for himself and his son.

Twelve years later, James' relationship with the Douglases was strained. William Douglas had formed an alliance with two of the most powerful men in Scotland: the Earl of Crawford, known as the Tiger Earl, who ruled in the North East, and the Earl of Ross. The Earl of Ross was head of the MacDonald clan. His other title was Lord of the Isles, and he could trace his ancestry back to Viking times. These men were as powerful as kings in their own lands, and they saw James II as a lowland king with no authority to dictate how they ran their lands and affairs.

James knew that he had to split this alliance. He invited William to join him at Stirling Castle for feasting on Shrove Tuesday, 1452. William was issued with a letter of safe conduct and joined the king for the feasting before the start of Lent. There was no political discussion that night. The next day was when James II approached the subject of the Douglas' bond with Crawford and Ross. He asked William to break it. He responded saying "I might no, I will no." The King replied, "False traitor, since you will not, I shall."

He stabbed William in the neck and the shoulder twenty-six times. One of his courtiers, Sir Patrick Grey, then 'struck him with a poleax and struck out his brain.' William's body was then unceremoniously flung out the window into the garden below.

In response, the Douglas clan marched on Stirling with the letters of safe conduct pinned to a horse's tail and disavowed their oath to James. The months of conflict that followed was tantamount to civil war. James II kept hold of the Crown and the Stewart dynasty would continue. In the aftermath of William's murder, James set out to remove the Douglas's power from Scotland, resulting in the family's ultimate destruction in 1455.

William Douglas's murder was said to be the inspiration for 'The Red Wedding' in George R.R. Martin's *Game of Thrones*!

Read more about the incident here:

https://blog.stirlingcastle.scot/2021/02/22/douglas-murder/

https://www.medievalists.net/2013/02/king-james-ii-of-scotland-a-reign-of-murder-and-mayhem/

In this novel, we also have a masquerade ball. These events began in the late Medieval period and were a feature of the Carnival season in the 15th century. They involved increasingly elaborate allegorical Royal Entries, pageants, and triumphal processions celebrating marriages and other dynastic events of late medieval court life.

I've set a few stories at Stirling Castle now. It was a royal residence during the 15th Century—and indeed, the 'Douglas Window' and the 'Douglas Garden' are named after the incident that took place in 1452.

Later in the novel, we spend some time at Kilchurn Castle. This castle was indeed built by Colin Campbell. The first castle comprised the five-floor tower house, with a courtyard defended by an outer wall. At the time, Kilchurn was on a small island scarcely larger than the castle itself—at the northeastern end of Loch Awe—and would have been accessed via an underwater or low-lying causeway.

Iver's stronghold, Dun Ugadale, is an iron age fort on the promontory near Ugadale on the Kintyre peninsula. Although it's now a ruin, the fort was owned by the Mackays from the 14th century and was passed through marriage in the 17th century to the MacNiels. The *Ugadale brooch* was allegedly given to the Mackays by Robert the Bruce near Crois Mhic Aoidh (Mackay's Cross), after transporting Robert to Arran.

In this novel, I explore the repercussions of illegitimacy. Being born out of wedlock in the Middle Ages was a scandal indeed. A 'bastard' carried a stain upon their name and were seen as 'morally faulty'. Much of this belief was spread by the church. According to the fifteenth-century abbot Walter Bower, illegitimate offspring were likely to grow up to be 'insolent, degenerate and depraved.' That said, lairds and even royalty could and did acknowledge their illegitimate children, even daughters. It seems that the treatment of children born out of wedlock varied considerably, and depended much on the class you were born into and attitude of your family.

If you're interested in discovering more about illegitimacy in Medieval Scotland, here's an interesting blog post on the subject: https://notchesblog.com/2021/07/15/illegitimacy-in-medieval-scotland-1100-1500/

REBELLIOUS HIGHLAND HEARTS CHARACTER GLOSSARY

Main characters

Iver Mackay (Mackay chieftain—laird of Dun Ugadale)
Bonnie Fraser (chambermaid at Stirling Castle)

Other characters

Ainslie Boyd (head laundress at Stirling)
Alba and Morag (Lorna's twin daughters – Bonnie's cousins)
Angus Boyd (chatelaine of Stirling)
Athol MacNab (steward of Kilchurn)
Colin Campbell (the Lord of Glenorchy)
Cory (cook at Dun Ugadale)
Davina Campbell (Colin Campbell's daughter)
Duncan Stewart (seneschal of Stirling Castle)
Lennox, Kerr, and Brodie (Iver's younger brothers)
Lorna Fraser (head cook at Stirling – Bonnie's aunt)
Malcolm Sutherland (the Sutherland clan-chief's son)
Rory Comyn (blacksmith's apprentice at Stirling)
Sheena Mackay (mother to Iver, Lennox, and Kerr)
William Douglas (8th Earl of Douglas)

DIVE INTO MY BACKLIST!

Check out my printable reading order list on my website: https://www.jaynecastel.com/printable-reading-list

ABOUT THE AUTHOR

Multi-award-winning author Jayne Castel writes epic Historical and Fantasy Romance. Her vibrant characters, richly researched historical settings, and action-packed adventure romance transport readers to forgotten times and imaginary worlds.

Jayne is the author of a number of best-selling series. In love with all things Scottish, she writes romances set in both Dark Ages and Medieval Scotland.

When she's not writing, Jayne is reading (and re-reading) her favorite authors, cooking Italian feasts, and going on long walks with her husband. She lives in New Zealand's beautiful South Island.

Connect with Jayne online:
www.jaynecastel.com
www.facebook.com/JayneCastelRomance
https://www.instagram.com/jaynecastelauthor/
Email: contact@jaynecastel.com

Printed in Great Britain
by Amazon